FRIENDS FOR ∞ INFINITY

THE DETECTIVE JOHN HOLLIS SERIES

JENNIFER GELLEL

Friends for Infinity
Copyright © 2022 by Jennifer Gellel

All rights reserved. No part of this publication may be reproduced, distributed, or transmitted in any form or by any means, including photocopying, recording, or other electronic or mechanical methods, without the prior written permission of the author, except in the case of brief quotations embodied in critical reviews and certain other non-commercial uses permitted by copyright law.

Tellwell Talent
www.tellwell.ca

ISBN
978-0-2288-7963-3 (Hardcover)
978-0-2288-7962-6 (Paperback)
978-0-2288-7964-0 (eBook)

For my wonderful family, and for my friends for infinity, who have consistently supported me in all of my endeavours . . .

CONTENT WARNING

This book contains references to the sexual solicitation of a teenager.

PROLOGUE

(April 2000)

With a few blinks, her eyes opened only as slits, desperate to keep the morning sun at bay. Disoriented, she recoiled at the blinding pain that shot through her skull. She floated somewhere between consciousness and oblivion as fear and anxiety rose in her chest. She felt weak, weighed down in the forest floor by the few inches of soil and damp leaves piled on top of her. Her shoulder burned, but she pushed through the pain and elevated one arm, extending it through the muck, its consistency mirroring cold molasses. Her clothes were soaked through, and she felt the autumnal chill seep through her bones.

Before she could gather her thoughts, she heaved her body to a sitting position, her achy, slender arms barely able to assist in what should have been a simple task. Now upright, she took a moment to think back, but her memory was not yet intact, unable to piece together how she had wound up in this shallow grave. Her mind flittered with dread, wondering how long she had been lying there. *Minutes? Hours? Days?* By God's grace, she was still alive, so she figured it could not have been very long.

Opening her eyes a touch wider, still unfocused, she peered around the forest where she had been left for dead, unsure if she was alone. Rotating her stiff neck and inhaling a deep, cool breath to alleviate her panic, she looked for a lurking predator, but thankfully, there was no one in sight. Calmer now, she took in the area encompassing her. In the distance, through the tall, looming maples, stripped bare from the hearty winds, she could see the ashen, skeletal remains of the house where she once lived. Her racing heart began to settle as her surroundings became familiar. Though she was frightened and, presumably alone, she knew where she was, and in a small way, that gave her comfort.

She shouted for help, though painfully aware that no one would come to her aid. Tears streamed down her face, and she wiped them away in an attempt to gather herself, but they kept coming in furious waves. Confused and overwhelmed, she tried to scramble from the interment, only to fall to her knees. Her head still searing, she ran her hands over the gash on the back of her skull and returned them to her eye line. Staring at her bloodied fingers, she clenched them into fists and pounded the ground below her, begging helplessly for an explanation. Minutes dragged like hours, slumped over, shivering in the seasonal gales. She could smell the acrid odour of smoke, a grey haze billowing through the air in the distance. Then, from nowhere, like vicious slaps, they hit her, flashbacks from the evening prior. One recollection after the next, and she gradually began to gain clarity. Bitterly swiping a sleeve clear across her muddy face, she steeled herself, a wave of indignation driving her to her feet. She grabbed for the nearest tree branch for balance, and, in that moment, attaining some composure under the dawn's sky, she looked up to the heavens and made a promise that one day, that girl would pay for this!

CHAPTER 1

The Investigation

(APRIL, 2021)

The brilliant, rotating cherry red lights lit up the evening sky like a beacon. The blinding glare came as a warning to the area's inhabitants that something dreadful had occurred right here in their usually charming and serene neighborhood. It was a marked departure from the monotony of Greenville, a small town in Maine, ordinarily offering stoicism, tranquillity, and incontestably law and order.

But today the yellow caution tape that rippled in a gentle breeze affirmed that a crime had occurred here. But what crime? What had happened in the playground usually filled with screams of laughter from rowdy children hanging from the monkey bars? What had brought police officers in white coverall suits to this cordoned area searching for God knows what? A hair, a footprint or a droplet of blood?

Officers swarmed the area, Detective John Hollis from the local police department leading the investigation. He was in his early fifties with salted black hair, his stern expression giving off a hard-boiled image that stated he was a no-nonsense man, shrewd and methodical, the sort who painstakingly checked off boxes in his head as he sifted through the helter-skelter. He was tall and he wore a dark grey, two-piece suit that didn't quite fit him anymore. The belt he was wearing cinched at his waistline, gathering material, and the shoulders of his expensively made jacket sagged.

Rumor had it that Detective Hollis had only recently arrived in this otherwise dull, now seemingly beleaguered town, from Los Angeles, California where he'd surely worked through dozens, if not hundreds of crime scenes. The look of familiarity Hollis wore on his face gave confidence that he wouldn't waste time creating theories and perhaps have this whole thing wrapped up in a nice, neat bow by the day's end.

A crowd grew while curious spectators stood on their toes, peering passed the tape and over Detective Hollis's shoulder, hoping to catch a glimpse of what was so interesting that it had sent eight Greenville Police vehicles, sirens screaming, to their location. To most of the residents, it was inconceivable that Greenville even had eight police cars in its fleet.

It was whispered among the onlookers that they had seen a figure covered with a white sheet with long, dark hair spilling out from underneath, indicating the delineation was probably that of a woman's body, and in all likelihood, deceased. They all had read their share of crime novels.

Mrs. Havasham, who held the position of Greenville's lead gossip for years, encircled the cul de sac with Archie, her Bernese Mountain dog, pretending not to relish in the frenzy that had descended upon the suburb. She was a heavier-set, elderly woman, recently widowed and had acquired this gargantuan tail-wagger for companionship, exercise, and, as a reason to get out and insert herself into other people's business. But then, she had always been a busy body, involved in every neighborhood committee and function for ages.

Mrs. Havasham stopped for a moment, running her pudgy fingers through Archie's luxurious coat as she discreetly listened in, trying to pick up clues that may reveal the identity of who lay under that sheet. She'd fancied herself as somewhat of a Miss Marple; but didn't have her shrewd investigative prowess. She was simply a woman with too much time on her hands.

"Good evening Mrs. Havasham," she heard called out from a distance. Without having to look, Mrs. Havasham recognized the voice immediately. It was her neighbor, Rita Morrison whom she had known for years. "I'm not the least bit surprised to find you here under the circumstances."

Rita was a younger woman in her mid-to-late thirties who, two years prior, had given birth to her first offspring, Benjamin, after being in a childless relationship with her husband, Rory, for almost two decades. She was now seven months pregnant with her second baby and starting to feel the general malaise and irritability expectant mothers commonly experience. Rita spent most of her days doing laundry, changing diapers and preparing meals, never being one to resort to the neighborhood tittle-tattle to occupy her time. She seemed to enjoy the tedium of being a stay-at-home mom. Rita had joined a committee or two to be neighborly, but she generally kept to herself. She certainly wasn't the woman of resource that Mrs. Havasham was, but today, she was intrigued.

"Good evening to you too, Rita," Mrs. Havasham shot back, rolling her eyes before turning to face her, feigning a smile. "You're looking well, considering." She paused for a moment as she pointed to her expanded midriff. "It seems Augusta has bequeathed upon us some of its overflow of criminal activity."

Rita nodded in agreement as she wiped her forehead with her cuff. Her ankles were nearly as swollen as her belly, causing her to sway as she pushed Benjamin towards the commotion to get a better look. Both ladies watched on in a state of tenterhooks, waiting for the mystery to unfold.

It was springtime in Greenville. The air was cool and it was beginning to get dark. The chaos made the small town look and feel different, lending an ominous vibe to its usual propitious feel. The bright lights of the police cars and the possibility that someone had been murdered right under their noses had shattered the evening calm.

Those who were not on the street rubbernecking were moving for cover inside of their homes, contributing to the sombre ambiance. Parents hid their children inside, away from the unimaginable terrors that now invaded their street. With very little information being given, it seemed like a favourable idea to err on the side of caution.

As dusk set in and shadows became long, the streetlights popped on offering more light to the investigators who were searching for clues. Detective Hollis walked out from the other side of the tape, lifting it up over his six-foot frame and towards the uniformed officers, his mouth moving. However, unless you were a lip reader, there was no way to know what was being said, but surely, he had been spouting off orders as the officers nodded and hurried to their assignments. As they dispersed, the detective spotted the two women gawking and took a few steps toward them.

"Good evening ladies," he said, calling out to Rita and Mrs. Havasham, both women appearing as though they had been caught red-handed. They stared at the detective wordlessly as they scrambled for a reply.

Rita elbowed Mrs. Havasham gently and lifted her chin towards the man, prompting her to answer back. She finally acknowledged him. "Good evening, detective . . .?" She dangled her reply as a question, leaving the man standing before them to fill in the blank.

"I'm Detective Hollis", he said, holding out his hand, "and you ladies are?"

Mrs. Havasham took the detective's hand in hers, giving it a firm shake. "I am Mrs. Havasham, but you can call me Doris, detective. And this is Rita Morrison. We've both lived on this street for years, and we've never seen this kind of commotion around here, have we Rita?"

"Ah, no, we haven't," Rita replied, staring past him, apparently intimidated by this very official man with the shiny metal badge suspended from his neck, advertising his lofty position with Greenville's police force.

"I mean . . ." Mrs. Havasham cleared her throat and continued moving closer to him. "Is there any way you can tell us what happened here?" She whispered with a little grin and a quick wink hoping this would encourage him to satisfy her inquiry.

"Well, um, Doris. That's a very good question. One that we're hoping, with the help of people like you and Rita here, we may be able to answer sooner than later," the detective replied with an obvious, and deliberate obfuscation of any details she was hoping to reap from him.

Mrs. Havasham began to lose hope that they may glean any information at all as to who might be underneath that sheet or how she had ended up there. Her spine tingled at the possibility of murder. Mrs. Havasham looked intently into the crowd. She had heard once that a killer would often revisit the scene of his crime and she cast her eye over the many faces lining the street. She caught sight of a young man with a shaved head and an unkempt beard, a middle-aged man with a bit of a lazy eye, and an older man wearing a toupee that didn't quite sit right. "It could be any one of them," she thought and smiled at herself admirably, reaffirming her belief that she had a nose for this kind of thing.

"How can we help you, detective?" Mrs. Havasham asked, directing her attention back to the detective, feeling flushed with importance.

"I was wondering if either of you ladies were in your homes around three o'clock this afternoon?"

"Yes," Rita said, nodding at Mrs. Havasham. "I mean, at least I was. I was making Rory's dinner. He likes it on the table when he comes home from work. You see, I'm a housewife and, well, since he's the breadwinner..."

Mrs. Havasham slapped Rita on the shoulder with the back of her hand, making her quit speaking mid-sentence, finally aware that she'd been babbling.

"Well, in that case, Rita," Detective Hollis said, "is it possible that you may have seen or heard anything out of the ordinary, you know, something that may have seemed unusual to you?"

"Unusual?" Rita asked.

"Yes, you know, like maybe you heard a scream, or perhaps a commotion, or a loud bang. Something that may have caught your attention?" Detective Hollis paused briefly, allowing Rita time to think but then continued in her silence. "Was there anything that may have caused you look outside, towards the park?" He asked this with hope that she would be able to give him a jumping-off point.

Detective Hollis maintained eye contact with Rita putting perceivable pressure on her to think hard. But, to the detective's dismay, she could not remember anything significant to share with him. Rita simply shook her head slowly from side to side, seeming disappointed in herself and answered, "No detective. Nothing."

"How about you Doris? Can you think of anything suspicious you may have seen or heard?" While the detective had his best men and women working in the park, he was eager to get something he could sink his teeth into, a small clue that would lead him in the right direction.

As Mrs. Havasham mulled over the afternoon, she wore several different faces. At first, her eyes rolled upwards, and she tilted her head slightly as though she was earnestly trying to jog her memory. Then, she pressed her lips together tightly and nodded like she had recalled something significant. Finally, she shook her head with utmost confidence and answered, "No, detective, sorry. I wish I could help. It's like she just appeared out of nowhere."

"Well," the detective interjected, "she did not just appear out of nowhere, that's for certain. And wherever she came from, we will soon find out. Do you know if there are any CCTV cameras around here, Doris?"

"I'm not sure which houses have cameras installed," Mrs. Havasham replied, "but I'm sure if your officers went door to door, the residents who have surveillance, if any, would be happy to share the footage with you, detective. You might even want to try some of our local businesses. I think I've seen a camera out front of Nick's hardware store."

Detective Hollis seemed content with this bit of information and jotted it down on his notepad.

"Well, ladies, thank you for your help," the detective said, reaching into the inside pocket of his ill-fitting suit jacket to pull out some business cards. "Here, take these," handing one to them both. "My number is on there. If either of you thinks of anything, you can call me at any hour. Okay?"

"We certainly will, detective," Mrs. Havasham responded, looking down at the wording on the card. *Homicide Detective.* Now it was official. Detective Hollis's arrival on Sycamore Lane was indeed in search of a killer. And that woman, underneath the sheet, had died under murderous hands.

Rita accepted the card and tucked it into the diaper bag suspended from Benjamin's stroller, offering him a perfunctory wave goodbye.

Detective Hollis nodded and thanked them both before walking away. He immediately headed back toward the mayhem and ducked back underneath the tape, eyes boring into him.

The wind blew through the red maples that stood tall in the park, small clusters of bright red flowers hanging high from their limbs. It was an indicator that fresh leaves would soon arrive, marking new life in Greenville. This seemed indubitably ironic, considering what lay at the foot of those trees.

Rita looked at her watch, surprised at the time, and bid Mrs. Havasham adieu. "I'd better go," she said before turning on her heel. "Rory will be home soon, famished from the long commute back from Sangerville."

Nodding goodbye, Mrs. Havasham watched her walk away. Now in her third trimester, and with Benjamin in tow, Rita waddled off, her pelvis tilted forward, her stride slow.

Mrs. Havasham lingered. Her curiosity hadn't dampened, if anything, her interest had escalated, her breath coming in shorter bursts. She had never spoken to a homicide detective before. She, in fact, had never spoken to any sort of detective before. It was thrilling.

Darkness descended upon Greenville, but the community was buzzing as they indulged themselves and each other, with their assumptions and conjectures, each meddler believing they had had the whole case solved.

"It must be Lionel MacKenzie's son. What's his name? Colin. That's it. Colin. That boy's been in trouble since he first drew breath," one of the men in the crowd argued.

"I doubt it. Murder is a far cry from petty theft and vandalism. It would be quite a stretch," another answered.

"What about Bobby Lennox? Wherever that boy goes, chaos follows."

"Now that's a theory I can get behind."

The chatter grew and before the locals knew it, no resident in the small town of Greenville was left unscathed. Each of them was guilty, each of them with a motive and means. It was Professor Plum in the living room with a candlestick, like a board game. Although, this wasn't a game, it was real life. There were no dice, cards or miniature plastic weapons.

Truthfully, not fifty feet away from where they stood, an actual human being was lying unmoving, slumped sideways, her hair sweeping the cold, damp ground. Someone somewhere would be missing her, looking for her. Maybe she was a mother, an aunt, or someone's wife. She was definitely someone's daughter. Her parents had probably already contacted their local police department, pleading for their help. Yet, the novelty of the predicament had everyone outside of the tape dismissing all of this, hanging around to get a better look.

The conversations of hearsay and slander pursued as the forensic officers scoured the park for evidence, and Detective Hollis continued to interview the urbanites. His posture was beginning to crumble while dark circles formed beneath each of his eyes. After closing his notepad, he helped himself to a coffee at the command post, dumping extra packets of sugar into the cup to give him an energy boost. He stirred his steaming, muddy brew and looked towards the sheet under which several mysteries lay.

Who was this woman and where did she come from? Who did this to her and why? As far as he could gather, no one had reported anyone missing locally, and the hours were passing quickly since the 911 call came in.

She was first discovered by a teen-age girl coming through the park on her way home from school. Initially, the dispatcher could not make out what the caller was saying as she babbled on incoherently, quite obviously in hysterics. Finally, the woman on the receiving end of the line shouted, "A body? Where? I'll send the police!"

The local duty officer was notified immediately, and with a sharp tongue, he barked, "What the fuck? Are you sure?" This was more than he had bargained for when he set out to work this morning, expecting an effortless day that would see him into the long weekend. "God damn it! Send everyone we've got."

With the caller laid out in shock, Detective Hollis would have to interview her later. For now, he would keep working with what he had.

The coroner, who was still bent over the body, jotted down a few more observations before he began to pack up his bag, indicating that his investigation was complete. He noticed that the detective had been hovering and curled his index finger at him, beckoning him to come forward. Hollis walked eagerly towards the body, desperate to have a closer look. This was old hat for the detective, and he showed no signs of distaste when the coroner pulled back the sheet. He'd seen many corpses and was familiar with the hideous optics of a dead body.

"She's all yours, detective," the coroner said without offering any pleasantries, removing his gloves while elevating to a standing position. "Good luck." The coroner extended his hand to Detective Hollis, passing off his report, including a death certificate. He turned away, exiting the crime scene instantly, seeming to be in a hurry to get out of there. Detective Hollis looked sharply at the coroner's notes. Taking his time, he read each and every detail carefully.

At last, he shone his flashlight toward the woman, lying face-up on the damp grass. The unidentified woman was pretty, well, from what he could tell anyway. She was not bloated or bloody. She could have simply been sleeping. A far cry from some of the decaying corpses he'd seen in his past.

She was Caucasian and approximately thirty-five years old. She didn't have a wallet or a purse with her. "Perhaps it was a robbery gone wrong," he pondered. But even without identification Detective Hollis suspected that she may not belong to this area, judging from her clothing and possibly some track marks located on the cubital fossa of her left arm. She was wearing a pair of worn jeans with holes in both knees, a hooded sweat top and a pair of beat-up running shoes.

Around her neck, Detective Hollis noticed an oval-shaped locket hanging from a long, thin silver chain. He snapped on a pair of his own latex gloves, careful not to disturb the scene and crouched down beside the body. He delicately opened the locket and inside, he observed two images; a photo of herself on one half and one of an older woman on the other, possibly her mother. She would be looking for her, worried, likely frantic. Unfortunately, being a parent, he knew that emotion all too well, but subconsciously, Hollis elected to ignore the anguish of familiarity. He continued on with his investigation and removed the locket gently from the woman's neck. He decided that he would show the images around to neighbors in hopes that someone might recognize one of them.

The coroner's report estimated that the victim had been deceased for about four or five hours judging from her skin's pallor and temperature. Rigor mortis had begun to set in, just starting to affect the larger muscle groups. Lividity had not yet begun, confirming the timeline suspected. Her lips were coloured a dark shade of blue under what was left of her pink lip gloss. The coroner had noted the welts on the woman's forearms, along with a number of scratches. This woman had put up a fight. Whoever it was that did this to her would certainly have Jane Doe's DNA under his fingernails, and his under hers.

Detective Hollis lifted the unidentified woman's sleeve to get a better look at the scratch patterns when he noticed a tattoo on the inner portion of her right wrist. It was one of those infinity symbols that looked like a sideways number eight, adorned with the letters *RM* underneath. *RM? Her initials?* Or more likely someone she was or had been close to. Detective Hollis removed his cell phone from his pocket and took a quick snapshot of the tattoo on his camera before tucking it away.

Finally, there was significant bruising around the woman's neck, the pattern resembling that of someone's hands squeezing tightly around her. Between that and the obvious petechiae in her eyes, the coroner was ruling her cause of death as manual strangulation. Of course, he would have to wait for the autopsy to confirm this.

Detective Hollis, still kneeling beside the body, stared at her face, remnants of mascara smeared across her cheeks. Not to his surprise, he felt a pang of sadness for this lifeless woman lying alone in front of him. It was never easy for him to imagine what these victims went through during the final moments of their lives. It was a heavy pack he wore on his shoulders, the memories of so many lives that ended morbidly and much too soon. At times, his thoughts haunted him, and he wondered what they were thinking as they gulped their final breath. *Did they have regrets? Did they beg for their lives?* He owed it to them to uncover the truth.

Detective Hollis was nudged from his trance when he heard his name being called. Through the dim light, he could make out the silhouette of Mrs. Havasham, still lingering at the periphery of his crime scene with Archie, waiting for news along with the rest of the neighborhood.

"Detective, I'm sorry to be a bother, but I was wondering if there was any new information. Anything at all, something to help us sleep tonight?" Mrs. Havasham asked as she made her way toward the detective, hopeful of sneaking a closer peek at the body.

"Doris," the detective said, welcoming her with a hint of a smile, realizing that he could try his hand once again with this nosey parker. "I thought you'd have gone home by now. Unfortunately, I don't have anything new to share; the investigation is very premature. But I do have another question for you if you could spare some more of your time."

"Another? I'm not sure how I could possibly help."

"The woman in the park was wearing a locket when she died. Inside the locket there are two images, one of the victim and the other of an older woman. If I showed you the photos, is it possible you might recognize either of them?"

"I guess that may be possible, that is, if they are from around here," she answered, reaching out her hand. Detective Hollis frowned. Earlier, he thought that the woman was likely not a local, but just the same he turned over the locket to Mrs. Havasham, placing it into her palm. She took the glasses that sat gingerly on top of her neatly piled, gray hair and placed them on the bridge of her nose. "I'll be needing these."

She looked at the images presented to her with scrutiny, deep in concentration, but she did not recognize either one of them in the least. She held out her arm, returning the locket to Detective Hollis and said remorsefully, "I don't know these people."

"Are you sure? The lighting isn't great. Maybe it would help if you had another look? Take your time." He pushed the locket back toward her, encouraging Mrs. Havasham to gaze at the photos once more. She peered at the faces briefly and answered with authority, "Detective Hollis, if either of these people were from around here, trust me, I would recognize them. I've lived in various parts of Greenville my entire life."

"But you couldn't possibly know everyone, could you?"

"Detective, I know that in a large city like Los Angeles, people crave anonymity and enjoy keeping to themselves, but in this town, we are community-driven. We get involved in our churches, schools, and spring garbage pick-up," Mrs. Havasham continued to speak, extending the locket towards Detective Hollis, indicating that she was sure of her answer. "These people could be from Guilford, Willimantic, or any other town in Piscataquis County, but I can guarantee you they are not from Greenville."

Detective Hollis begrudgingly took the locket from her, tossing it into an evidence bag and into his jacket. "Well, Doris, I appreciate your candor," he replied, disappointment trailing in his voice, understanding his efforts had come to naught. Frustration rose within him; he was not getting anywhere with his potential witness.

In fact, things had just gotten more complicated, now dealing with two unidentified people.

But returning to his main focus, the corpse lying stiffly in the grass, he looked to Mrs. Havasham, hoping the mystery would sustain her interest, and said, "You have to admit, it's odd. How and why does a woman from another town turn up dead in a park in Greenville? We'll have to start checking databases from surrounding towns. It won't be long before this woman is reported missing."

"Well, detective, I do love a good mystery. I've read all of Agatha Christie's. I really wish I could have been more helpful." It was getting late, and Archie was becoming restless at her heels, hungry for his raw protein dinner.

"Before you go, Doris," the detective said, clearing his throat, "do the initials *RM* mean anything to you?"

Mrs. Havasham turned over the initials in her mind's eye. *"RM. RM."* She repeated the letters slowly, out loud several times, considering whether or not they were familiar to her. She took several seconds before shaking her head. "My apologies detective, but I believe I have let you down again. I honestly wish that I had something for you. Now if there's nothing else I . . ."

"What about this tattoo?" Detective Hollis asked, cutting her off, making a final and desperate attempt. He grabbed his phone from his pocket, tapping on the photo album icon and scrolling to his most recent picture. He held up his cell for Mrs. Havasham to see. She accepted the device and squinted fervently at the image before she drew a quick breath. To the detective's surprise, a look of recognition crossed over her face.

"What is it, Doris? Have you seen this before? Tell me!"

Mrs. Havasham nodded slowly, meeting the detective's eye. She knew she had seen the tattoo and exactly where she had seen it.

Mrs. Havasham opened her mouth to speak when, from nearby, she was interrupted by the sound of a booming voice.

"You old fool!" It was Rita. She had been lurking in the shadows, listening in on Mrs. Havasham's conversation with the detective. "You couldn't keep your nose out of this, could you? Always meddling in other people's business!" Rita appeared bedraggled and completely out of sorts.

Mrs. Havasham looked at her with surprise. She had never heard Rita speak so obstinately. Sure, she could be a bit sarcastic, even disparaging at times, but she was sheepish, and not one to cause a scene.

"You couldn't leave well enough alone could you, Doris?" Rita cried, anger stirring within her.

"Good heavens, Rita, control yourself! Getting this worked up is not good for that baby," Mrs. Havasham answered back, trying feverishly to connect the dots. *The dead woman. The tattoo.* It was the same one she had seen on Rita's wrist, save for the letters, the one she had always wondered about. It couldn't be a mere coincidence. Then suddenly, it clicked, the initials printed beneath the photo of the tattoo she was shown.

As the entire neighborhood watched in bewilderment and awe, Mrs. Havasham, thrown by the turn of events, had a brief moment of clarity. *"RM."* She mouthed the letters to herself and then shouted out the name, "Rita Morrison!"

Benjamin cried in his stroller as his mother mutated into a scary form before their eyes. Rita balled her fists. Her face appeared distorted, like a reflection of herself in a funhouse mirror. This was not a case of pregnancy hormones; it was blind rage that was quickening her blood. Then, without hesitation, she raised her arms in surrender and revealed her hand as the crowd stared slack-jawed, "I killed her!" She spat. "I killed her! And I would do it again."

CHAPTER 2

The Investigation

(April, 2021)

The interview room was a cold and confined space with bare walls, reminiscent of something you'd see in the movies. It was silent except for the humming sound emanating from the ceiling fan above. There was a table in its center, and Rita sat on one of the two uncomfortable, rickety chairs placed at opposite sides, her hands tightly bagged to preserve trace evidence. Her wrists were cuffed to the front, a luxury not often afforded to most criminals, much less self-confessed murderers. It was usually strict protocol to have arrested parties handcuffed to the back, restricting their movement and access to weapons of opportunity. But Detective Hollis had considered Rita's current state and taken pity on her.

Still astonished by the chain of events, he wondered how he had missed her complicity. He had been a little rusty since his sabbatical. He didn't know Rita, but looking back, he remembered that she seemed on edge, reluctant to offer help, but he had passed off her fidgety demeanor as just nerves. He knew from experience that not everyone was comfortable speaking to the police.

On the opposite side of the one-way mirror, Detective Hollis studied Rita. He always believed this activity gave him a bit of an upper hand. Even before he got the opportunity to question his suspect, in this case his penitent, he was afforded the advantage of scrutinising their behavior, a technique he had learned at the academy. He looked for simple things like how they sat in their chair, slouched or upright, signs of anxiety such as perspiration or restlessness and even overstated emotions such as crying or screaming.

But unfortunately, Rita's actions weren't giving him anything more to work with. She seemed calm and at peace, a far cry from the Rita he had seen only a couple of hours ago having a meltdown on Sycamore Lane. Oddly, he thought, she looked as though the weight of the world had been lifted from her shoulders, which was strange considering the secret she'd been harboring was no more than six or seven hours old.

In any case, the detective had already received his confession, and as a bonus, he had several eyewitnesses to Rita's admission of guilt. At this very moment, Mrs. Havasham was in the next room giving her full statement to the police; something Detective Hollis knew she would be relishing in. If he was being honest, for a mere neighbourhood snoop, she had been instrumental in uncovering Rita's involvement, for which the detective was very grateful. Unfortunately, only half of the mystery had been solved as, so far, there was no further information about the woman found beneath the maples. Rita exercised her right to remain silent, and no new missing person reports had been filed. However, Detective Hollis was confident that once he had established Rita's motive, he would then be able to identify his victim.

Unfortunately, she had not reached her husband yet, a lawyer, who would presumably be representing her, although, from what he understood, the man had never taken on a murder case before. His main focus of law had been representing greedy divorcees hungry to cash in once they were traded in for a newer model.

Still evaluating Rita on the other side of the glass, he made a mental list of everything he knew. Having Rita's initials on the victim's wrist meant that the woman was definitely not a stranger to her, which was common for female killers, being more likely to target someone they were acquainted with. Additionally, the matching infinity tattoos likely indicated that she was not only known to Rita but that the victim had been someone close to her, a friend or a relative perhaps. Detective Hollis had seen the identical tattoo himself as he handcuffed Rita, but the ink was faded, and it had been a rudimentary job. Unfortunately, the letters imprinted had been smudged and really could have been anything, lending another piece to the dismantled puzzle.

What Detective Hollis found peculiar was the method Rita had used to kill this woman. From a criminal profiler's point of view, manual strangulation was a sadistic technique more commonly used by men requiring a great deal of strength, whereas women would commonly take a more covert approach, like poisoning or suffocation. He considered numerous possibilities. "Could it have been that Rita's motivation to kill this person was born of so much hate that she had consciously chosen this violent end to the woman's life? Or was it that Rita's hand had been forced, and in that split second, with no other means, had chosen this cruel yet effective way to kill another human being? And where did she find the fortitude given her physical condition? She may well be covering for someone," he concluded. Hopefully the neighborhood canvas would tell him if someone else, aside from Rita, had been seen in the vicinity at the time of the murder.

Being held in the cramped area for over an hour, and of course, being seven months along in her pregnancy, Rita was beginning to look wearisome. This was the moment at which the detective would often begin his questioning, when the suspect would tire, rendering him, or in this case her, more vulnerable and inclined to talk.

Rita had been given her Miranda rights and knew she wasn't required to answer any questions without counsel present, regardless, he decided to try his hand. It was time for him to start fitting this jigsaw together.

After taking a long, deep breath to bring him back to life, the detective turned the door handle and entered the austere room, primed to get answers. However, he was always steadfast in creating a gentle, non-aggressive presence in order to develop a positive atmosphere, one where he was more apt to gain trust.

"We meet again, Rita." He began, greeting her with a soft voice as he closed the door gently behind him. Detective Hollis pulled out the vacant chair, opting to sit rather than stand, avoiding the illusion of being overpowering.

Her striking blue eyes, puffy from crying, stared absently at the detective who also looked worse for wear. Holding back her reply momentarily, doubtlessly considering whether she should wait for Rory to arrive before engaging in casual conversation, Rita acquiesced and responded slightly mournfully, "Yes, I suppose we do." Immediately deflecting from the fact that she was currently being detained following a murder confession, she asked with an abundance of concern and a heavy sigh, "How is Benjamin?"

"He's fine. He's with a neighbour and Rory is on his way. I take it he will be representing you?" Detective Hollis asked, acknowledging how handy it must be having a lawyer for a husband.

"Yes. I mean, I guess so. I haven't spoken to him yet. I've only left him a message. How much does he know?"

"At this juncture, he only knows as much as you have told him in your message," the detective answered truthfully, and in an effort to be as transparent as possible, Detective Hollis gave Rita her secondary caution.

"I must inform you that even though you have made a statement," he cleared his throat and continued, "meaning your confession, you should not feel influenced by that to make any further utterances. And anything you do say could be used against you in a court of law."

Rita nodded, confirming what the detective had already known, that she would be familiar with her rights, being married to a lawyer. Beads of sweat trickled from her forehead, prompting Detective Hollis to pass her a handkerchief from his jacket pocket. Placing it between her bagged palms, she used it without hesitation, removing the drips of perspiration. Offering a nod of thanks, Rita tried to hand it back, but he raised his hand, bidding a gesture that implied, "You keep it." She dropped it onto the table and the two of them sat in silence for a few moments.

He was comfortable with the rapport he was building with Rita, so, in a further attempt to appease himself that he wasn't manhandling a woman, just weeks away from giving birth into an unrepresented interview, he offered her something to drink. "It's getting awfully hot in here Rita. Can I get you a glass of water?"

"No. No thank you, I'll just wait for Rory," she answered.

"What about something to eat? Or maybe one of the matrons can escort you to the restroom?"

"I said no," Rita bit back, Detective Hollis receiving the message loud and clear. She understood his tactics, offering her items of comfort with the intention of softening her, but she would not be jostled into giving the detective any more information until she had an opportunity to speak to her husband.

Aware that the interview was being recorded and that he had no other recourse but to back off, Detective Hollis stood slowly and assured Rita that he would let her know the moment Rory arrived. He exited the room and slipped some coins into the nearby vending machine. Much to his surprise, a cold ginger ale tumbled from the innards of the ancient contraption, landing with a thud. Grabbing the can and pulling back the tab, he handed it to the guard outside the door and said, "Give this to her," acknowledging that the rendering would be better received coming from anyone other than him.

Grateful for the peace offering, she accepted the can awkwardly, and she gulped its entire contents down.

Also beginning to feel the aftermath of a long day, Detective Hollis slumped lazily in a chair parked opportunely in the corridor, watching the minutes on the clock tick slowly into the late hour. It had been a while since he had run a murder investigation following his unforeseen sabbatical from the Los Angeles Police Department. He had taken a leave of absence to get his head on straight. Detective Hollis had been labelled by his therapist with a diagnosis of Post-Traumatic Stress Disorder, stemming from either a manifestation of cumulative trauma having worked twenty-five years with the worst of humankind, or perhaps, just the one single traumatic event that, even now, was still festering.

Either way, the department had forced him to take a break, to regroup. Afterwards, he was offered the job in Maine, and he accepted it, hoping that the change in pace, the scenery, and the distance would do him some good. But apparently, he had jumped from the frying pan and into the fire, being handed a homicide case just a week following his arrival in Greenville. Maybe he was just bad luck.

Staring at the moving hands on the clock was beginning to have a hypnotic effect on the detective until, finally, the spell was broken when a man dressed in a fitted, seersucker suit entered the police station taking long strides toward him and demanded in a commanding voice, "I want to see Rita Morrison right now!"

CHAPTER 3

The Investigation

(April 2021)

Detective Hollis showed Rory to the interrogation room, where Rita fumbled from her chair and fell into his arms. Stifling a sob, she lifted her head from his chest and looked to his bolstering face, her eyes begging for absolution.

"I'm sorry, Rory. Can you ever forgive me?"

He stroked her long, chestnut hair, kissing her softly on the top of her head and assured Rita, "We'll get through this together, I promise." He held her for another moment longer before letting go and expeditiously set the ball rolling. He threw his briefcase onto the table and removed his jacket like he was preparing for a fight, taunting and intimidating. "Now, let's get down to business."

Rory didn't want to waste another moment. His wife, the mother of his son and unborn child, was behind bars and it was going to be up to him to find a way to get her out. Rita nodded affably at his suggestion.

Allowing Rita some privacy with her attorney, Detective Hollis excused himself and exited the dank room. He continued to watch them closely through the glass as his curiosity was getting the better of him. He looked on as Rory opened his case and grabbed at a steno pad and a pen before he began to take notes. He scribbled intensely as Rita spoke, recording the details and planning his strategy. He wondered how much Rory knew prior to Rita's telephone call this evening and if he, himself, had known the woman whose toe tag currently labelled her as Jane Doe.

Eyes still prying, the detective noticed that Rory appeared confident and upbeat, and he admired his certainty in himself, despite fighting an uphill battle. After all, Rita had already confessed. *What loopholes could he possibly find?* But Detective Hollis was familiar with this type of man; his overconfidence compensating for something lacking, in this case, his proficiency. He was a divorce lawyer with little to no experience in the criminal courtroom. Nonetheless, he was giving off the impression that he was on top of the world, the same one his wife was currently being crushed by, waiting to be formally charged with murder.

Hesitantly, Detective Hollis made his way to the officer's break room. He sat cross-legged on a wooden fold-out chair, hands intertwined and clasped over his knee. But before he could get a moment's peace, he was suddenly interrupted, the door pushing open behind him. He sat bolt straight, adopting a neutral expression, careful never to let his face give away what he was feeling. He looked to the intruder, a uniformed constable he had yet to meet. She stood with one arm extended, pensively offering the detective a cup of coffee.

"A penny for your thoughts Detective," she said, provoking a half-smile from Detective Hollis.

"Thank you. . . Miller," he replied, gazing at her nameplate that was pinned to the right side of her pristinely ironed shirt. Gratefully accepting the young woman's much needed refreshment, he grabbed the mug by its handle and took a quick sip. "You're working late," he noted, looking up at the clock, the hands now showing after eleven pm.

"I'm on the overnight shift sir," Miller answered, pulling out a chair next to him and taking a seat. "How are you holding up?"

It was the same question he had been asked a million times in the last two years, which should have elicited a predefined, automated response, but he took his time before answering. "I'm good thanks. It's been a long day," he asserted, rubbing the sprouting bristles on his face. Taking another sip of the bitter coffee, he gestured his chin across the hall toward the interrogation room, and he commented, "What I wouldn't give to be a fly on that wall."

Miller peered toward the window getting a good look at the pregnant woman's face. "With all due respect sir, I thought this one was a slam dunk," she said, shifting in her seat. "I mean, I heard that the suspect has already confessed. Everyone is talking about her meltdown in the park."

"Yes, but twenty-five years of experience is telling me there is a lot more going on here," the detective contested, knowing that leaving his intuitions unchecked earlier in his career had led him to poor decision making. It was her eagerness to concede that had seemed so off beat. Surely with her understanding of the law, she would know that the tattoo was just circumstantial evidence, and, currently, with no witnesses to the crime coming forward, it would be difficult, if not impossible, to make a case solely based on that.

"So, you're saying that you have a hunch detective?" Miller asked greenly.

"It's not a hunch Miller," Detective Hollis protested hotly, his fatigue allowing him to become untamed. However, quick to acknowledge that he was dealing with an unseasoned officer, he gathered himself and lowered his tone. "I just meant that sometimes your experience tells you something's off."

"Sorry detective. I'm new at all this," she confessed, "still taking people's word at face value I suppose. Rookie mistake."

"You're forgiven Miller," he assured her. "Don't beat yourself up. It's a skill you develop over time. Eventually, you'll know when something seems hinky."

"Hinky, sir?"

Coming to the understanding the job's slang was as new to her as the position itself, he explained, "Yes, hinky. You know, suspicious. I mean, why does a woman like Rita, with an unstained record, and not to mention very pregnant, end up killing someone in broad daylight in a neighborhood park?" He paused for a moment, deep in thought, and then coming to his point, he stated, "You're a woman Miller."

"Thank you for noticing, detective," she replied sarcastically, though partly sincere, often feeling very masculine in the boxy, polyester and cotton uniform.

"What makes a woman kill? It's rare, but not unheard of. I'm sure there are at least a dozen women in Maine's Correctional Centre serving sentences for the same thing," Hollis said, rising to his feet and turning on his heel to meet Miller's gaze. "What would it take to make a woman snap?"

"That's a good question sir. I'm not sure. Jealousy? Financial gain?" She suggested.

Shaking his head, he countered, "I think it's more than that Miller."

"Is that what your hunch is telling you?" She smiled derisively.

"Touché Miller," he replied grinning back, the irony not being lost on him. "Any other suggestions?"

She shrugged and put forward, "Vengeance?"

"Maybe," the detective replied falteringly, temporarily considering the idea but dismissing it. For a moment, the two of them sat quietly, lost in thought as Hollis traced the grooves of the graffiti etched into the lunchroom table with his finger.

"Well, good luck detective," Miller responded, rising to her feet and letting out an audible yawn. "You're a highly trained investigator. I'm sure you'll figure it out." Standing now, she ran her palms over her thighs, attempting to eradicate the creases in her slacks. "My break is over; I'd better get back out there With nearly all the on-duty officers guarding the scene, the calls for service are piling up."

"Be safe Miller," Detective Hollis said as she opened the door and walked away, the scent of her perfume lingering in her wake. She left the detective alone, immersed in his doubts. Shrouded in more questions than answers, he set down his mug and returned to the observation window to find Rory and Rita whispering conspiratorially. He thought about how drastically their lives had changed in the last few hours. He found himself wondering if their relationship could sustain such a catastrophe and how their children would grow up without a mother.

Detective Hollis was not a sentimental man. If anything, a quarter century on this job had left him cynical and sharp-edged. But Rita was unlike the depraved and disreputable felons he had dealt with in Los Angeles, and, even with the dead woman's face still fresh in his mind, he felt unusually empathetic toward her.

At long last, the detective watched as Rory rose from his seat and moved hastily to the door. He heard the knob turn a second before Rory emerged imperiously, leaving an agonised and despondent Rita behind, resting her head on the grimy table. Speaking in an imposing voice, illustrating the same bravado that overflowed earlier as he entered the police station, Rory insisted, "We're ready to commence the interview."

"Well then," Detective Hollis answered, "let's start at the beginning, shall we?" dragging in an extra chair behind him.

CHAPTER 4

(The Confession)

My first vivid memory was of my father as he walked out the door for the last time. He held a small, red suitcase at his side that was nearly bursting at the zipper. It carried everything he owned. Without saying goodbye, he simply looked at me, his eyes vacant, and said two words, "I'm sorry." My mother threw something heavy at him as he hurried out into the cold, the door slamming shut behind him. I cried because even at the age of ten, I understood that it would be the last time I would ever see him.

My parents constantly battled, mostly just yelling, but sometimes it came to blows. The alcohol consumption would induce my mother's fury, and she would always hit my father first. And when they fought, it frightened me. I was a child with no siblings I could rely on for comfort. So when the yelling started, I'd run to my room and hide underneath my blankets. I would place my hands over my ears to protect them from the things that a child should never hear. Eventually the hysteria would stop and things in our home would return to normal. Our normal, I guess. And only for a while.

My mother, Laura Morrison, was very much an alcoholic. Vodka, sometimes straight from the bottle, replaced most of her meals. And for dessert, some kind of pill that would thankfully cause her to pass out. Most nights, she would not even make it to her bed. I'd wake myself up for school, when I went, and find her collapsed on the couch. I was always careful not to disturb her because I knew waking her was more trouble than it was worth. It was not like she would prepare my lunch or be in any condition to get me to class. I would tiptoe out of the house and not return until the streetlights came on. Occasionally there would be dinner on the table, but often there was not. And sometimes, there would be an insincere apology accompanied with false promises, "I swear Rita. I'm going to turn my life around; things will get better." At first, I would believe her, but later, I learned to take the apology with a grain of salt as I discovered that she, for lack of a better term, was full of shit.

My father, Ray Morrison, was a kind-hearted man with a good work ethic. He earned a measly income at a job he hated so he could put food on the table for me and alcohol in my mother's glass. He woke up every day before dawn and made the trip from Waterville to Augusta, rain or shine. We didn't have a car, so it was public transit for my father, an hour and a half each way. He welcomed overtime hours when he could get them, and, while he said it was for the money, I suspected it was an excuse to keep him away from home, away from my mother and perhaps even me. I was young and naive and quick to take some of the blame for his absence. He worked tirelessly and was beginning to look older than his years.

Before Ray met my mom, from what I was told by those who knew him well, he was full of life. He had lots of friends and was always up for a laugh. He was easy to talk to and his charming personality drew others to him like moths to a flame. He would tell stories, make grand gestures with his hands, drawing a crowd. He told jokes and belted out punch lines, slapping his knee while listeners roared. "Oh, Ray, tell us another one," they'd beg, and he'd always oblige.

When Ray left, life in our house was never the same and I entered into a very dark place. I spent sleepless nights hating him for leaving me with this monster of a mother. I prayed to God, although I wasn't a believer, that Ray would suffer a hideous consequence for abandoning us. I experienced persistent, ghastly nightmares, the kind you wake up from in a cold sweat, trying to scream, but nothing comes out.

Years went by and I had to raise myself, and obviously, I made very bad decisions. I started hanging out with kids who came from families like mine, and we would pass time committing petty crimes like stealing and truancy. I even started drinking a little, but who could blame me? I had come by it honestly and I believed if it was good for Laura, it would be good for me too. It allowed me to forget the things that were wrong with my life, and I figured it did the same for her.

I entered my teenage years with so many questions and didn't have a reliable source to turn to. Ray was gone and my mom was unreachable. I had no more teachers to lean on since I stopped attending class in the ninth grade. I ended up getting the answers to my questions, the wrong ones, from the kids I hung out with who had as little, or even less, life experience than I did. I made so many mistakes, and needless to say, my errors in judgement brought police and social workers to our home, time and again, wondering what kind of show Laura was running. Luckily, officers took pity at the sight of our home and no charges were ever laid.

Eventually though, our unseemly family dynamic caught up with us. With an absent father and an incompetent mother, I was placed into the foster care system. Laura was so badly off by then that I'm sure she hardly noticed that I was gone. Sure, she fought for me at the beginning, again with her empty promises, this time to the court, that she would change. But ultimately, she stopped fighting. The last time I saw her, Laura had shown up to the courthouse intoxicated, and when they deemed her an unfit parent for good, she declared loudly, "It was not my job to make her life bearable," as though absolving herself from the parental responsibilities she had signed up for. After that, I bounced around from foster home to foster home, each time being too much of a burden for the parents who took me in.

Finally, I ended up with Mr. and Mrs. Russell. They lived in a beautiful, two-storey, Victorian home in Cooper's Mills, a quiet village in Lincoln County. It was nothing like I had ever seen. On the outside, there were turrets and dormers and a gabled roof. On the inside, it was complete with decorative woodwork, bright colours and large windows. They were known for taking in misbehaved kids like me, though I proved to be a challenge, even for them. But there was something about them; they knew how to rein me in. I got away with less, and this made me want to please them more. It was the first time in years that I had discipline and instead of rebelling, I delighted in it, knowing I was in a home where people cared. The Russells were not like the other foster parents before them. They weren't taking in kids for the payoff. They had money. They were good people who truly wanted to help. In their home I found a healthy and righteous environment, where there were no loud arguments or intoxicated parents, at least, not at the beginning.

Luckily, I had arrived before I had become too far gone, and basking in their kindness, I started to thrive. I went back to school, and I actually got good grades. I helped out around the house, even laughed at times and slept dreamlessly, half forgetting about my previous life with Ray and Laura.

Trust me; this didn't happen overnight. I was enrolled in therapy as part of my rehabilitation and I started to work out my demons.

I was sixteen years old by this time and as I healed, my heart softened. With counseling, I decided to forgive Ray for leaving. I could see that being married to Laura had become a heavy anchor that was dragging him, slowly pulling him beneath the water's skin as he gasped for air, fighting for the life he'd once known.

Ray had come to an impasse. He could either drown in a cold, dark sea of pain and resentment, or he could leave. I figured that he loved me and must have considered my well-being, but he had a choice to make and he settled on the latter. Believe me, I know Ray was selfish, leaving me there to fend for myself with my alcoholic mother, but time is an excellent healer. I had made peace with his decision, knowing that we had both been offered a second chance. As for Laura, I remained indifferent. It was going to take a lot more therapy for me to absolve her from the sins of her past.

***

In the months I had been with the Russells, my neatly appointed room housing two other single beds, many girls came and went, their stays never long. Some of them became old enough to move into group homes while others were placed back with their parents, or had been moved to other foster care facilities. But, in June of 1999, a girl my age, Sarah, had come to live with the Russells, veiled in the same despair and bitterness that all of us prior to her had arrived in. She stood in the doorway, saddled with heavy baggage. Not the kind that came in the form of a suitcase like Ray's, but the kind that invaded and burdened a kid's heart.

Sarah kept to herself, and I was careful to give her the time and space she needed to assimilate to her new surroundings. I was curious about Sarah and was craving her friendship. She seemed lonely, but then, so was I. As a child, I found it difficult to make friends, and as a teenager, it was no different. Sure, I had acquaintances in the past, the local riffraff, but I wanted a true companion, someone I could talk to, a person who would listen and support me and show loyalty. Sarah, unfortunately, had been reluctant in pursuing a relationship with me, but I didn't hold this against her. I had been in her position once before, so I waited patiently, making a conscious effort not to push, careful not to open old wounds. Instead, I'd distract her with conversations about *Destiny's Child* and *Alicia Keys*. She'd nod and give me a shy smile, but then she would carry on with her own business.

Eventually, July came, and while school was out, I immersed myself in reading anything I could get my hands on. I knew how to read when I arrived, but I'd never found joy in it, besides which, we never had any books lying around our house. On the contrary, the Russels had shelves of novels, and I'd allow the written words to transport me to many lands in different eras in time, past and future, away from the banality of the lonely summer days. But thankfully, through the summer months Sarah remained an occupant of one of the beds and for a long while, it was just the two of us; that's when the transformation began.

Sarah emerged from her shell. The privacy and time that I'd allowed her seemed to have paid off as our earlier, one-sided chats about current musicians turned into conversations that lasted for hours. I talked to her about Ray and Laura, and she told me about her life before coming to the Russells. As it turned out, our histories were similar having grown up in households tainted by alcohol abuse and where routines, rules and support did not exist. But in Sarah's case, it was Becky, her mother, who had fled into the night, leaving her alone with her father, Martin, who was emotionally and physically abusive. With every insult and lift of his hand, Sarah's internal brokenness grew increasingly broad as she longed for a way out. Luckily, he was never prudent of where he left the bruises, nor was she careful to cover them up. Sarah hadn't been brave enough to report the abuse herself, but she'd hoped that someone would notice and call the authorities. Eventually, someone did notice, a teacher, if I remember correctly, and she was finally relieved of the life she so desperately wanted to escape.

In no time, it had reached September, and we were back at school. Gratefully, the two of us were placed in the same classes. I helped her with her reading and writing, and she showed me how to apply makeup and style hair, something, among the many things, Laura had never taught me. Our friendship became a two-way street that thrived, not only on our common experiences, but on our differences as well. Sarah remained bitter, but her rough edges began to smooth. Unfortunately, her foul mouth had gone unaffected.

Late into the night, we'd fill the room with secrets and the many shameful stories of our past. As we unburdened ourselves of our trauma, it felt like the walls surrounding us had absorbed and freed us of their cumbrous weight. I wondered how many more painful tales the drywall could take before it collapsed before our eyes. We continued on like this, relishing in the relationship we'd forged, more like sisters than friends, until one Sunday afternoon, late in October, well after the green leaves on the maples had turned bright orange and red and had fallen to the ground, there was an urgent banging at the door.

Surprised by the explosive knock, Sarah turned to me and exclaimed, "Who the fuck could that be?"

CHAPTER 5

The Confession

(October 1999)

Gazing down from our bedroom window, I could see a nondescript, four-door, navy blue sedan parked out front of the Russell's Victorian. "Shhhhhhh." I held a finger to my lips trying to quiet Sarah, while I eavesdropped on the conversation going on downstairs. Having recognized the vehicle, I put my ear up to the wall and through the insulation, I could hear a female's voice speaking to Mrs. Russell. Over the muffled sound, I confirmed that the visitor was Miss Davies from the Child Welfare Department. She was the appointed social worker for the Russells. She had been the one to bring Sarah and me here, but also came from time to time to pluck the girls away. Worried that she had come for one of us, I cracked the door open an inch to listen more closely.

"You've always been so wonderful with the children we've sent to you, Mrs. Russell and we've recently received word from the school that both Rita and Sarah are coming along quite well in their studies."

"Thank you, Miss Davies," she replied with a genuine tone of gratitude, delighted the efforts that she and Mr. Russell put into the kids had not gone unnoticed. "We get so much joy from watching the children flourish in our care."

"That's very good to hear, Mrs. Russell," she paused briefly. "Which brings me to the reason that I'm here," Miss Davis continued, able to segue right into her request. With both enthusiasm and a morsel of apprehension, she came to her point. "We were wondering if you had the time and space for one more girl in your home?"

With a pang of relief, and a bit of sadness that the vacancy being filled would likely put an end to my cherished late-night chats with Sarah, I closed the door, dismissing the rest of the exchange. While filling Sarah in on what I'd overheard, Mrs. Russell came to our bedroom door announcing that a girl named Suzie Hutchinson would be coming to stay, and that we should make her feel welcome. Without being given a choice, we agreed reluctantly and before we knew it, Miss Davies had returned with the strange girl. She must have been waiting in the car, which would explain the desperation in Miss Davies' banging at the front door.

Suzie's complexion was ghostly, her eyes bathed in dark makeup and lips drenched in a bright red shade lending to her gloomy pallor. She didn't speak as she entered the bedroom, tossing her filthy bag on top of the pristinely made bed. Sarah and I looked at each other, hesitant to engage with the interloper, who was giving no indication that she was remotely interested in making small talk. But the sadness in her eyes had brought me back in time to my first day in this house. I considered the loneliness I had felt, fiercely longing to make a connection with someone, and I decided to make the first move.

"I like your T-shirt Suzie. It's very retro," I shot out in the moment, thinking of nothing more intelligent to say.

"It's *Pink Floyd*, you moron. They're a psychedelic pop group, not retro," she answered facetiously, rolling her eyes like she had never heard anything more ridiculous.

I changed the subject promptly, waving off the slight as first day jitters, extending one more olive branch, and asked, "Are you from Lincoln County?"

But I was met with the very same derision as she responded sneeringly, never taking her eyes from her bag, "What are you, a cop?"

Deciding to abandon the mission and leave Suzie to unpack her things on her own, I grabbed Sarah's elbow, leading her out into the hallway.

"Where are we going?" Sarah asked, annoyed that she was being forced from her room by the newcomer's indignity.

"Let's get out of here, give her some space," I suggested, understanding that we were getting nowhere with Suzie at this point.

"Okay," Sarah sighed, "but that zombie girl better not mess with my shit while we're gone."

Making our way to the mud room, we punched our arms into our coat sleeves and waved goodbye to Mrs. Russell, who was, as usual, fussing in the kitchen, a tartan apron draped over her neatly pressed clothing. The two of us stepped outside into the blustery winds that ravaged the autumn day in Coopers Mills. The nearly bare tree limbs offered a clear view of the crisp blue sky, and I'm not sure if it was the fresh air or just being away from Suzie, but I could sense that our moods were beginning to lighten. Wrapping our jackets tightly around us, we strolled, carefree through the streets, taking in the musty, sweet smell of the decaying leaves as they crunched under the rubber soles of our boots, briefly forgetting about Suzie's arrival.

CHAPTER 6

The Confession

(November 1999)

Four weeks passed quickly, and Suzie still hadn't warmed up to Sarah and I, but not for our lack of trying. We invited her out with us several times and tried to introduce her to people at school, but she consistently brushed us off and never very kindly. Her bad attitude and dismal presence in the house were making her impossible to be around. I was tempted to go to the Russells with this, but then thought better of it, hoping a little more time would be the answer to breaking Suzie in. Despite everything, the three of us had more in common than one would think, all of us being only children from broken homes.

In the meantime, we did our best to avoid her, spending as much time as we could outside of the house. It was finally the weekend, so the two of us decided to take in a movie at the Tinsel-Town theatre. We'd heard *Clueless* was not to be missed.

We sat side by side in the theatre, sharing a bag of popcorn drenched in melted butter, sipping our single jumbo soda from two separate straws. We laughed and we cried. I think we even cheered at the end and stayed seated for the credits, prolonging our stay in the comfort of the theatre. It was rare that the two of us got to see a movie, so we dragged out the experience until the lights came on and the custodian picked up the discarded trash.

Sarah and I exited through the heavy glass doors following the show. We walked, arms entwined, relishing in our time together, away from the house and away from Suzie.

"I want to be Cher Horowitz," I shouted, staring up at her very chic image on the marquee, her character's desire to do good deeds appealing to my kind nature.

"Well, if you're Cher, then I'm Tai, friends for infinity," Sarah smiled, and I felt the warmth of my best friend as she leaned in close to me.

"You know the movie was adapted from Jane Austen's novel *Emma*, right?" I said smartly, waiting for Sarah's response.

"How the fuck do you know so much shit, Rita?" Sarah exclaimed in her usual profanity, to which I had become accustomed and now found strangely endearing.

Mockingly, I waved the periodical I had picked up from the theatre's lobby and replied, "I read it in this magazine."

We laughed as we trudged along the sidewalk, the light snow blanketing last month's mulched leaves. But suddenly, we came to an abrupt pause, passing a sullen figure on the road. It was Suzie, cloaked in a dark hoodie that was covering the majority of her pale face, though she was still recognizable. She marched past us, unaware she had been seen, so playing sleuths, we decided to follow her.

She led us off the main street to a menacing laneway where we thought only stray animals and tweakers ventured to go. We stood back, spying from the shadows, as Suzie entered the back street, wrapping her arms around a man whose figure was difficult to make out. As our eyes adjusted to the dim light, we could see that he was older than Suzie, with black, wavy hair and a jutted chin. She thrust her pelvis wildly against his groin as their lips met, the view making us feel uncomfortable, but at the same time, captivated and reluctant to look away. He unbuckled his belt and unzipped his pants before reaching around her waist to unbutton her jeans. He pulled back her hood with his free hand, brushing her hair to one side as he kissed her neck. He guided her urgently toward a dark-coloured, larger sized vehicle and opened the back door, pushing her in.

Very quietly, Sarah took another step closer, hoping to get a better look at the man, while I hovered closely behind, spying over her shoulder. Awash in puzzlement, Sarah tilted her head while I squinted my eyes as the illumination from the car light shed momentarily over his face. Our brains were slow to process the visual information, but, eventually, our jaws dropped in unison, staring open-mouthed into the alley. Initially, stunned and unable to react, we stood frozen until Sarah knitted her brow and screeched, "Is that . . .?"

Cupping my hand over Sarah's mouth before she could finish, I pulled her in the opposite direction towards the main road as we heard the car door slam behind them. Hoping we had gone undetected, we ran quickly, and unable to catch our breath, we didn't speak the entire way home. When we finally reached the Russell's, we opened the door and fell inside, meeting a succulent aroma coming from the kitchen.

After removing out boots and making our way into the front hallway, we saw Mrs. Russell as she entered the dining room, placing a tray of roasted chicken with all the fixings onto a beautifully set table. "I hope you girls are hungry," she grinned.

"We ate popcorn at the movies," Sarah replied quickly, neither of us having an appetite after what we had just seen.

Mrs. Russell looked disheartened, her amusement disappearing abruptly from her face. So, in an attempt to ingratiate her, I immediately interjected, "Well, we could always eat," elbowing Sarah, willing her to take a seat at the table.

We took our chairs and dug into the feast with as much enthusiasm as we could muster up, the grotesque image still knocking us sideways. Sarah lifted the serving tongs, plumping for the dishes stacked with sweet potatoes and cheesy cauliflower. Placing just enough food on her plate to satisfy Mrs. Russell, Sarah asked as casually as possible, "Will Mr. Russell be joining us tonight?"

I kicked her under the table.

"I don't think so dear. He's been called to a late meeting," she claimed, stabbing the gravy-soaked chicken with a sterling silver utensil and then shoving a forkful into her mouth. "It seems like business is multiplying these days, which I suppose is not a bad thing," she smiled, her facial expression so obviously not in tune with her emotions.

Sarah and I sat muted, awkwardly feeding ourselves with small bites from our plates. My mind began to flood with doubt and denial, though I was certain of what I'd seen. With no idea what to say next, Mrs. Russell broke the uncomfortable silence and asked, "Did you girls enjoy the movie?"

CHAPTER 7

The Confession

(November 1999)

The three of us padded the remainder of our dinner together with hollow conversation, recapping the film and discussing our plans for Thanksgiving. Mrs. Russell, barely eating as she pushed her food from one side of the plate to the other, told us she would make a proper holiday feast and that it is tradition to spend the day watching the parade and our team play football. On any other day, this idea would have seemed inviting, unmatched by anything Sarah or I had experienced growing up. However, today, the notion of all of us sitting down together after what we'd seen was making my stomach feel uneasy.

"That sounds great Mrs. Russell," I gushed, counterfeiting my current distaste.

"For heaven's sake, dear, how many times have I asked you to call me Grace? Mrs. Russell makes me sound old," she said, patting my wrist before getting up to clear the table.

Grace wasn't old; she was only twenty eight, just eleven years our senior now, both Sarah and I having celebrated our seventeenth birthdays in August, another thing we had in common. She was stunning with her huge brown eyes, unblemished olive complexion, and long, shiny black hair that she usually wore in a flawless up-do. And, of course, she had great taste, having graduated with a degree in fashion design, and was always impeccably dressed in the newest trends.

"I'm sorry Mrs . . . I mean, Grace," I answered, trying desperately to mask the disquiet roiling inside me. Until today, I'd always found it so easy to speak with her, but with my head still in the alley, I was blundering, trying to find my words.

Abruptly, the door opened, and after cleaning off his shoes, Mr. Russell entered the dining room. "Hi everyone. I'm home," he greeted us cheerfully, removing his coat and throwing it onto a wingback chair. "It smells delicious in here," he added, then apologized for being late, articulating himself so remorsefully that if Sarah and I hadn't known better, we'd have believed he was actually sincere.

Grace entered the front hall to greet her husband, Mr. Russell pulling her close. He gave her a respectful kiss on the cheek, a blatant transition from his animalistic behavior earlier that evening.

Letting go of her waist, Mr. Russell asked us, "What did you girls get up to tonight?" While he waited for our answer, he shuffled through a tall stack of mail, mindlessly staring at each envelope before tossing them aside.

"We saw a movie," Sarah answered nervously, still unsure whether we'd been seen in the alley.

"Where's Suzie?" Mr. Russell inquired, looking up as he peered around the room.

"She left earlier, but she didn't mention where she was going," Grace answered, sounding concerned. "Did she mention anything to either of you girls?"

"No, she didn't say," I said, fidgeting with a spoon left on the dinner table. "She was in our room when we left." Sarah and I exchanged a discerning look and I wondered if either of the Russells had picked up on it. I suspected that Mr. Russell would be anxious, discovering that we had been in town, but if he was, he certainly didn't show it.

"Well, let's hope she'll be home soon. It's starting to get late and very cold out," Grace fussed, looking at her watch and then at her husband. "You must be hungry love. Let me fix you something to eat," she insisted, hurrying back towards the kitchen.

Stopping Grace in her tracks, he answered, "I ate at the office, darling, but thank you. I think I'll head upstairs and have a shower before turning in. Let me know when Suzie gets home. The girls really shouldn't be out this late, Grace."

With that said, Mr. Russell climbed the steps, disappearing into his bedroom, closing the door behind him. I immediately felt the tightness between my shoulder blades release; his presence caused the muscles in my neck to become rigid. It was unnerving hearing him lie to Grace, but worse still, scolding her for letting Suzie stay out so late, seeing it was him who had kept her out. I felt like a loose cannon, ready to break free with the truth. But I inhaled deeply, releasing a long breath, and selfishly, with it, any ideas of jeopardizing our home with the truth.

Embroiled in the dark thought of Mr. Russell and Suzie together, I felt a mingling of emotions twitching inside of me, pity for Grace for being lied to, but also bewilderment at the entire situation. Grace was kind and good-natured, but then, he was too, well, at least I thought he was until this evening. *"How could Mr. Russell be interested in Suzie,"* I wondered silently, picturing her ruddy, pale skin, earnestly aware of her ominous demeanor that was truly unalluring. She was the complete opposite of what he must have seen in Grace. She was an incredible foster mother, and it made me wonder why she never had any children of her own.

Shaking my head, I remembered Laura telling me once in her slurred, intoxicated speech, never to be fooled by men, that they were all pigs and only after one thing. I thought, at the time, that she was just spouting off her usual drunken rhetoric, but now I was beginning to believe that she was onto something.

Sarah and I returned to our room following the excruciating dinner, relieved that it was only the two of us as Suzie had yet to return home. We remained speechless for a few minutes, addled by Mr. Russell's evident lack of concern for what he'd done, until Sarah spoke up. "I'm scared, Rita. Has he ever tried anything like that with you?"

"God no! I'm as shocked as you are. He's never been anything but respectful towards me. I'd always thought he was really cool."

"What about the other girls that were here before me? Did any of them ever mention anything about him being, like, fucking offside?"

"No, not to me anyway," I replied, but I couldn't help thinking that Suzie would not have been the first girl he had done this with, just perhaps the first time he had been caught.

"Do you think Grace knows?" Sarah pressed, remembering Grace's odd reaction to her question regarding Mr. Russell's whereabouts.

"No way," I countered in disbelief. "I mean, if she had any idea, she would have said something to him, right? She wouldn't let this go on. She was just pissed that he was going to be late, again!"

I momentarily scrutinized the notion of Grace knowingly allowing Mr. Russell to carry on like that with one of the foster girls, but immediately dismissed the idea as ridiculous. "Certainly, she wouldn't," I exclaimed, answering my own question, then posing another. "Could we have been wrong? Maybe it wasn't Mr. Russell after all."

Sarah looked at me incredulously, as though I was trying to cover for his behaviour. "Of course it was him, Rita, don't be stupid! We saw him with our own eyes."

Maybe I was being naive, or maybe I simply didn't want to believe it, having finally felt, for the first time, safe and at peace under anyone's roof. "I know, I know," I interjected. "I'm still just trying to make sense of it all," my words lingering in the air.

We remained quiet, submerged in our dingy thoughts until Sarah finally voiced, filling in the gap, "What could we possibly be missing?"

CHAPTER 8

The Confession

(November 1999)

Grace sat at the edge of their bed, biting nervously at her fingernails, unsure how she would broach the subject of her husband's late arrival home. Mr. Russell emerged from the shower, entering their bedroom with a towel wrapped around his lean, armored waist, leaving his broad chest exposed. His posture always emanated confidence, and most times, Grace could not help feeling like a shrinking violet in his company. Though she, herself, was a very attractive woman, she didn't radiate the same self-assurance that her husband appeared to.

Deciding to quash her uneasiness, she pasted on an artificial smile and in a higher octave than her normal pitch, she asked, "Did she show up?"

Circumventing her inquisitive gaze, Mr. Russell turned from Grace, desperately trying to avoid the discussion they were about to have. Grace knew all along that her husband was uncomfortable with her ghastly request, referring to it as insanity and a last-ditch effort from an unstable woman. But begrudgingly, she believed, he assented to her proposal as a means to an end.

Feeling her eyes fixated upon him, he grabbed at a T-shirt, throwing it on to cover himself. Silence hung between them for a few moments before he answered, "Yes Grace, you know she did."

"And?" Grace asked, eager for more information.

"And what?" He answered, shrugging his shoulders.

"Did everything go, you know, as planned?"

"Do you want all of the sordid details?" He asked sarcastically.

"No, I mean . . ." She hesitated. "No, I don't. But what did she say?"

"What do you mean what did she say? She didn't say anything!" Mr. Russell said, wearing an amused grin, reminding Grace that his clandestine meeting with Suzie in the alley wasn't intended for conversation.

"You know what I'm asking, Grant," she answered, looking at him now with a hardened focus. "Do you think she'll tell anyone?"

"No Grace," he sighed. "You know that she needs this as much as we do," Mr. Russell reminded her. Relenting, he took her hand and gave it a reassuring squeeze.

Grace bowed her head and exhaled deeply, releasing the heightened anxiety that had built up furiously in her chest. She removed a tissue from her pocket and dabbed the corner of her eyes as she started to sob. She wasn't quite sure if the tears that fell were of relief, her plan in motion and their secret safe, or ones of dismay at the idea of Grant having sex with another woman, or in this case, a teenager. She shuddered at the thought of it and shook her head, trying to remove the aberrant image from her mind, choosing to focus solely on her goal.

It had been almost two years since she and Grant had began trying to conceive a child, her friends all beating her to the punch. She had sat miserably through baby shower after baby shower, putting on a good face for the absurd party games, always trying to be a good sport. Grace had lived a charmed life, but it seemed as though her luck had run out. She'd been told by the fertility specialist that her chances of becoming pregnant were low after the two of them got tested following months of failed attempts. Of course, it was her problem, not his, which did not surprise Grace in the least. It was just another reason for her to feel inferior to her husband.

They had tried a couple of rounds of in vitro fertilization but, again, had no success. Unfortunately, surrogacy wasn't an option. Grace had done her research and heard that it could run them over a quarter of a million dollars with all the medical bills and so on, and, while they did do well for themselves, with a heavy mortgage, and her not working, they didn't have that kind of cash.

She came up with the idea of fostering children to fill the emptiness in their home and was taken aback when the agency asked if they were willing to take in a teen aged girl. She ruefully agreed, figuring a flat-out *no* would ruin her chances of being considered for a foster-to-adopt home should an infant need placement in the future. Grace had set up the master bedroom like a dorm, getting carried away as she made space for three foster children.

There was an influx of girls who turned up and left following the arrival of the first young lady, and their home became a revolving door for teenagers, all with their sad stories, all desperate for love and attention. Grace happily immersed herself in caring for these troubled souls, fastidiously catering to their every need and desire. She was vigilant in helping with homework, serving healthy meals, taking them to their appointments, all the things a mother would do for her own children. Although she enjoyed looking after the girls, sometimes, the long hours and the efforts she'd put into them would burn at her, her one dream of having her own baby still not being met.

Then one day, doused in self-pity and nearly at her breaking point, Grace had a fleeting thought that sent a shiver up her spine. With her belly fluttering, she earnestly tried to push the idea from her mind, but slowly, it grew until it consumed her, and she could think of little else. *"Could one of these girls possibly be the key to what she ached for?"* Grace calculated. In that moment, she'd felt an equal measure of hope and shame at the thought of it. However, her desperation obviously outweighed her good sense and she allowed her mind to run with her idea.

Not long afterward, on a Friday night while their girls were out at their very first high school dance, she hesitantly proposed her plan to Grant, introducing it slowly and meticulously to him over a bottle of wine. As she expected, the idea landed like a lead balloon, her request causing him to spit up the expensive cabernet and to just about tumble from his chair.

"Have you lost your mind?" he asked bitterly.

Grace was aware that her unrelenting desire to have children had developed into an obsession, but she was incensed by her husband's accusation that she had seemingly gone off of her head.

"No, I haven't lost my mind! Can you think of a better idea?"

"Yes Grace, I can. What about no children at all?" he answered facetiously, her ceaseless thirst to have a family now driving a wedge between them.

Grant had been content with the way things were before becoming foster parents, a childless couple, able to get up and go on a whim. Grace knew this. It was what they talked about, even before marriage. It was what they had agreed upon. But, soon after their vows, he could see she was slipping into a dark place, watching her sorority sisters of Glendon College having babies, sending family Christmas photos, and slowly drifting away, busy with their families. He thought he had given Grace the world, a beautiful home, vacations in Cabo and fine jewelry. But it wasn't enough to snuff out her maternal yearning.

When he agreed to start trying and they had had no luck, he'd hoped Grace might let the whole idea go. But then visits to the fertility clinics started, and good money after bad was spent, still rendering a negative outcome. And when that didn't work, she brought up fostering a child, to which he was opposed, but eventually gave in, expecting a baby, not nearly full-grown adults.

Now, almost a year later, she had yet another supplication. "Just hear me out," she begged. Grant, worn down by her insistence, and a bit tipsy from the wine, agreed reluctantly to tune in. He listened to Grace intently as she went through her plan from A to Z, the who, the what, the where, and the when. He already knew why. And for all of Grant's questions, she had the answers.

Currently sharing their third bottle, the alcohol lubricating the conversation, Grace noticed her husband staring attentively at her over the rim of his glass, looking more relaxed as he sipped slowly from the goblet. Then, at long last, to her surprise, Grant, now inebriated, she found him grinning warily in compliance.

The next morning while Grant slept off his hangover, and before he could change his mind, Grace began to set her plan in motion. She'd have to choose the right person to make a party to her fiendish proposal, acknowledging that selecting the wrong girl would likely land her, and also Grant, in jail. She'd have to be a bit older, of legal age to consent; seventeen in New York State. Someone with no hope of reunification with her parents, a person incapable of rehabilitation, and finally, someone who would do anything for cold, hard cash.

But since the hatching of her unspeakable plan, the girls who came to stay were either too sweet, or too young, or too gossipy. She had considered me as a prospective candidate when I arrived, but I didn't satisfy Grace's qualifications. I was too innocent, too bright. Later on, there was Sarah, who had been closer to the image of whom Grace had had in mind. But despite her edginess and her foul mouth, she was sensitive and kindhearted in her own right. And then, Sarah and I became inseparable, constantly whispering in our room at all hours, sharing our secrets. No, neither of us would do. She was looking for more of a loner, a person who kept to themselves, uninterested in making friends. Someone who would go out on a limb, keep her mouth shut, and whose moral values were far less than questionable.

Finally, Suzie had come along, a teenager with an extensive rap sheet who, coincidentally, had been no stranger to the back pages of the newspaper, experienced in selling herself. While her history was unfortunate, a young girl with such a bleak past, and a long record of solicitation, this elated Grace. She was ideally suited for the task. Cautiously, she observed and studied Suzie's behaviour until she finally knew. This girl was exactly who she'd envisioned.

Now, still settled at the edge of their bed, Grace poised herself. She stuffed the wet tissue into her sleeve and sat upright and spoke with conviction. "You know I wouldn't have asked you to do this if we had another option."

"Enough!" Mr. Russell bristled with an audible tightening in his throat. His face reddened as he paced the chenille carpet back and forth, aware his temper had gotten the better of him. Lowering his voice, he forced a calm confidence and said, "Enough now darling. It's done. Now we wait."

Hopeful, Grace rubbed at her midsection, nodding effusively at her husband in agreement and repeating his words with optimism. "Yes, now we wait."

CHAPTER 9

The Confession

(November 1999)

After everyone had gone to bed, Suzie finally returned home. Pushing the door open, she stood in the dimly lit foyer and removed her coat and her boots. She called out in a resonating voice, "I'm home," her words echoing in the empty space. After receiving no answer, she bowed her head in relief, sighing with satisfaction at the moment to herself. She hung up her coat and ventured into the kitchen where Grace had left a foil-wrapped dinner plate in, set out almost as a thank you.

Suzie took the dish adorned with pink flowers on its edges, piled heavily with chicken and sweet potatoes, and tossed it recklessly into the microwave. She set the timer for two minutes and pulled up a chair at the kitchen table, guided only by the internal light flooding from the cooker. It was nearly ten-thirty, and she was delighted that no one had waited up for her. Suzie wasn't in the mood for the line of inquiry she expected from Grace or for any of my mindless attempts at conversation. She just wanted to enjoy the moment alone, an opportunity so rare for any of us at the Russells.

She watched the plate rotate around in the microwave, the food on top starting to bubble, emitting the aromatic smell of yams throughout the kitchen. She sat in the quiet, immersed in her thoughts, when the timer let out three rather loud beeps in a row, broadcasting that her dinner was sufficiently heated and ready to eat. Suzie hoped it hadn't woken anyone up and for a second or two, she listened at the foot of the stairs but didn't hear anyone stirring. She opened the door to the microwave quietly and reached in with dish towel for the hot plate.

She had gone to a bar outside of Cooper's Mills after her surreptitious rendezvous with Mr. Russell. She was only seventeen years old, but already looked twenty-one, her life experience prematurely ageing her. She'd fancied a drink and disregarded her curfew. But as far as Suzie was concerned, with the enormous secret that she was holding over the Russell's heads, she could break a few house rules now and again. Although she was feeling smug, she figured, she wouldn't push it too far just yet, still months away from her pay-out.

Miss Davies had given the couple high praise as she drove Suzie to the Russell's house. "They're different from most of the foster parents you've met. They're empathetic, honest and stable people. And there will be other girls there your age. Maybe you'll make some friends."

Miss Davies always tried to over-sell the homes she was bringing Suzie to, likely in hopes, she supposed, that it would give her motivation to behave and possibly turn her life around. Sadly, her efforts were habitually made in vain as each set of placement parents would eventually call and suggest that she'd be better off in another type of environment. Miss Davies always knew what these words meant...that Suzie was no longer welcome.

Suzie didn't take in much of what Miss Davies was saying that afternoon. She was going to be eighteen next year, and she knew this would likely be her last stop before going out on her own. But for that, she needed money. She stared out the passenger side window as they drove through town toward the Russell's. The houses looked a lot nicer than what Suzie was accustomed to which piqued her interest. Even if they were as annoying as the people previous to them, they would probably have a few expensive things that she could pocket and hawk.

Miss Davies parked the car while Suzie watched on as she ran towards the Russell's door. Miss Davies had been hopeful that the Russell's wouldn't deny her request, and had already tucked away Suzie's bag in the back seat.

During her initial few weeks at the Russell's, Suzie could sense she was being watched, perhaps even scrutinized, by Grace. It made Suzie feel uneasy. She didn't appreciate being spied on and wondered what Grace was up to. She was young, but she wasn't stupid;

far from it. Being out in the world had sharpened her survival skills, and part of that was learning how to read people more carefully. Perhaps Grace didn't trust her, or maybe spying on Suzie was her way of getting to know her better, but what happened next was not what she'd expected.

Less than a month had gone by since her arrival at the den of iniquity when Grace, surreptitiously, approached her with her wild proposal. In that second, Suzie had thought the whole thing was some kind of sick joke, a way to test Suzie's integrity. Holding her side, doubled over with laughter, she looked into Grace's eyes and snickered, "You can't be serious?"

But Grace wasn't laughing, and in a bid to camouflage the sound of their voices and Suzie's laughter, she grabbed at her sleeve and pulled her into her bedroom, closing the solid oak door tightly behind them. Grace sat her down on the bed and, speaking in a hushed tone, meeting her eye with a stern gaze, an indication that this was no laughing matter, she gave Suzie a very detailed explanation of what would be expected of her, finishing off with, "And at the end of it all, you will walk away with twenty-five thousand dollars! Take it and disappear . . . go anywhere you want, far away from Lincoln County."

Confused, but intrigued, Suzie stood up and took a few steps backward, still facing Grace head-on. Sizing her up, she eyed her from head to toe. *Does this crazy woman really want her to have Mr. Russell's baby? Is she completely insane? Can she even be trusted to make good on her promise?* With the experience of her past stacked heavily in her memory, she knew she was better off not relying on anyone's word.

Suzie was placed in the foster care system at five years old by her mother who vowed that she would be back for her. "Don't cry." she breathed into Suzie's ear. "Mommy loves you and as soon as I am feeling better, I'll come for you." She wiped the tears from Suzie's cheeks, kissed her on her forehead, and then turned and walked away, ultimately placing her in the arms of strangers. Suzie didn't know why her mother didn't feel well or where she was going, but she felt confident that she would, indeed, return for her.

Months went by and Suzie waited patiently, believing with her entire heart that her mother's word was gold. Every time she heard the sound of a car sputtering up the long, gravel driveway of her first of many foster homes, she would run to the window with a wide grin to greet her, each time, withering in disappointment. Even after several years passed and Suzie had bounced from one placement to another, she never gave up hope that her mother would find her.

But as she grew, her mother never came for her and Suzie's memories of the woman gradually began to fade until she could no longer remember the scent of her skin, the shape of her face, or even the colour of her eyes. Finally, the only thing Suzie had left of her mother was her unmet emotional needs, leading to her lack of self-worth and other abandonment issues.

Suzie's father was more of a cliché, a one-night stand who had never been in the picture. Learning more of her mother through the years, Suzie figured he was just a source of income for her, someone to hook up with in exchange for money or even drugs. She tried in desperation not to follow in her mother's footsteps but soon fell into her legacy, realizing that there was little to no way of escaping her wretched circumstances without the aid of some money in her pocket.

However, this offer from Grace was completely different from what she was used to, a few bucks in exchange for a hand job in the back seat of some dirty old man's car. It was a huge sum of money in the swap for a baby. Suzie refused to think of herself as a prostitute this time. She considered herself more of a businesswoman. A person who now had a sense of purpose, a girl who was going to take back her power. She had something that the Russells wanted and for all the times she had given herself away for a pittance, she was now going to collect her due with Mr. Russell. It wasn't dirty; it was transactional.

Once Grace had baited Suzie with the princely sum, she explained how the scheme would work. Grace laid it all out for her, when and where Suzie and Mr. Russell would meet, what Suzie would tell people, namely Miss Davies, when she fell pregnant, who would be responsible for her health care, and even what she should eat and drink. "And no weed," Grace demanded after detecting the skunky odour on her clothes just days before. "And above all," Grace emphasized, "You cannot tell anyone!"

Suzie didn't have to think about the proposition very long, it was a life-changing amount of money. Quid pro quo. The money in exchange for a child. She wasn't worried that she would become attached to the baby, she had no desire to be anyone's parent, and this was strictly business. Suzie had agreed to Grace's terms, but she had one condition, she wanted some cash upfront. Grace didn't hesitate. She agreed to five thousand dollars to start, but would dangle the final payment like a carrot in front of a horse to ensure the deal would get sealed.

Following the negotiations, Grace handed Suzie a calendar, asking her to map out her cycle. It was vile for her to think of Grant with Suzie, and she had hoped that if they tracked things correctly, it would only mean them 'hooking up' a few times at most. She thought of all the couples she knew who were years apart in age and tried to convince herself that what she was asking was not a big deal. Just eleven years between the two. But in the cold light of day some things would never be acceptable, and she knew that this was one of them. As a foster parent, in the eyes of the law, Mr. Russell was in a position of authority, and as such, the legal age to consent didn't carry any weight. Notwithstanding, it was already out there, and the wheels were in motion, and in the end, everyone would get what they wanted.

In the darkness, Suzie sat at the table for a few more moments, blindly scraping the last bites of her meal from her plate and shoving them into her mouth. *"Grace may not be able to have a baby, but she sure can cook,"* Suzie thought.

She also thought about what had happened earlier in the evening and felt not even a little remorse. Mr. Russell was a relatively handsome man, and she was nearly an adult herself. Besides, it was nothing she hadn't done before and he was much classier and more attractive than the pigs she'd been with prior him. And, of course, he came with a much larger payout. Maybe he would take her to a more suitable place next time, assuming there would be one, the car parked in a menacing alley made her feel a little cheap, despite her contentious history. Finally, she thought of the pot of gold at the end of the rainbow and smiled to herself. She had finally found a way to get out of there.

Suzie left the dirty plate on the counter before climbing the winding, oak staircase to our bedroom. She carelessly flung the door open without knocking, catching Sarah and me completely off guard as we lay in our beds in the blackness. She could have listened at the door first, but that wasn't her style. She was never concerned about what we had to say about her or even thought about her. We bored Suzie and, besides which, she had a lot to think about.

She flicked on the lamp beside her bed, paying us no mind, believing we considered her to be a third wheel, which surely, we did, especially now. Suzie attended to her business, fussing through her things, a mop of dark hair falling over her face, strategically blocking the two of us from her view.

Lifting myself up from the twin mattress with an elbow, I wiped at my eyes, pretending to have been asleep. I blithely acknowledged Suzie's intrusion and asked the question for which I knew there would be a contemptuous answer. "What have you been up to, Suzie?"

Tucking her bangs behind her ears, she lifted her head briefly to meet my inquisitive gaze. Not surprisingly, Suzie flung back with the same acidic inflection she had commonly used and answered, "None of you Goddamn business, that's what."

A feeling of rawness stretched through my stomach, and I rolled my eyes at her before plopping my head back down on the down-filled feather pillow. Sarah, who had no interest in engaging with Suzie, lay motionless in her bed, sensing my irritation. The two of us closed our eyes, hoping to find that a good night's sleep would bring some clarity in the morning.

Suzie dropped on her bed, seemingly unfazed by the exchange. She let some time pass, staring impatiently at the ornate clock on the wall that hung above my bed. When she was convinced we were both asleep, she grabbed at a diary that was strategically hidden from all of us, including the Russells, beneath a loose floorboard next to her bed. Reaching for her nightstand, she took out a pen and began writing. Suzie was many things, but she was not a fool. This diary was going to be her insurance policy should either of the Russells decide to double-cross her and not fulfil their end of the proposed agreement. She laid it all out, Grace's request and the specifics of her secret meeting with Grant. She designed it like a manifesto, complete and concise with every last detail, including times, dates and, most importantly, names.

CHAPTER 10

The Investigation

(April 2021)

Becoming restless, Detective Hollis rose from his chair for what seemed like the tenth time that hour. With his head bowed, he paced the minuscule length of the interview room, rubbing at his temples as he tried to process the new details. Lifting his eyes to meet Rita's, Detective Hollis asked with uncertainty, "You mean to tell me that Mrs. Russell offered to pay Suzie to have her husband's baby?" His eyebrows lifted high as he shifted his gaze back and forward, from Rita to her husband, waiting for an answer.

"Yes, she did. She wasn't the person we all thought she was," Rita responded after Rory gave her a nudge.

"And what kind of person was that?"

"Nurturing, caring. The kind of person you could have trusted to raise your own child. Obviously, everyone was wrong."

Detective Hollis cringed at her words. He hadn't seen this loathsome information coming. *What kind of monster would pay her foster child to bear children? Furthermore, what kind of person goes from zero to sixty overnight?* He questioned Rita's version of events, wondering whether this had been Grace's motivation for fostering children from the get-go. Perhaps she had spent months lying in wait for her prey. It seemed more likely that Mrs. Russell had been unbalanced from the very beginning, fooling Miss Davies and everyone at the childcare center into thinking she had the girls' best interest at heart. That it wasn't really the emptiness of her home that persuaded her to bring in the young ladies, that they had a designated purpose all along.

"Where is Mrs. Russell now?" the detective asked, bouncing on his feet.

"She died. Twenty years ago," Rita answered with no remorse, confirming it was not Grace who was currently lying in the morgue.

"And Mr. Russell?"

Rita raised her shoulders with a languid shrug. "Nobody knows."

While he tried to calm his frenzied thoughts, an officer pushed open the door and entered thoughtlessly, carrying a black, plastic forensic kit.

"Is this a bad time?" he asked unapologetically, disregarding his obvious intrusion.

"Your timing is perfect," Rory replied before the detective had an opportunity to chastise him for barging in. It was quite obvious that his client, his wife, needed a break and having those bags removed from her sweaty hands would serve as a welcomed comfort.

Detective Hollis held his tongue temporarily and nodded in agreement. After all, the faster he could get the samples to the lab, the faster he'd be able to confirm Rita's confession. "Take as much time as you need . . ." The detective paused, picking up the business card that the officer had thrown mindlessly on the table. "Constable Moran." Hollis called out his name and time of arrival for the recording before politely taking his leave.

Detective Hollis entered the hallway outside of the interrogation room, checking his mobile for messages. There had been one text from his wife, "Call me," time-stamped just after midnight. His index finger hovered over the keypad as he wondered if this call could wait until morning. But, deciding he owed his wife an explanation for his absence, he veered toward an empty interview room for privacy and dialled her telephone number.

"Hello, Patti," he said, managing to make his voice sound more upbeat than he'd felt.

"It's late," the woman noted with regard.

"I know. What time is it?" Detective Hollis asked, having lost track of the hour absorbed in Rita's story.

"It's two o'clock in the morning. Let me guess. You've caught a case," Patti answered acrimoniously.

"Yes, I'm interviewing a murder suspect." Detective Hollis justified himself, feeling guilty after having promised his wife that things in Maine would be different. He'd listened to the psychologists who had warned him about the effects of burnout, but being a cop was in his blood. Begrudgingly, he'd accepted the position in this sleepy town, figuring he could appease his wife and the doctors who had suggested that the dilatory pace would do him some good. He would still be in the game, just in the minors. But here he was, just weeks into the move, diving in, headfirst.

"How long will you be?"

"As long as it takes," he said, unintentionally losing his cool. The detective immediately apologized to his wife and carried on more civilly. "I'm going to be a while still."

There was an awkward pause in their conversation while Detective Hollis waited for an argument to come.

"Then I won't wait up," she huffed, immediately ending the call.

"Hello?" Hollis said into the static phone line, but there was nothing, only silence.

He looked at his mobile and shook his head, *"I'll deal with this later,"* he thought, rubbing the back of his neck, alleviating the tension that had been building up since he'd arrived at the park yesterday afternoon.

He leaned against the wall for support, his knees threatening to buckle beneath him, but at the sound of footsteps approaching, Detective Hollis forced himself to stand rigid as he turned his focus from his mobile to the man walking towards him from the other end of the hall.

Suddenly, he found himself staring at a man he'd once known very well, his face now worn and slightly weathered, an indication of a hard life lived in the trenches of this job. It was Detective Sergeant Wade Banks, his former colleague who had also moved to the hollows of Maine just a couple of years ago, hoping to ride out his remaining time with his feet propped comfortably up on a desk before his pension would kick in. They had been partners in the Robbery and Homicide squad, where they worked tirelessly, for several years, putting LA's most dangerous street thugs behind bars until Banks had climbed the ranks and they eventually lost touch.

"You look good, John," he grumbled wryly, the corners of his mouth giving a slight, but noticeable rise.

"Thanks."

"Who's your undertaker?" Banks laughed.

"Hilarious," Detective Hollis answered. He was accustomed to this back-handed banter between co-workers and had developed a thick skin, shielding him from the countless insults he'd met throughout his career. Just the same, he rubbed his palms against his face, trying to bring colour to his pale cheeks.

"I'd heard you'd come to the place where good detectives go to die, but I didn't want to believe it. Sorry I missed the welcome wagon, John. Carol and I just got back from holidays."

Detective Hollis didn't like being reminded that he'd taken a step down coming to the jerkwater town, but again, he decided to let the Detective Sergeant's indignant remark roll off of his back.

Pragmatically, he answered, "Yep, it's true, but it seems like there is no rest for the wicked, is there?" He stuck out his one empty hand, the other still clutching his mobile, to meet his superior officer's grip, which had gone flaccid and lifeless, a sign of what the passing years would have in store for him.

"Listen John," Detective Sergeant Banks replied, this time speaking with empathy. "I am truly sorry to hear about what happened in Los Angeles."

"Thank you, Wade," Detective Hollis answered, letting go of his old friend's hand.

"Any leads?"

"Not yet, but I'm keeping the lines of communication open with the department. Hopefully they'll catch a break."

"Well, you know I'm here for you and Patti if you need anything." Aware he had brought up a painful, distracting memory, the last thing Detective Hollis needed in the middle of a murder investigation, he quickly decided to change the subject. "So, what do you make of all this?" he asked with a fragment of excitement in his voice, the memories of big-city police work beginning to jostle his enthusiasm slightly.

"Honestly? I'm not sure yet. I don't know if you've heard, but there's been a confession."

"A confession?" Banks smirked. "Up to your old tactics I see."

"It's not like that," Detective Hollis grinned, aware of what the Detective Sergeant was inferring. This wasn't the time for old-school policing, phone books and dehydration. He hadn't forced anything. "Rita Morrison's admission came from her own free will."

"Hmmm, you've gone soft," Banks said, lifting a brow. "Well, in that case," he shrugged, thoughts of unreliable confessions at the forefront of his inquiry, "Is her confession solid?"

"I think so," the detective answered sceptically. "But I'm not through with her yet."

"Then keep digging. In the meantime, if you think she is telling you the truth, get her in front of a judge in the morning."

Detective Hollis wished it could be that simple. He had witnessed Rita's confession, along with everyone else in the park, and had patiently listened to her story in the interrogation room. But he was only halfway to where he wanted to be before parading her into a courtroom. He needed to know why Rita had killed the still, unidentified woman, decade's after she had left the foster home. Hopefully, Constable Moran would not be long. Detective Hollis felt the brevity of a long night ahead of him.

"Good to see you again John. Again, if there's anything you need, just let us know." He patted Detective Hollis on his shoulder, and then, placing his hands into his pockets, he turned, making his way back to his office.

"Thanks, Wade." Detective Hollis called out, watching his old friend straggle away, an unruffled air about him following close behind. He'd been on the job for nearly thirty years and Rita's case was not going to keep him up at night. He'd given up; that much was obvious. But Detective Hollis hadn't. He needed to uncover the truth.

He peered through the window at Rita, her husband and the forensics officer. Rory was rubbing Rita's back, trying to invigorate his exhausted wife while the officer took swabs of her hands and dug under her fingernails. He noted that Rory also looked in poor condition, staying up all night being a young man's game. There was a discernible age gap between them; he was at least ten years her senior. But he put the observation out of his mind when he felt a buzzing in his pocket.

He reached for his phone and looked at the message. "I'm sorry. I'm just worried about you." Detective Hollis felt relieved. He didn't want to continue with the investigation while in a row with his wife, especially since she'd been so supportive. He knew that this move was difficult for her and that she was hurting as badly as he was, perhaps even more so, but she always had his back.

He was about to send Patti a text, apologizing for being curt, when Constable Moran opened the door. "I'll have these back as soon as humanly possible."

"How long?"

"Between six to twelve hours. I'll make sure they make it their top priority at the lab."

"Well I can't imagine there being anything more important than solving a murder, is there?" the detective asked caustically.

"As I said, it will be a priority." The constable ran off with several bags carrying the microscopic proof that would corroborate, or perhaps disprove, Rita's confession. DNA was always strong evidence. Things were starting to move forward, and this pleased the detective.

Rory fell in line behind the officer. He drew in a breath before speaking and persevered. "Let's get this over with," he said, his weariness evident both in his voice and his deportment.

Detective Hollis slid his mobile back into his pocket and looked squarely into Rory's face. "I'm ready," he answered back.

He needed to get through this swiftly, figuring his relationship with his wife depended on it. But his gut instinct told him to take his time, to listen to the facts carefully, although he wasn't sure he was in the right mindset. Regardless, he took his seat at the dilapidated table, elbows perched, waiting in thirsty anticipation.

CHAPTER 11

The Confession

(November 1999)

Thanksgiving arrived and Grace made her finest turkey feast, complete with stuffing, potatoes, and pumpkin pie which she served atop a beautifully adorned, merry table. She liked to make all of us feel at home, but more importantly, she yearned to feel maternal. She dreamed surreptitiously of the day she would have her own family to whom she would serve a holiday meal to. She was even starting to secretly knit a few baby things in both pink and blue wool while she waited for the good news.

At times, however, she fretted with uncertainty, worried her plan may not pan out as she'd hoped. But Grace pushed herself to think positively and batted away her feelings of doubt, allowing herself to become carried away, daydreaming about her future with Grant and their new baby, who, she assumed, would arrive in the new year.

As the weeks went by, the entire household carried on with their routines. The three of us went to school, or at least Sarah and I did. Mr. Russell was busy at work, and Grace studied the calendar, hoping to find that Suzie had been late. By now, as far as she knew, the two of them had been together twice. She scheduled these meetings herself, like a secretary booking a dental appointment. She aligned the hook-ups perfectly with Suzie's estimated ovulation dates, as she was familiar with these things from when she had tried desperately to get pregnant, turning her sex life with her husband into a timetable.

She could barely look Grant in the eye when he casually sauntered home after what should have been their second encounter, pretending like it had been a regular day at the office. Following their conversation in their bedroom last month, she hesitated to ask how *it* went, refusing to, again, be reprimanded for her incredulous ask. Instead, Grace waited impatiently for a moment where she might get Suzie alone, anxious for updates, to get her to pee on a stick. But it appeared that lately, she had been avoiding Grace. Silently, however, she prayed for the best, heedless of the potential consequences of her actions.

***

In an effort to keep the family dynamic in our home in play, Grace suggested that we have a movie night, to which Sarah and I were very receptive. With a fire roaring in the alcove, we gathered around the big screen, draped in blankets, waiting for Grace to serve dishes of popcorn. The house was decorated to the nines in Christmas cheer while snowflakes swirled through the air outside, illuminated by twinkle lights that were wrapped tightly around the maples.

For over a month now, the sight of Suzie and Mr Russell together had consumed us, so the movie night was not only a much-needed distraction for Grace, but for Sarah and I as well. However, having decided to put the incident in the alley behind us, and enjoy our cozy night at home, we could not help noticing Suzie's, as well as Mr. Russell's, absence.

Grace placed the overflowing bowl onto the table in front of us, kernels falling from its edges. She seemed to be in good cheer, appearing more relaxed than she had been in the recent weeks which added to the lightheartedness of the evening. We switched the television set on after selecting a movie from their large coolection of DVDs. We settled on a movie that none of us had seen, placing the disc into the machine and clicking the play button.

The hours passed quickly and before we knew it, the credits rolled over the screen, jolting me from a brief sleep. My eyes darted around the room as I woke with a start, catching sight of Grace looking nervously at her watch. In the few minutes that I had been out, there seemed to have been a sudden and discernible change in her mood. She appeared preoccupied. Her husband hadn't made it home yet and she was beginning to look distressed. Sarah and I exchanged a flash of concern.

"How about another one, girls?" Grace suggested mindlessly as she rolled her fingers over her necklace and her eyes veered toward the window, framing mounds of glistening snow icing Haskell Hill in the distance. Sarah remembered that Grace once said she'd received the jewelry, a gold chain with a pendant that caged a solitary, full karat diamond, as an anniversary gift from her husband, her behavior suggesting, Sarah believed, that Mr. Russell, and possibly, their marriage, had been consuming Grace's thoughts.

"Sure, why not?" Sarah answered, hoping another film would take Grace's mind off Mr. Russell's absence.

"Do we need more popcorn?" I asked in a light voice as I leapt from the couch, swinging my arms mirthfully while I hurriedly made my way toward the kitchen, disturbing Grace's trance.

Grace pursed her lips and lowered her brow. "On second thought, why don't we call it a night? It's getting late. I promise we'll do this again soon." Moving reluctantly toward the stairs, she paused once more to glare outside before making her way up. "Goodnight, girls."

I waited until I'd heard her last footstep on the landing before speaking. "What was that all about?" I asked Sarah, crossing my arms over my chest.

"What do you think?" Sarah took a step back. "Suzie and Mr. Russell are still not home. It's ten o'clock! Tell me you're not thinking what I'm thinking?"

"She said she was going out with friends."

"What friends? She's a fucking loner. No one even talks to her at school," Sarah said, waving a hand at me in dismissal.

"Maybe Mr. Russell had a late meeting," I suggested naively.

"He's been having a lot of those these days."

"But why would Grace be concerned? She doesn't know what we know."

"How can you be sure? I don't think she believes that he's at the office this late on a Friday night."

"Well, if she suspects that Mr. Russell is lying to her, and possibly having an affair, I'm sure she doesn't imagine it's with Suzie," I answered, my voice firm, shaking my head decisively. "Should we go after her? Maybe she needs to talk," I suggested, indecisively swaying on my feet, hopping from one foot to the other.

Sarah grabbed at my hand firmly. "No. Let's just sit on this for now, wait it out, do some digging of our own."

Feeling flanked between a rock and a hard place, I nodded my head in agreement as the mudroom door swung open. We listened keenly, holding our breath as footsteps crept around the corner.

"What are you losers doing up? I mean, isn't it past your bedtime?" Wearing a smirk on her face, ostensibly pleased with her disparaging comment, Suzie stood in the hallway, soaking the floor with her dripping wet feet.

"Why do you always have to be so mean Suzie?" I scowled, my eyes cold and my feet firmly planted on the ground as I prepared for the quarrel that I knew was inevitable.

"Oh, did I hurt your feelings?" Suzie laughed as she bent over to unlace her boots.

"Where the fuck have you been anyway? You know we have a curfew!" Sarah demanded, determined not to back down from the altercation. As it currently stood, it was still two against one.

"I don't owe anyone any explanations. And if I were you, I'd mind my own business," Suzie replied, puffing her chest as she moved closer to Sarah.

I stood between them, tenaciously trying to keep the two apart while Sarah pushed up her sleeves to her elbows. Restraining them wasn't easy, but the last thing any of us needed was to have all hell break loose in the Russell's living room, turning over their expensive things.

"Keep your voices down! Grace is upstairs. She'll hear you!" I whispered.

"I don't fucking care," Sarah yelled "This is going to stop right now. You walk around here like you own the place, Suzie. You come and go as you please, make your own rules. Everything was great before you got here. It'll take one phone call from me to get you tossed. Missing school, missing curfews. Though I think being unwelcome is something you might be used to by now. Am I right?"

"Enough," a pyjama-clad Grace abruptly yelled from the top of the stairs, throwing her arms into her robe and tying the belt tightly around her waist as she descended briskly. "What's going on? Who started this?" she asked, primed for answers.

"It's Suzie's fault," Sarah insisted. "She's always so crude, and she made a mess in the hallway with her boots. She didn't even bother to clean it up!"

"I'm crude? You can't complete a sentence without using a four-letter word," Suzie contended.

"Enough of your wrangling! Both of you!" Grace said, pointing her finger in Suzie and Sarah's direction. She looked to me and urged, "Tell me what happened."

"We just asked Suzie where she'd been, and she freaked out."

"I freaked out?" Suzie hollered back and took a step toward me this time.

"Okay, okay. I said enough. This animosity between the three of you has got to stop! All of you, go to bed and we'll continue this discussion in the morning. In the meantime, if you can't say anything nice to each other, don't say anything at all. I don't want to hear another peep from any of you tonight."

Suzie gave both Sarah and me a hard look, suggesting this discussion was far from over. I walked in line with Sarah and headed up the stairs, Suzie trailing a few steps behind.

"Suzie," Grace called out, the three of our heads turning in unison to look behind. "Before you go up, I'd like to speak to you for a minute."

Sarah and I, both curious, but wanting no part of this conversation, slinked quietly to our bedroom, shutting the door tightly behind us.

CHAPTER 12

The Confession

(December 1999)

Grant sat on a bar stool, shoulders bowed, in the county's local dive bar, *The Bear's Paw*, as he took the last sip of his watered-down scotch. Without hesitation, he raised his hand to the blithely unconcerned young man behind the counter, indicating he was thirsty for another. In the wake of what he had gotten himself into the last time he overindulged in alcohol, the erroneous amount of wine he'd shared with Grace just over two months ago, he planned to make the one tumbler of scotch his limit. But, tonight, he was not ready to return home to his wife, where he knew he'd be faced with an interrogation regarding his whereabouts. He was aware he had been pushing his luck, his late nights out with Suzie, but he couldn't help himself. He was given an inch, but he was taking a mile.

The guileless, fresh-faced bartender who appeared barely old enough to be serving alcohol, placed the neatly poured drink onto a coaster in front of Grant.

He lifted the glass and said, "Cheers," not meeting the servers eye.

"What are we drinking to this evening?" The barkeep asked, whose name tag read Chris, as he freely poured a shot of the amber liquid for himself as well before raising his glass to meet Grant's.

Grant tilted his head slightly and thought about the question for just a fleeting moment. "How about to new beginnings?"

As their glasses clinked together Chris repeated the phrase, "To new beginnings," then quickly swallowed the contents of the glass and moved on to his next customer.

Contrarily, Grant sipped slowly, starting to feel the numbing effects of the alcohol wash over him. As his tension gave way, he eagerly began to take stock of his life. He tried desperately to remember at what juncture his world had taken this perilous turn, leading him in the direction to where, not long before, he had no inclination to go.

He and Grace had married young, and though she was the one he'd envisioned himself growing old with, something was changing within him. He barely recognized this desperate, troubled person anymore with whom he was sharing his home. This *new* Grace was an imposter, and Grant wondered what had happened to the woman he'd fallen in love with, the woman who was teeming with confidence and aspired to great things. The woman who wanted to be well-read, well-travelled, someone he would spar with intellectually. His distinguished, young wife, with whom he would share a bottle of fine wine and then make love to in every room of the house.

Conceding, he had come to accept that this person was officially gone and in her place was a stranger, a pariah with the willingness to do anything to achieve her goal of starting a family. In a small way, he felt sorry for this person, but unfortunately, her irrational behaviour and poor judgement were dragging him down the stormy path with her, to which, now, he could no longer resist. He had become just as deranged as she was. Suzie did not have Grace's class or privileged upbringing, very far from it, but there was something exciting about her. He was enamored, or perhaps, one would say, infatuated.

At the start of all of this, though the idea of indulging freely in extramarital sex excited him, he figured his initial rendezvous with Suzie would be unpalatable, that it would leave him feeling grimy and ashamed. But to his surprise, it didn't . . . not in the least. Soon after their first visit in the alley, more, unscheduled clandestine meetings followed. He couldn't help himself, the illicit encounter left him craving more. He found himself cornering Suzie, suggesting they meet at various hotels to which she was receptive. After all, Grace was paying her for a job, and they decided to take advantage of the situation.

But after a few weeks, he was made to believe that Suzie was so much more than what she appeared to be behind her inflexible surface. Her difficult childhood had forced Suzie to build an ironclad wall around her in order to protect herself from being hurt again. But inwardly, she was softer and deeper than she seemed. Or so he'd thought. All Suzie wanted was to get out of the city and create a new life for herself, explore new and exciting things, some place where she could leave her painful memories behind and start afresh. And now, he wanted to go with her. *But what could he do? Give Grace the slip while he initiated his vanishing act?* "No", he thought, giving his head a shake. "No, he owed her better than that."

Grant tried in earnest to reason with himself. Perhaps this growing fascination with Suzie would peter out, and he would completely forget about disappearing with her. Maybe with time he would outgrow this thing that was tearing him away from his commitment to Grace, but he had become addicted to the high he experienced while being with Suzie. It made him feel vital and alive again. Not just the sex, although that was a big part of it. For a young person, she was certainly experienced and far more adventurous than Grace had ever been. He also loved talking to her and learning new things about this girl. He'd missed out on the dating rituals, having married his first crush and he seemed to be making up for it with Suzie.

Eclipsed with feelings of guilt and despair, he quickly decided to blame Grace for his infidelity, as it was, after all, his wife who had put this abominable proposition into motion. However, though the concept was beginning to release him from his culpability in all of this, he was well aware he was making excuses for himself. When he had agreed with Grace's insane plan, it was just supposed to be only, once, or at least only as many, or as few, times it took until Suzie became pregnant. He was not supposed to fall for her.

Clasping his hands together, Grant's eye caught a glint of his wedding ring, and it knocked him with a punch of bitterness. He felt stuck and he wanted out; that was the truth. He was only twenty-eight years old and the thought of being with Grace for the rest of his life soured him. He took a gulp from his scotch that burned at his throat and decided it was time to face the music at home. He worried Suzie had spilled the beans, revealing that she no longer was on side with Grace, but he immediately thought better of that. Suzie was a tough match for Grace; not as intelligent, but she was street smart. She wouldn't allow herself to be outwitted, not when she was so close to getting what she wanted. But, if this was going to work, they needed to bide their time and remain discreet until they could leave town together and go where they wouldn't be recognized. The very thought of it was exhilarating.

When Suzie first took up Grace on her offer, she had been committed to fulfilling her end of the bargain, having the baby and then, before leaving town without a trace, conveying her wishes to Miss Davies that Mr. and Mrs. Russell become the legal parents of her unwanted child. But now Grant had given her a rebuttal offer that was impossible for her to refuse. Leave with him, and they would start over, together. He smiled to himself at the thought of double-crossing his wife, but, of course, this wasn't the first time he had pulled one over on

Grace. No, he wasn't just harboring this one secret, but another that he had buried years ago, which he hoped Grace would never unearth.

He grabbed his glass and drank greedily from it, then exhaled deeply, motioning to Chris for the cheque. He placed the empty glass on the bar and threw down a few bills. He wrapped his cashmere scarf securely around his neck and grabbed for his coat, heading out into the cold, snow fallen night.

CHAPTER 13

The Confession

(December 1999)

In the vestibule at the bottom of the staircase, Grace held on to Suzie's elbow. She was attempting to break away, frenzied to avoid the battle she was about to have with Grace. But Grace pulled her closely, jerking her forward until they were face-to-face.

"You've been avoiding me, Suzie," Grace insisted, trying to manage a less accusatory tone than she felt. But her voice was not as cathartic as her normal pitch, a prick of confusion and a tinge of jealousy giving rise to the change in her timbre.

"I haven't been avoiding you, Grace. It's a big house. I guess we've just been missing each other," Suzie came back, fluffing off the accusation.

She squeezed Suzie's arm even tighter while eagerly trying to hold herself together. She took a few deep breaths and counted to ten before speaking again. She knew she had to deal with this in a more mature, rational fashion. After all, Suzie was her last hope at giving Grace what she wanted, and they had come too far to turn back now.

"Suzie," she paused, "what's going on? I mean, tell me, honestly. Have you been meeting with Grant without telling me?"

"Don't be ridiculous, Grace," she answered sharply, ripping her sleeve from Grace's rigid constraint. "You're a complete nut job who's letting her imagination run wild. Now back off!" Her teeth, now exposed, caused Grace to recoil, quickly coming to the understanding that she was merely a house cat who'd come across a tiger in a mangrove swamp. She could feel her cheeks flush, and her underarms dampen.

Grace dropped her arm to her side, her words soft and distant; she whispered, "Well then, maybe I was mistaken," her confidence momentarily degenerating under pressure. But Grace was a stubborn woman; she couldn't hamper her curiosity. Smoothing out her ruffled feathers, she regained some control, continuing her inquisition, imposing more urgency in desperate chase for answers. "Well then, If you haven't been out with Grant, then where have you been going?"

"Listen, Grace," Suzie huffed. "I intend to hold up my end of the deal we've made, so don't you worry about where I've been and who I've been with. But I will tell you right now, I'm not joining in on your wacky movie nights, sitting around like we're one, big happy family. Do you even have any concept at all of what you've asked me to do? We're one hell of a long way off from being a happy family, so stop acting like it. A single word about any of this to Miss Davies or to the police and this place you call home topples over like a house of cards. So back off."

"There's no need for threats, Suzie. I just wanted to . . ."

"You just wanted to know if I'm having an affair with your husband."

"Well, are you?" Grace knew it was the wrong thing to ask, but her uncertainty was getting the better of her. She had come this far, so why not go all the way? She kept her tone level, but unyielding and braced herself in case Suzie decided to get violent.

More infuriatingly than Grace had imagined, Suzie answered the question, her face contorted, "Is this really necessary?"

"Is *what* necessary?"

"This third degree you're giving me. You're paying me for a job and I'm doing it. If you're really concerned, why don't ask your husband?" she asked, thwarting her opposition.

Suzie hadn't answered Grace's question, once again, leaving her incertitude unsupported, that the two of them had been meeting outside of the agreed-upon parameters. It would definitely explain the odd hours he was recently keeping, but, perhaps, she was better off not knowing the truth. However, if her suspicions were correct, was it strictly for pleasure or an affair of the heart? She shook her head. The thought of Grant's possible betrayal sickened her, but Grace, with a full understanding that she was beholden to them to carry out the requested task, swallowed her diminishing pride, electing to play the long game.

With her decision made, she tamped down her anger and frustration, fearing that one more ill-conceived comment may put a shrieking halt to the entire operation. But Grace had one final request. "All I ask is that you keep me in the loop and to keep it professional," handing her a small, pink and white carton she extracted from the pocket of her robe.

"What's this?" Suzie asked with a huff, grabbing the packet out of her hand.

"What do you think it is? It's a pregnancy test. It's been a week; that should be enough time," Grace answered, hoping the result would render two distinct lines indicating a positive result.

"Good night, Grace," Suzie said, turning on her heel, immediately leaving Grace to feel like the bad guy.

She made her way up the steps feeling equal measures of victory and ambivalence. She had won this battle, but would she win the war? She had quieted Grace's misgivings for now but questioned whether or not she could keep Grant on side. She shivered at the idea of going anywhere with him, but she considered this new opportunity far more attractive and less daunting, than the idea of having a baby, messing up a year of her life. Besides, she wouldn't stay with Grant very long, just until she had enough money to go out on her own. He was a 'get out of Lincoln County free card', providing he didn't waver.

But time was not on her side and Suzie questioned how long she could keep up this facade. She wasn't getting pregnant and Grace, as well as Grant, would soon question why. She thought it odd that Grant had never brought up the possibility of them starting a family even though their sex was unprotected. They spoke at length about their future together while snuggling beneath cozy blankets in hotel rooms following their dirty deeds, but he never acknowledged the idea of her becoming pregnant. Grant had once mentioned to Suzie that the fact that she was needed in the first place had nothing to do with his 'swimmers', that it was his wife's inadequacy that had brought them to these crossroads, not his. She didn't know why he had told her this, but she suspected that it made him feel more masculine.

Frankly, she couldn't have cared less whose problem it was, the notion of Suzie having a baby coming to a swift halt when she opted to forsake Grace and backhandedly accept Grant's offer instead. Unknown to either of them, weeks ago she had gone to a free clinic out of town where she knew that she wouldn't be recognized and received a six-month supply of birth control pills that she kept tucked away with her insurance policy, the journal, and the money, where, she thought, no one would look. She took advantage of this new opportunity where she could still get out of town but not have to give birth in exchange.

Grace's rising suspicions worried Suzie, but she was determined to get what she wanted. She had this under control; she just needed a little more time. She grinned at how pathetic the two of them were, putting their hopes and dreams in the hands of a seventeen-year-old girl who had no intention of giving them anything. Suzie had always been a taker, and as it stood, without either of them knowing, she had pitted the couple against each other, each with their own agendas and Suzie held all the cards.

So up to her room she climbed, walking without urgency in the attempt to convince Grace that she wasn't one bit intimidated by her line of questioning. She was, in the grand scheme of things, in control but, unfortunately, equally as desperate.

***

When Suzie reached her bedroom, she braced herself for a second skirmish with Sarah, who she believed may have been waiting up, eager to continue their conversation. But the room was in darkness, the sounds of gentle snoring buzzing through the air. Relieved, the battle with Grace surprisingly taking the wind from her sails, she crawled into her bed, reaching for the journal and a small pen light she kept in her night table. Careful not to wake anyone, she wrote down all of the details of her night with Grant. Where and when they met, what they'd discussed and what had happened between them in unsavoury detail. She even wrote about her altercation with Grace. And as she penned these words, she silently thanked whatever mystical force decreed that she be sent to the Russell's home. *Was it a happy accident? Her destiny?* She didn't know, and she didn't care. A distinction without a difference. All she knew was that it had been her first stroke of lady luck she'd been given since the day she was born, and she was grateful for how this chance meeting would inevitably determine her fate.

CHAPTER 14

The Confession

(New Year's Eve 1999)

Grace hurried into the kitchen, her arms nearly giving way to all of the bags weighted heavily in her grip. When she finally reached the countertop, she placed the bags down with a sigh of relief and stood leaning against the breakfast bar as she caught her breath. She took a moment of rest before plucking one item at a time from the bags, placing each of them on the counter with precision while she went over the menu for this evening's dinner party in her head.

The bags, empty now, she reached for a recipe book from a shelf that had been collecting dust and leafed through the pages until she found what she was looking for. It had been weeks since she had made a proper, sit-down meal, our makeshift family opting to order pizza for Christmas dinner instead of leaning toward the traditional holiday dinner.

"An odd choice," Grace had said, but it was what everyone had agreed upon becoming tired of turkey following endless leftovers from Thanksgiving.

We sat on the sofa, piling slices onto paper plates, licking our fingers, ridding them of sauce and grease, wiping away tears as the credits rolled on *It's a Wonderful Life*, everyone from the mythical town of Belford Falls belting out the lyrics to *Auld Lang Syne*. The vibe felt relatively calm, everyone silently conceding to leave their differences behind for the holidays. Sarah curbed her use of expletives, Suzie kept her mouth shut for once and Grace and Grant seemed to be getting along much better, the dynamics between them having curdled in the last few months.

But even with the newly found civility, it was obvious that Grace had sensed the cold vibe coming from Sarah and me. She wasn't entirely sure if it had been her imagination or if she was over thinking things. She had done everything she could think of to make our entire Christmas nothing short of magical, including stocking stuffers and an abundance of elaborate gifts. *"Still,"* she thought, *"something is off."* She immediately blamed Suzie, having done something to dampen our moods. She wasn't wrong, but Suzie was only half of it. The other half was what Grant had done and the lingering guilt we felt, deciding not to come forward with the news of their involvement. But Sarah and I had agreed. We were comfortable, despite Suzie's intrusion, and we didn't want to take a chance on being separated. We were young and foolish, with no inkling of how their affair would affect our foreseeable future and decided to look the other way. We put our comfort and wellbeing before anyone else's. What can I say? We were kids.

Grace quickly glanced at the ingredients listed on the dog-eared pages, then scoured the cupboards and the refrigerator. When she was satisfied that she had all the items the recipes called for, she got to work. Wrenching herself into her comfortable role as wife and foster mother, she was determined to put our lack of warmth towards her, as well as the negative pregnancy test Suzie had so maliciously and carelessly placed outside Grace's bedroom door following their heated discussion, out of her head for the evening.

Grace had thought of Suzie's words tirelessly since that night. "Ask your husband." *But how could she?* Grace knew that she was in no position to question his loyalty and told herself to let it be, at least for the time being. It was now New Year's Eve, a time for new possibilities, a fresh start that would finally bring her what she wanted, a baby.

Puttering around the kitchen, Grace prepared a medley of dishes that included all of her party favourites, like crab cakes, spring rolls, and cheese fondue, for the celebration ahead. She wanted everything to be just right, and she hoped that, with a bit of effort, she could maintain the Christmas cheer they'd found just a week ago.

Grace had also picked up party hats, horns, noise makers, as well as masks and headbands to celebrate the occasion. She laid them all out on the table with quiet contentment. She threw up banners and blew up balloons, trying to make everything perfect. It brought her back to a time when she used to have parties with all her old friends, before they became busy with their own families, eventually turning down invitation after invitation to celebrate birthdays and other special occasions, and this burned slightly at her. *"But next year things will be different,"* she thought, immediately fluffing off her preoccupations. She hummed softly as she rolled up her sleeves, getting to work on the menu.

After doling out the spring rolls onto the baking sheet in neat rows. she poured out sweet and sour sauce into small ramekin dishes and cut up some lemons and parsley for garnish. The familiarity of doing what she had always enjoyed relaxed her. As she cooked, Grace thought solely of what lay ahead, donning a smile that she vowed would occupy her face for the rest of the day. This time next year she would have her own child, just her and Grant and whomever God would bless them with. A girl or a boy, she didn't care. She tossed around names as she stood over the stove, mixing the crab in with some breadcrumbs and thick cream. Charlie? Rose? She would have to wait and see. Placing one of the hats on her head, she tied the elastic band securely around her chin. 'Happy New Year', it read, and a happy new year is what she was determined to have.

***

Up in our room, Sarah and I got ready for the big night, applying the make-up that Grace had bought us from Ken's local pharmacy. We sprayed perfume on our necks and threw on the beautiful dresses we received from Santa. I glossed my lips and smiled at myself in the mirror, rubbing my finger along my front teeth to remove the excess product.

"Are you excited, Sarah?" I asked, watching her place huge, hoop earrings into her single pierced ear lobes.

"Of course, I am," she replied with a massive grin, "It's not every year you get to celebrate a millennium."

"Are you nervous at all about the bug? What is it again? Y2Q?"

"It's called Y2K knucklehead," Sarah laughed, "and no, I'm not. I'm looking forward to the madness it might bring, a once-in-a-lifetime thing."

"Nothing's going to happen idiots," Suzie blurted out from her end of the room. "It's just a myth."

I rolled my eyes at Suzie's rude remarks as I passed a crimping iron through my frizzy, dry hair, a film of steam rising from the heat.

Suzie laughed at the sight and yelled, "You're going to burn your hair clean off with that thing," but we continued to primp as the minutes passed.

Sarah had picked up a Polaroid camera and a pack of film to commemorate the special occasion. It wasn't often that we got the opportunity to dress up. Suzie didn't wear anything special, just her usual uniform of black jeans and a black t-shirt. She mocked our outfits as she slid her feet into her dirty, worn-out boots that made her look like she was going into combat.

When we were finally ready, there was a knock at our bedroom door and suddenly we could hear Mr. Russell's voice coming from the other side.

"Is everyone decent?" He asked and waited for us to answer before turning the knob. He stood in the doorway straightening out his bow tie and asked, "How does the old dad look?" Raising his hands to his sides and twirling around once in a counter-clockwise circle.

"You look great," Sarah answered, and she meant it. In spite of her feelings toward him. Grant was a handsome man and he looked like a movie star in his tuxedo, ready to walk a red carpet. If it weren't for knowing his dirty secret, she may have even been a bit smitten with him. She had always wanted a put together, well-dressed boyfriend.

Seeing us formally dressed, he looked at Suzie and asked, "Aren't you going to change?"

Choosing boldly to ignore his question, Suzie remained muted, her booted feet kicked up, on to her bed now, staring blankly at the pages of a red, leather-bound, book.

"I'm speaking to you Suzie."

The sound of her name prompted her to lift her head briefly, and she answered, "Sorry, what?"

"I asked you if you were going to change."

"No, is that a problem?"

"Not at all," he answered immediately, choking on his words. "I mean, it's fine. Just that all of us are dressed up, including Grace. I wouldn't want you to feel out of place."

It was the first time that he had ever commented on our appearance. I didn't think he noticed what we wore. But, of course, he *had* noticed Suzie, and for the umpteenth time, I wondered what he had found attractive about her. A bitch of the highest order.

Grant spotted the camera on Sarah's nightstand and asked if we would like him to take a picture of the two of us. We smiled at one another and I answered, "If it's not too much trouble."

"It would be my pleasure," he assured me, grabbing at the camera while he waited for us to strike a pose. We stood alongside one another, our faces beaming. In that instant, I was unable to remember the last time I felt this happy. The excitement of it all, the possibilities of what the New Year would bring ignited an inexplicable warmth in my chest and I could not stop smiling. "Say cheese," Grant said as he looked through the viewfinder and then clicked on the shutter button. We asked him to take another so we would have one for each of us. He graciously obliged our request and snapped a second photo.

Taking both films in either hand, Sarah waved the negatives, and slowly images appeared. *"Magic"*, I thought, stifling my awe. She handed me one of the photos and I held it to my chest, vowing I would keep it forever. And I meant it.

"How about you, Suzie?" Grant asked. "Would you like your picture taken?"

She looked up at him, away from the pages of her book and glared, "No, thanks," she answered, simulating a yawn.

"Well then, I'll leave you to it," Grant said, handing the camera back to Sarah. "We convene downstairs in just a few minutes," he continued, lifting his sleeve as he looked to the face of his fancy watch. "See you there." He closed the door behind him gently and made his way down the stairs to the dining room.

"Are you ready?" Sarah asked me, glancing at her reflection in the mirror one last time.

"As ready as I'll ever be," I told her, as the two of us withdrew from our bedroom, arms linked together, leaving Suzie behind to do whatever it was she did when we were not around. Balancing carefully on our shiny, patent leather pumps, we held onto each other as we descended towards the penetrating smells whirling from the kitchen.

***

Music played, and the aura felt truly upbeat. Neither Sarah nor I had been to a New Year's Eve party before, so we followed Mr. and Mrs. Russell's lead, dancing in the kitchen as we sipped from our mocktail beverages. Grace looked beautiful; her gorgeous hair hung long and was combed straight. Though she always looked perfect, it was a far cry from her usual up-do. She wore a blue, silky dress. The hem would have reached the floor if it weren't for the four-inch heels she wore on her feet. Grant took her hand in his and twirled her around the makeshift dance floor, and if we hadn't been the wiser, we wouldn't have guessed that anything untoward was going on between them.

"Where's Suzie?" she asked as the song playing on the radio came to a close and they let go of their grip.

"She's upstairs," Sarah answered. "She'll be down shortly."

And then, as though she was waiting for her cue to join the party, Suzie suddenly appeared in the doorway, looking so obviously out of place in her drab clothing, calling out, "Here I am."

"What happened to the dress Santa brought you for tonight?" Grace asked cutely, trying not to make her feel uncomfortable.

"It didn't suit me. I guess Santa didn't receive my list this year," she answered, blatantly disregarding the efforts Grace had put into the evening or into picking out a dress for her.

"No matter," she called back, ignoring Suzie's obvious attempt at being aloof, and told us to make our way to the dinner table.

The dining room looked like something out of a fairy tale, decorated like a proper storybook. All of us took our seats and I reached for the cone-shaped hat that stood on the charger plate in front of me. I put it on as Grace began to serve. Mr. Russell placed his top hat on his head making himself look more dapper than he already had.

The night was full of cheer, with great food and great music, none of us seeing the hours fly by as we approached midnight. We could hear the disc jockey announcing the time, "One minute," he yelled, and the countdown began. Sixty, fifty-nine, fifty-eight . . ." We all sat quietly, listening to the numbers for that long minute at the table, our eyes shut tightly, half scared of the pending disaster of the Y2K and half excited about what a new year, decade, century, and millennium, would bring.

For all of us who sat at the table, the possibilities were endless. After observing Mr. and Mrs. Russell as they danced earlier in the kitchen, Sarah crossed her fingers that the New Year would bring that well-dressed boyfriend she'd envisioned for herself. I thought of the blooming friendship I had made with Sarah and hoped it would continue to flourish. Grant imagined what life would be like once he disappeared with Suzie and the havoc it would bring about. Suzie thought of the money she had stashed and where it would take her once she left Grant for good. And Grace, of course, dreamed of her new family, the one who would replace this unusual group, the one that would be sitting around this very table in one year's time. How very foolish we all had been.

"Five, four, three, two, one! Happy New Year!" We braced ourselves for a power outage and worse, but then, somewhat to our dismay, nothing happened. The lights remained bright, and the clocks kept ticking. The Millennium had arrived without any disturbances. It was finally here, and everyone was safe.

We picked up our glasses and touched them together, yelling, "Cheers!" Large grins covered our faces, even Suzie's. I leaned over and hugged Sarah snugly and she whispered in my ear, "Happy New Year."

Grant raised from his seat and took Grace in his arms and kissed her on the cheek. At the sight of the two of them embracing, Suzie sneered, feeling something unfamiliar grinding in the pit of her stomach, something she was not expecting, jealousy.

CHAPTER 15

The Confession

(January 2000)

Well beyond midnight, after the table was cleared and everything had been put neatly away, everyone heaved themselves up the stairs, straight to bed, our bellies weighted down from an abundance of food and drink. But though the evening had been a success, Grace hadn't failed to catch sight of the biting look Suzie had given her at Grant's embrace come midnight. The hideous glare sent Grace's head swimming, once again, in an ocean of suspicion, leaving her to wonder whether her intuitions about Grant and Suzie carrying on an affair behind her back were not merely conjecture. The thought of this treachery caused her to become slightly destabilized and Grace felt that she could no longer hold her tongue, ignoring her earlier concessions to let it be.

As they got undressed and prepared for bed, in the privacy of their room Grace confronted Grant, choosing to deploy an altruistic approach to her fact-finding mission. She didn't want to outright accuse him, but she needed to get to the bottom of what was happening under her nose.

"Listen Grant," she started in a soothing tone, careful not to ruin what had been an otherwise perfect evening. "I've been thinking. I haven't been fair to you. You've been trying for a couple of months with Suzie, and it doesn't seem to be, um, working out. Maybe it's time we gave up on the whole thing and put another bug in Miss Davies' ear, you know, find out where we stand on the whole adoption business."

"Are you serious?" He questioned, sounding befuddled and slightly defensive. "We've been housing these teen age girls for over two years, and never once has Miss Davies or the institution even mentioned the possibility of honouring us with a baby of our own, in spite of our good deeds. Do you really want to risk having a future with no children in our home? You're being impatient."

"Well maybe it's time for *us* to start trying again," Grace cringed, the possibility of her husband wanting to continue having sex with this young meddler lending to her mind's unrest. She and Grant clearly were not being intimate anymore, and this thing with Suzie had been his only means of satiating his appetite. Or maybe, she'd hoped, he had truly come on board and wanted this baby as much as she did. She'd prayed for the latter, but perhaps she knew better.

With the cracks in her armor beginning to show, she wrestled through the murky waters she had seemingly stirred up and, not as rigidly, she suggested, "Maybe we could see a different specialist, get a second opinion."

Grant was apparently all too aware of the possibility his excuses of late meetings to explain his recent absences from home were not being accepted by Grace at face value. He was conscious that his protests may have seemed a little over the top considering he'd been against the idea of having children from the onset, so he began to backpedal and replied, "I mean, if this is what you really want, then yes, I'd be happy to put an end to these shenanigans. It was an absurd idea from the start."

With almost no effort, Grant had turned the table on her, leaving her with little to no options. Without Suzie, there was not going to be a baby. *What could a new specialist do or say?* She knew flat out that she could not conceive a child, and no new opinions would state otherwise. Her suggestion of putting an end to his meetings with Suzie was intended merely as an attempt to gain information, but it had backfired. She hadn't wanted the operation to come to a grinding halt; she had just worried that he was enjoying himself too much, or even worse, starting to fall for Suzie.

But now, even if what she suspected was true, she hadn't gained any new insight and was admittedly out of options. She'd backed herself against a wall, Grant's compliance being her only hope of having a child. How stupid she had been to take on this exploratory task? Yes, she had become jealous, but what did it matter at this point? After all, her commitment to having that baby had far outranked her desire to have a faithful husband. Besides, she rallied, Suzie would eventually be gone, and the baby would bring them closer together. She could kick herself.

Frustrated at the pivot that this inquisition was taking, Grace asserted, "It was not absurd, it was practical." Immediately shifting her ground, she hinted, "Maybe, we could give it another month . . . if you're willing?"

"Not if it is making you uncomfortable, Grace. Just give her the money you promised, and she'll vanish. She won't become a problem. I can guarantee it," he answered, appearing unshaken, grabbing at the duvet and pulling himself into bed.

"I'm not uncomfortable," she bristled and then steadied her emotions once again. "Maybe you're right. I am being a little too eager, darling. One more month won't kill us. It might be worth it."

"It's not a bad idea," he countered, relieved at her sudden change of heart, but considering the time constraints he was now under. A month was a very short time to get his affairs in order. But just the same, he reasoned, even if he had been given a wider berth, Grace would eventually have further reservations, not just regarding whether or not he was falling for Suzie, but about why she was not getting pregnant. Suzie was in the prime of her child-bearing years and he had been proven quite virile at the fertility clinic. He was beginning to fear that the truth would catch up with him sooner than later.

In point of fact, Grant wasn't getting any woman pregnant, that was reality. Unknown to Grace, who had spent their entire union with the wool pulled over her eyes, he had chosen to have a vasectomy as a very young man, before their marriage, adamant that children would eventually hold him back. When he finally found a physician that would even perform the questionable procedure, the surgeon had begged him to reconsider his options, certain he was being rash, but he was steadfast in his decision.

He knew he could never impregnate Suzie, that it was never an option. His head spun the idea of Grace suggesting a second opinion. A year ago, before attending the fertility clinic with Grace, desperate to keep his secret, he had furtively purchased a semen donation from a cryobank. Slipping the plastic vial from his pocket and spilling its contents into the vessel provided when he was sent to the restroom to do his thing, he handed over the bogus sample to the lab. When they found nothing wrong with his counts, in an unsuspected, but welcomed turn of events, Grace was found to have a problem conceiving. Endometriosis was the diagnosis, leading him into a false sense of security that his deception would never be revealed.

When Grace had approached him with her plan, though hesitant at the start, secretly, he became a more than willing participant, knowing this pregnancy would never happen. He'd be in it for the sex only. God knows he had become tired of Grace, and she with him, and after all, he was still a man with needs. He just hadn't anticipated falling for this girl, and now, things had gotten complicated.

Grant quieted his anxiety, opting to leave his planning and scheming until morning when he would have a clearer head after drinking all that champagne. He decided that reassuring Grace may buy him a little more time and, instead of performing his usual nightly ritual of turning his back on her, he dimmed the lamp and leaned into his wife, throwing his arm around her waist, and pulling her close. "Maybe this month you will get what you want after all," he whispered. Thankfully, she relented and the two of them slept undisturbed, like they hadn't done in months.

CHAPTER 16

The Confession

(February 2000)

Already a month into the New Year, I woke to the shattering sound of heavy winds cracking at our bedroom window. Neither Sarah nor I had remembered to set our alarms. Looking at the digital clock on my nightstand in a daze, I jumped out of bed quickly, shaking Sarah's shoulder, forcing her from a deep sleep.

"What time is it?" she groaned, the room still dark, trying to pull the blankets over her head in order to drown out my voice.

"It's seven-thirty. We slept in," I answered, playing a game of tug of war with her, each of us grabbing either end of the sheets.

It was Saturday morning, and we were going to be late for work. That winter had been an exceptionally brutal one, even for Cooper's Mills, notorious for its heavy snowfalls and cold temperatures. Sarah and I were beginning to feel a little contained. Needing to get out of the house, we had landed ourselves part-time jobs at a local coffee shop that was earning us a bit of money, of which we saved none. We had blown our first cheques at the mall on stuff we didn't need, but felt we'd earned. Spending our own money was liberating and it felt good to be independent.

Sarah crawled begrudgingly from her bed when she heard me call out the time, splashing some cold water on her face. We moved quietly but diligently, trying not to wake Suzie as we threw on our uniforms and brushed our teeth. I realized, just then, that I hadn't heard her come home last night and was half surprised to find her lying in her bed. Preoccupied with our tardiness, we rushed past the kitchen where Grace sat at the coffee bar, unnoticed.

"Good morning girls. Off to work?" She sat upright, wearing her hot pink snow pants, taking a sip from the tea cup in her hand.

"Oh my God! You startled us. What are you doing up so early?" I asked, looking at Grace as I clutched at my chest.

"I couldn't sleep any more. I shovelled the driveway. We had another heavy dumping last night. Just trying to warm up."

"Isn't that Mr. Russell's job?" I asked curiously. He'd always be the one out there, digging in with the shovel and tossing it over his shoulder, making his work seem effortless.

"He's still in bed," Grace answered lightly, not seeming put out. "Sound asleep. He was very late getting home from his meeting last night. "Listen," she continued, placing her teacup back onto a saucer, "I am very proud of the two of you," she said, smiling at the sight of us clad in our brown and red polyester uniforms. "Try and have a good day and stay warm out there."

Sarah and I smiled and thanked her for the kind words. Then, grabbing our coats, scarves and gloves, we headed out into another cold and dreary, winter day.

Shuffling through the snow in our winter boots, we had barely reached the foot of the cobblestone driveway when a beat-up old, green truck came splashing through the slushy mess on the road, almost spinning out before stopping immediately in front of the Russell's house. Suddenly, a woman in her forties, with a leathery, grey complexion, jumped out of the driver's seat. She stood triumphantly in front of us like she'd been searching for something she had finally found.

Sarah remained still at the curb while a surprising look of recognition swept across her face.

"Becky?" she asked suspiciously in a barely audible tone, thinking her eyes had been playing tricks on her. She took in the woman's slender figure clothed in crumpled garb, waiting for an answer.

"Yes, it's me. Your mom. The woman at the agency said that I'd be able to find you here. Look at you, all grown up. I barely recognized you." She held out her arms as she made her approach, as if fooling herself that Sarah would jump right in, putting aside the fact she had left her years ago, and with that monster, Martin, eventually forcing her into the foster system.

Sarah deliberately took a few steps backwards, avoiding Becky's attempt to embrace her. Part of Sarah was delighted to see that her mother was alive, but the other part was extremely cautious not to dive in, head over heels, given the history between them.

"What are you doing here?" Sarah asked, rattled but stern. Considering the circumstances of her departure, she thought it was a fair question.

Becky's shoulders sank at the chilled greeting, causing her to lower her arms to her sides. "Look, Sarah. I have some news," Becky said in a cheerless voice but cleared her throat and carried on with her message. "Martin has passed away. The fool was found a month ago at the side of the road, a half-empty bottle frozen in his hand. Hypothermia they say. If you ask me, the bastard got what he had coming to him."

Sarah could not argue with that, but in the grand scheme of things, it was her father they were talking about, and she could not help but feel emotions that confused her. Pity, anger, and perhaps, even a little sadness. She was content to have gotten away from Martin in the long run, but she never wished him a miserable death. Sarah stood in the cold, mulling over her feelings as pristine flecks of snow started to form a thin layer over the mucky slush.

She forced her thoughts from Martin to Becky, determined to push the image of Martin lying iced in the snow out of her mind. Becky had shown up after playing hooky from motherhood for nearly six years. She'd disappeared, leaving her alone with an abusive father. *Why had she shown up after all this time? Why today? She must want something.* While her mind raced with contemptuous sentiments, Sarah decided quickly that self-preservation was her best option and instead of hearing her out, she cursed, "You left me with that fucking asshole!"

There was no chance for Becky to respond. Seeing the alarming car out front of her house, Grace emerged from the doorway, her arms wrapped around her, fighting off the bitter chill of the sub-zero temperatures. "What's going on out here?" she asked, demanding an explanation. "Get away from my girls! Who are you?"

Sarah met Becky's gaze and then turned to Grace. She hesitated, struggling to say the right thing. After all, even in the short time she'd been at the Russell's, Grace had been more of a parent to her than Becky had ever been. She wanted to choose her words carefully, but with the evident look of discontent on Grace's face, Sarah finally blurted out, "This is Becky . . . my mother."

Following a brief moment of uncertainty, her eyes darting back and forth from Sarah to Becky, Grace finally challenged. "Your mother? But I thought . . ." Grace didn't know how to react to this news, cutting herself off. She knew that, like most of the girls who came to stay under her roof, Sarah had been abandoned, but she had never broached the subject with her, careful not to open old wounds. Grace had taken for granted that Becky was not coming back for Sarah. She felt blindsided. None of the parents had ever shown up here unannounced. Her first instinct was to grab at Sarah, run inside and lock the door behind them. But she thought better of it and decided hearing this woman out would be the best course of action.

"Yes. I'm Becky. And you must be Grace," extending her hand apprehensively towards her, aware that her sudden arrival at the Russell's would likely not be well received. Grace, fumbling for her words, took Becky's hand in hers and gave it a genial squeeze.

"Nice to meet you, Becky. Would you like to, um . . . come inside?" she asked motioning towards the front door as Sarah and I exchanged a jittery glance. "We'll all freeze out here," Grace murmured as she rested a protective hand on Sarah's shoulder.

"We were just headed off to work," Sarah said, faltering, unsure if she was ready to enter into a big to-do with a woman she hadn't laid eyes on for several years.

"Nonsense, Sarah!" Grace exclaimed. "I'm sure Rita could justify your absence to the manager," Grace suggested unequivocally, as though Sarah's life should stop on the spot because this virtual stranger had popped up out of nowhere. "Rita, you run along. Make up some excuse why Sarah couldn't make it in today.

Now the two of you," she insisted, "get in the house; we have a lot of sorting out to do."

Sarah nodded toward me reassuringly, indicating that she would be okay, despite the very current upheaval in her young life. I gave Sarah a wry smile, turning on my heel as I headed towards the coffee shop and the three of them ambled towards the front entrance. But before shutting the door behind them, I caught sight of Sarah while she gazed at my silhouette that was now fading in the distance, nervous that this would be the last time she would ever see me. A chill crawled up Sarah's spine at the familiar feeling of loss that so closely mirrored the despair she had experienced when she watched Becky parade so selfishly out of her life all those years ago. Finally, she shut the door and hesitantly followed Grace and her mother into the kitchen.

CHAPTER 17

The Confession

(February 2000)

The Russell's house seemed colder and less welcoming to Sarah that morning, her head still swimming in bewilderment. Sarah and Becky sat wordlessly while Grace poured two more cups of tea from the pot, thoughtlessly filling them to the brim. Placing the urn back on the burner, Grace took a moment to clear her head, thinking decisively of how she would handle Becky's unannounced arrival. Extending the invitation to Becky to enter her home rattled Grace, but her eagerness to understand why Becky had shown up out of nowhere overrode her immediate instinct to shut her out. She grabbed the teacups and set them on the counter in front of them.

Settling into her seat at the breakfast bar, she sat tall, appearing authoritative, placing both palms firmly on the countertop to anchor herself. Grace picked up her cup, took a quick sip and asked the question she feared that she already knew the answer to, "So, Becky. What brings you here today?"

"Well," Becky paused, fidgeting in her seat. She looked as nervous as Grace felt but gained some composure and spoke assertively in her raspy voice. "Look, I'm not here to cause trouble for you Grace, but I'm not going to beat around the bush either. Sarah is my daughter, and frankly, I'm here to take her home."

"Home? What home?" Grace laughed outwardly. Judging from the truck she'd pulled up in today, the nearest thing to home she could envision was a dodgy trailer, at best, with no running water. "Does Miss Davies even know you are here? This seems very inappropriate; no parent has ever arrived without warning. I'm calling the agency." Starting to unravel, Grace placed down her tea cup with trembling hands as she grabbed the handset from the wall, punching in Miss Davies' telephone number.

"No wait," Becky petitioned, snagging Grace's hand. "Here me out, please."

Grace didn't know what to do. On the one hand, this was Sarah's mother and she had a right to be heard. On the other hand, she had disappeared years ago and wasn't sure Becky deserved an opportunity to explain. While desperation filled Becky's eyes, Grace allowed the building tension to loom over the three of them. Finally making the choice to end the call and rest the handset back on the receiver, she looked at Sarah, attempting to gauge her reaction to this decision. Sarah bowed her head, and then nodded her approval.

"You have five minutes, Becky, then you need to leave," Grace insisted, taking a seat.

"The truth is that the agency didn't tell me where to find Sarah. I did my own digging with a detective friend of mine. Well, maybe not a detective. He's a private investigator, but he led me in this direction, and now here I am."

"And what makes you think that you can just show up and leave with Sarah after all these years? There are procedures to follow, and miles of red tape to slice through. Have you ever considered whether she even wants to go with you? How you just showing up here like this would confuse her?"

"Of course I've considered all of that. Truth be told I wasn't even going to approach Sarah today. I just wanted to have a glance at my baby girl and see where she is living. But when I drove up, there she was, all grown up and right in front of me. I couldn't stop myself."

"Because you are selfish," Grace insisted, pounding her fist on the table, her eyes fiercely gazing into Becky's.

"No, Grace, I am not selfish. It was my motherly instinct forcing me to react, to reach out to her, to speak to Sarah face to face. She is, after all, my child. But from what I understand, you wouldn't have any idea about that, would you?"

The obvious slight at Grace, not having had children of her own, bit deeply at her, causing her to rise heatedly to her feet. Eyes wide, she pointed to the door in anger. "Get the hell out of my house! Did your so-called motherly instinct ever come into play when you abandoned your daughter?" she snapped. For a brief second, time stood still, and nobody moved. No one even dared to blink.

"What in God's name is happening down here Grace? What is all this fuss about?" Grant demanded as he made his descent from the stairs and into the kitchen where he was met by this total stranger so early on a Saturday morning. "Who is this?" he asked, baffled at the sight of this odd woman sitting in his kitchen drinking tea.

Reticent to answer, the room fell quiet, each of the women exchanging apprehensive glances.

Grant was growing impatient, now raising his voice. "Well, are one of you going to fill me in?"

"This is Sarah's mother, Becky. And she was just leaving," Grace sneered.

"Sarah's mother?" Grant questioned, demonstrating the same astonishment Grace had expressed just minutes earlier. "Where's Miss Davies?"

"The agency has no idea that she's shown up."

"Well then, what is she doing here?"

"She's come to take me home," Sarah answered softly.

"What? No! You are a stranger to us. This is inappropriate. I'm calling the police," Grant asserted, standing firm.

"No, please!" Sarah begged. "Don't call the police." Concern for her mother skyrocketed in an instant. She felt torn between the Russells and Becky. She knew that she didn't want to leave, but she didn't want to see her mother being dragged away by the cops. "Please. She's leaving, aren't you, Becky?"

Indignantly, Becky rose to her feet. Hoping to spare her daughter, but more so, herself, any more discomfort, she agreed to leave willingly. She knew that she wasn't getting anywhere today, and the sound of her only daughter addressing her by her proper name grated at her. It wasn't the right time.

"I am," she answered, pushing her chair backward, its legs grating along the solid wood floor. "I'm outta here! But this won't be the last you've seen of me," she swore. "Sarah is my daughter and if I have to go through the proper channels, so be it. I'd just hoped you would be reasonable, spare all of us the inconvenience."

"That's not the way it works, and you know it . . . now get out!" Grace scolded.

"Goodbye, Becky," Grant said, showing the pathetic woman to the door.

Sarah peered empathetically at this virtual stranger as she was guided toward the exit, feelings of pity starting to override her initial animosity. Regardless of her dubious past, this was the woman who had given birth to her. Sarah decided to extend a peace offering and gave Becky a chilled hug goodbye. Becky left their company without further incident and a sense of calm settled over the three of them as they stared at the image of the beat-up truck trudging away from their home through the growing mounds of snow.

"How dare she?" Grace asked, unsure at what she was more disgruntled by, the fact that Sarah's mother had shown up unannounced intent on taking Sarah home, or that she had insinuated that Grace did not know what it was like to be a mother. All things being equal, Grace believed she was a better mother to Sarah than Becky had ever been. If anything, this incident with Becky encouraged her, strengthening her willingness to proceed forward with her plan. There was no way that she would leave people as low as Becky, or anyone else, thinking that she didn't have the capability or the wherewithal to be a parent to a child.

Still angry, she reached for the phone and hit redial. Grace held the phone to her ear and allowed her careworn shoulders to drop when she heard a voice on the other end, "You've reached Miss Davies. How can I help you?"

CHAPTER 18

The Confession

(February 2000)

An hour later, there was a knock at the Russell's front door. Anxious to speak to Miss Davies in person, Grace ran to the foyer, swinging the door open with a jerky movement, Grant sauntering in behind, manufacturing the image of a united front. They greeted Miss Davies with a fresh waft of coffee percolating on the French press. Grace had sent Sarah upstairs earlier, hoping to keep the conversation between them and the social worker private. She explained to Miss Davies over the phone about Becky's unceremonious arrival at their home earlier that morning, but she needed the comfort of seeing her in person to discuss Becky's rights as Sarah's biological parent.

Unfortunately, she had not brought with her good news. Miss Davies decided that it was no use hiding anything from the Russells and broke it to them as gently as she knew how.

"If Becky can prove to the courts that she is a fit parent, she has every right to become a mother to her daughter once again. Sarah is only seventeen. But in August she will have the option of whom she would prefer as a parent, stay here, if the bed is still available, choose a group home or even go out on her own."

This news did not make Grace happy. Though she had become very fond of Sarah, the truth was that she needed someone to keep me engaged and out of their hair. She knew that I was eager to make friends, and if Sarah were to go, it wouldn't take much time before I began meddling in Suzie's business, asking all sorts of questions, and trying to build a relationship. I needed a distraction, and that distraction was and had always been, Sarah. Now, the possibility of her leaving hung in the air like a bad smell.

Grace began to pace. Turning away from Miss Davies. She tried to articulate her thoughts. Grace needed Sarah to stay, she was an integral part of her master plan, though, of course, neither Miss Davies, nor Sarah knew it.

Pressing her lips together until they became a shade of white, grasping at straws, she asked, "What if Sarah refuses to go?"

"That won't fly," Miss Davies countered repentantly, "if the court rules in Becky's favour, she'll have no choice. She's a minor and Becky is, for all intent and purposes, her biological mother."

There was that phrase again, biological mother, the words that made Grace feel inconsequential, almost defeated.

"Listen," Grace said desperately with only one card left to play in her hand, "Sarah is upstairs. Why don't I bring her down here and we can let her decide?"

"As I've said, it is not up to Sarah. You know this. You've had many girls come and go, it's not your first kick at the can," Miss Davies reminded her with a sigh. She was grateful to the Russells for taking in the older foster girls who were usually very difficult to place, but she was at a stalemate. Her chin temporarily dropped while she struggled to find her words, wanting to sound as tactful as possible. "Grace, I have to ask. Are you okay? I've never seen you become this attached to any of the foster girls. You know how this works."

"Yes, I'm okay, and I am offended by you insinuating otherwise. Why wouldn't I be okay?" Grace asked, raising her voice, her cheeks becoming flushed while Grant watched on silently as his wife began to unravel.

"I didn't mean to offend you Grace. It's just that . . ." Miss Davies stopped herself there. She knew another word out of her mouth would undeniably make things worse. She feared that maybe Grace's infertility was forcing her to become too connected to the teenagers, but given the circumstances, she thought it best to hold her tongue.

"She hired a private investigator and showed up here unannounced. She's obviously unstable. I guess we'll leave it in the hands of the court," Grace replied, listing her grievances, confident that the powers that be would not find Becky to be a suitable parent. "After all, she had left her once before. Who's to say she wouldn't do it again." Maybe the judge would see reason.

Miss Davies held Grace's elbow gently, trying comfort her, and replied, "Believe me, Grace, they will do what's in Sarah's best interest. You're not to worry, okay?" She offered Grace a reassuring smile as she reached for her bag of files, leaving the coffee behind.

Grace nodded, and before she knew it, Miss Davies exited through the front door, wishing her and Grant a good day. Grant closed the door behind her, but before he had a chance to have a discussion with his wife, Sarah suddenly emerged from around the corner. She had never gone upstairs. Instead, she hid in the den, neither of them aware that she had been snooping this entire time.

"So that's it then," Sarah insisted, "I will be going home with Becky."

"It's not over yet, Sarah," Grace said, pulling Sarah towards her with a caring embrace. "Becky still has a lot of work to do until the courts deem her fit, if ever. Until then, you'll stay here, and we won't lose hope."

Sarah found Grace's words encouraging, but she knew better. She had seen it all too often, parents reappearing out of the clear blue sky, children being plucked from the security of their newly found homes and friendships. Hopefully, Sarah thought, she would turn eighteen before the court would have a chance to preside over their case. She thought of leaving her friends, her school, her job, and a rush of unexpected tears rolled from her eyes, cascading over her rosy cheeks.

Her mother had come for her. It would be a dream come true for most children. Becky was alive and well and wanted to take her home. But she wasn't a child anymore, and the fantasy of her mother showing up and swooping her away from foster care had lapsed long ago. Sarah swallowed back the lump in her throat, letting go of Grace's clutches and finally replied, "You're right, Grace. There is still a chance."

They smiled at one another, and Sarah ran to her bedroom, away from the Russells, taking the steps two at a time.

***

As Sarah fell inside her room, she shut the door with a bang, securing herself in her safe space, forgetting about Suzie, who was, as usual, in fine form.

"What the hell?" she asked, giving her eyes a few blinks before scolding her further. "Thanks for waking me up."

As Suzie turned over, still half asleep, Sarah spotted the red book she had seen Suzie with on New Year's Eve, accidentally dropping open from the bed to the floor. Sarah stared at the pages filled with Suzie's written words. But before Sarah had a chance to react and make a play for it, Suzie leaned over and grabbed at her property urgently, taking it in fiercely in her hands as though the content meant life or death.

Sarah's eyes widened, focusing exclusively now on the red jacket. She knew instantly that it was not merely a book that Suzie was into, it was a diary, evidence, perhaps, of what Suzie was up to.

For a long-standing moment, the two girls remained like statues, neither of them moving an inch. But then, with her usual level of dominance failing her, Suzie finally buckled, rolling over on her face as she smothered her private thoughts beneath her like buried treasure. Savouring her minute victory, Sarah grinned behind Suzie's back. Eventually, one way or another, she would get her hands on that diary, she knew it, and it would answer all our questions. It was the ace up her sleeve.

CHAPTER 19

The Confession

(February 2000)

I arrived home from work later that day, barging into the house, frantically calling out for my friend.

"Sarah?" I yelled, hoping to find that she hadn't already packed her bags and whisked away by her mother. I hadn't a clue as to how these things worked, and for all I knew, she had already gone. "Sarah, are you home?" I called out unremittingly as I took on the flight of steps, still trying to catch my breath following my marathon sprint home. Much to my relief, Sarah was sound asleep in her bed, her things still untouched, set in their usual place.

Kneeling beside her, I whispered into her ear, "Sarah," trying to wake her, gently.

"Hey," she answered slowly, coming around from her deep sleep, "you're back." Sarah repeatedly blinked until her eyes finally opened wider, content to see a familiar face after the day she'd had. She sat straight up in her bed, giving me a firm embrace.

"What happened? Are you allowed to stay? Did Miss Davies intervene?" I assaulted Sarah with questions, the answers I had hungered for throughout my shift not coming quickly enough.

Sarah smiled, possibly the only one she had worn all day, her reaction to the overwhelming concern hovering in my voice. "One question at a time," she laughed as she swiped at her eyes and let out an undisguised yawn. Stretching her arms high to the ceiling and then allowing them to drop heavily on to the bed, she gave me the good and the bad news. "I can stay for now, but there's going to be a hearing."

"A hearing? What kind of hearing?"

"A competency hearing for Becky. To determine whether or not she is a suitable parent for me," Sarah explained.

"When?" I asked, unsure if I even wanted to hear the answer.

"I'm not sure. In the next few weeks, I'm assuming," Sarah shrugged.

We grabbed each other's hands and squeezed tightly. Sarah and I had come to be so close over the passing months. It was like we'd known each other all our lives, and neither of us could imagine how this huge change would affect our friendship. *Where would Sarah and Becky live? Would we even be able to see one another?* We remained still, looking into one another's faces until I decided to fracture the portentous aura that was now invading our room.

"Why don't we get out of here for a bit, head downtown?" I pulled out a couple of pieces of paper from my pocket and offered one to Sarah. "Look, more pay cheques. Let's do a bit of shopping," I suggested, donning a playful smirk. "It will make us feel better," I assured her, pulling her from her bed to her feet.

Raising her eyebrows, Sarah gave an agreeable nod, "That sounds like a great idea." With a new burst of energy, Sarah took a quick glance at herself in the mirror, carefully rubbing away the streaks from her stained cheeks while she prepared to spill her second volley of news before we hit the road. "Before we go, I need to tell you something."

"What is it?" I asked, my pulse immediately quickening, incapable of dealing with any more bad news.

"It's about Suzie. You know that red book she's always into? It's not a book, it's a diary. She's hiding it somewhere, right here in this room."

"Okaaaay?" Stretching out the word as I spoke, my response drawing out as more of a question than an answer.

"I think if we could get our hands on it, it would explain what is going on between her and Mr. Russell, about how it all started, and maybe if it is still going on."

"Where is she keeping it?" I asked, then brusquely began to rifle through her things with little to no care. The prospect of finding the diary incited me to manoeuvre nimbly and diligently through Suzie's personal space. But though I scoured through drawers and bedding and an old trunk of memorabilia with a fine-tooth comb, I came up empty-handed. "Maybe she took it with her," I sighed, my posture sagging in defeat.

"Possibly," Sarah concurred, "but let's not give up just yet." We carried on optimistically, tossing things about the room until it was clear that the diary was nowhere to be found. When we finally called off the fruitless search, we caught sight of Suzie in the doorway, fanning herself with the manila pages.

"Looking for this?" Suzie asked, waving the red diary in front of them. She knew that Sarah wouldn't be able to resist searching through her things once she was gone, but she thought it was atypical behaviour for me, always doing the right thing. Either way, she was clearly proud of herself, taking care not to leave her insurance policy behind.

"Gimme that," Sarah insisted, lunging forward and taking a swipe at the diary.

Suzie pulled it close to her chest and laughed uproariously. "Do you think I'm stupid?" she asked, placing the book securely into her cross-body satchel. She stood smugly for a moment, shaking her head, wearing a wide grin.

"Fuck you Suzie," Sarah spat and carried on without holding back. "We don't need to read your "memoirs", making air quotes with her first two fingers. "We already know what's going on."

"What are you even talking about?" Suzie interrupted, waving a hand at us, beginning to straighten her things.

"You're fucking Mr. Russell!"

A moment passed as the three of us allowed Sarah's accusation settle like specks of dust, but then, smiling at us unnerved, Suzie replied, "You know nothing, and if I were the two of you, I'd stay out of it. Do you understand?"

"We saw you, Suzie! We saw you in the alley with Mr. Russell months ago, so don't tell us we don't know anything. We know everything!" Sarah challenged.

Suzie stepped forward, narrowing the gap between us, her face now twisted "If you know everything, then you also should know what's good for you and keep your mouths shut!" She warned through gritted teeth; her eyebrows pinched together.

"Why would we do that?" I asked, curling my lip, unable to mask my growing frustration with her.

She ignored the question and silence besieged our room, the two of us waiting for an answer as Suzie went about her business like she hadn't had a care in the world. She strutted around as though Grace finding out about their affair was inconsequential as she tidied her up-ended third Embittered at being dismissed, I leaned in aggressively towards Suzie. My customary unruffled demeanour having gone by the wayside; I expelled a loud roar. "Answer me," I demanded, grabbing at Suzie's collar.

"Because she already knows!" Suzie snapped back, tearing violently away from my strong hold and meeting my contemptuous glare.

Confused by what I'd just heard, I shook my head and turned directly to Sarah, giving her a bewildered stare. It couldn't be possible. If it were, Suzie would have already been gone. Mr. Russell too. There's no way Grace would put up with that.

"You're lying!" I shouted back decisively, heading towards the door without a backwards glance, determined to spill the beans.

"I wouldn't do that if I were you," Suzie crooned in a carefree but heeding tone, causing me to stop dead in my tracks, fear of what beheld us if I were to confront Grace about what we'd already discovered months ago. If Suzie were lying, Grace would be angry at the idea that we had kept this secret from her. If she wasn't lying, I figured there must be some sinister reason why Grace was allowing all of this to carry on. I looked to Sarah, my expression begging for advice.

Sarah didn't say anything. She just closed her eyes and shook her head from side to side, a clear indication that she didn't think that going to Grace, or anyone else, would be the best idea. At least not for the time being, not with the looming competency hearing. So instead, I took a few steps back toward my bed and wrenched at my bag, gripping its strap tightly in hand and exited the room. I couldn't look at Suzie's face a moment longer than I had to, her admonishing glare sending a tingling sensation up my spine. Sarah picked up her cheque that I had left on top of the blankets and shoved it into her back pocket, following in line, close behind.

Fearing any interaction with Grace would surely send our tongues wagging at both ends, we scurried through the hallway, down a flight of stairs and straight out the door, shutting it quietly behind us. We kept our heads down, shielding our faces from the frigid north winds. We walked briskly towards the mall, full of shops where the two of us would joyfully blow our hard-earned cash. Mindful of the limited time Sarah and I could possibly have to remain together, we agreed not to speak of Grace, Suzie, or her admission for the rest of the day, but believe me, while we didn't speak of it, it was all we thought about.

CHAPTER 20

The Confession

(March 2000)

"All rise!" The court clerk called out, sending the entire room lifting to their feet. An official-looking family court judge clad in a black robe emerged from the side entrance, taking a seat at the helm of the courtroom. Judge Carrington would be presiding. She swung her gavel down hard on the desk in front of her, commencing the proceedings that would ultimately determine Sarah's fate. "Court is now in session."

She asked the participants to be seated, and in no time, she called Becky to the chair. She stood in the witness box, raising her right hand, her left hand placed firmly on the bible, swearing to tell the whole truth and nothing but the truth, so help her God.

Unable to attend as the hearing was held during school hours, from what I'd heard, Becky appeared slightly more gathered than when she initially showed up at the Russell's. She had put together a makeshift pantsuit and dabbed on a bit of foundation to soften her rugged complexion.

Along with Miss Davies, who was present to show her unwavering support, Grace and Sarah sat nervously in the front row as they listened to Becky's testimony. Grant's obvious absence dangled like a betrayal to Grace, however, with a hint of theatre, they presented as a united front, the three of them holding hands while Becky was peppered with questions from the Crown. *Why had she left? Had she been receiving counselling? Was she employed? Why did she believe that she could be a suitable mother to Sarah after all these years of being an absent figure in her life?*

In true form, Becky had said all of the things the court wanted to hear. She was not entirely self-righteous, admitting to her many mistakes as a parent. She wept as she gave her testimony, pleading her case to the judge. She painted a vivid picture of what she envisioned her future with Sarah would look like if they were afforded the opportunity. She was very convincing, making it impossible for the court to determine whether she would make good on her many assurances. Finally, Becky stood down and the judge thanked her for her frankness.

And eventually, it was Sarah's turn to enter the box, her palms becoming sweaty as her name was called. She shyly approached the bench, and like Becky, she promised to tell the truth. She fidgeted in her seat, the Crown urging her to remain calm, that she intended to ask Sarah just a few questions. *But whose side was the Crown on? Hers or Becky's?* She decided that she had no choice but to trust in the system, that the woman standing before her didn't have any particular agenda. She was merely acting as a nonpartisan agent who would have her best interest at heart.

Sarah took a deep breath and nodded her head, giving the courtroom a clear indication that she was ready for questioning. The Crown began; and speaking in a caring but curious tone, she asked, "Prior to your mother's unexpected arrival at the Russell's house, when was the last time you saw her, Sarah?"

Sarah conscientiously thought back to the last time she had seen Becky, her back turning on her as Becky made the decision to leave her behind, exiting their home without a thought. It left a bitter taste in her mouth, reliving that feeling of abandonment she had made the effort to forget.

She cleared her throat and answered honestly, "About six years ago."

"And in those six years, have you ever heard from Becky, even once, aside from when she arrived unannounced at your doorstep just weeks ago?"

The question stung like a bee's bite and Sarah swallowed the lump in her throat before answering, "No."

"How did that make you feel?" The Crown asked, sounding more like a child psychologist than a court-appointed attorney.

"Sad. Unwanted. Unloved." The three words stabbed Becky squarely in the chest like a sharp knife, each answer, another painful jab.

"And how would you characterize your experience in the foster system following your rescue from, Martin, was it?" She looked down at the paperwork in front of her to confirm her father's name. By all accounts, she hadn't done her homework. "Yes. Your father, Martin. Can you describe that for the court?"

"At first, it was rocky, I moved from one home to another until I ended up at Mr. and Mrs. Russell's house."

"How long have you been there?"

"About nine months."

"And how has that been going?"

"Well," she hesitated. Sarah wanted to tell the truth, but she also didn't want to hurt Becky's feelings. However, she had sworn on the bible, so she continued to answer candidly. "It has been like being a part of a real family." Again, Sarah's words hit Becky hard, causing a shameful tear to roll down her cheek.

"Can you describe your answer more clearly to the court? What do you mean by family?"

"I don't know." Sarah paused and met Becky's glare. "Like, I finally felt safe, cared for. I'm going to a nice school; I've made some friends. Grace puts dinner on the table. She takes responsibility for me. Does my laundry, takes me to the doctor when I'm not feeling well. You know, like a real parent would. I am encouraged to be a kid instead of feeling like an adult for a change," Sarah's voice began to rise as she let her answers spew relentlessly. It was a release. All the feelings of resentment she had bottled up inside of her for years, finally erupted like lava through the vent of a dormant volcano.

The room fell silent as Sarah was given a moment to collect herself. There was no need for the Crown to continue, her point of questioning being made clear given Sarah's answers.

Finally, it was Grace's turn, and as expected, she handled herself with poise. She spoke mainly about Becky's unorthodox visit to the Russell's house and the progress Sarah was making while under her and Grant's care.

With no more witnesses to call, the Crown rested her case and the judge ordered an immediate recess while she made her decision.

Sarah and Grace settled into the uncomfortable bench outside of courtroom number four. Hours felt like days waiting for the decision when suddenly, to Grace's surprise, Mr. Russell arrived huffing and puffing. "Sorry I'm late. I got stuck on the I-295. A pile-up of cars."

Grace gave him a blank stare, his apology, or better still, his lame excuse, for missing the proceedings, seeming inconsequential to her. She pursed her lips tightly before wrangling a bright smile, and replied, "It's all right darling. I think it went well. We're just in a holding pattern now. Judge Carrington is just going through the testimony."

Sarah was well-tuned to this act, Grace recoiling in her husband's presence, careful never to divulge her true emotions. She was forever loyal, though she wasn't sure that he had deserved her loyalty, silently questioning if it had been Suzie causing him to be late. A stretch, perhaps, but given what she knew, she wouldn't have put it past him, taking this opportunity while he knew everyone would be busy.

Sarah didn't have the answers, and, quite frankly, she didn't care all that much. Her animosity toward Mr. Russell, and admittedly, now toward Grace, no matter what she had said on the stand, had flourished exponentially since our argument with Suzie. If Sarah was being honest, she wasn't overly concerned about leaving the Russell's house; more so about leaving her school, her job and her best friend.

"How long has it been?" Mr. Russell asked with a measure of concern.

"A couple of hours. It could be promising," she answered, taking Mr. Russell's hand. Though Grace tried to remain confident, Sarah could hear the trepidation in her voice. Her husband stroked the back of her neck with his free hand in an effort to get Grace to relax. We all waited in silence until Miss Davies popped her head out of the courtroom, announcing that the Judge was ready to hand down her ruling.

The three of them followed her back in where Sarah would soon realize her destiny. They took their positions and waited patiently for the hearing to resume.

"All Rise," they were told and stood, hand in hand, waiting for her finding. It was time.

"I want to thank you all for coming today. In these types of cases, it is always difficult for me to make my decision, so your patience has been greatly appreciated." Judge Carrington stopped and made eye contact, one at a time, with all the stakeholders. She began again after a brief moment and spoke firmly and with confidence.

"It has been made obvious to me how the Russells have cared for Sarah and the good home that has been provided to her has not gone unappreciated by this court. It is people like them who make the foster system work, and for that, we are greatly appreciative." She extended a courtesy nod towards the Russells and Miss Davies, but kept the ball rolling.

"However, while everyone has offered dutiful testimony, this court always believes it is in the best interest, for all parties involved, to place a child back with their parents whenever appropriate." Sarah could see the muscles in Grace's neck tightening as the Judge pressed on without hesitation.

"And this, I dare say, is one of those times. Becky Belmont, could you please rise," she instructed. Becky lifted herself to her feet, her legs shaking in anticipation.

"It is this court's ruling that Becky Belmont has given ample testimony to award her custody of her daughter, Sarah Belmont. This granting will be given on a temporary basis, with the expectation that her court-appointed liaison, that would be you Miss Davies, make regular bi-weekly visits to ensure the proper standards of care are being met. Her reports will be forwarded directly to me for review. Thank you for your time." And with that, she hammered down her gavel, adjourning the room.

Shock covered their faces as Becky leapt towards Sarah. Taking her into her arms, she said, "I promise you things will be different this time sweetie. Are you happy?"

"Sure. I mean, I guess," Sarah replied. Still jolted by the decision, she offered Becky a loose hug in return.

They all hurried out of the courtroom, Grace most obviously frayed by the ruling. Her face hardened. Not even this court would find her to be an actual mother, despite all her best efforts. It hit her like a barbarous whack, adding insult to her already injured pride. There was nothing left she could say or do, so in her usual steadied fashion, out in the hallway, she turned to Becky and offered her congratulations.

While Becky made her way back to Waldoboro to get her house in order for her daughter's return, Grace drove Sarah back to their home to pack her things.

Grace sat in the car with Sarah, turning her thoughts over in her head. They sat in awkward silence as Grace wondered what to do next. With Sarah leaving, it would leave Suzie and me, alone in that room, countless hours in the night when the two of us would find all kinds of time to talk. Grace fretted that I would find a way to get through to Suzie, the same way in which I had broken Sarah's guard, encouraging her to spill all her secrets. She wasn't sure that Suzie could keep her mouth shut, but she hoped for the best, despite the setback, willing herself to remain in control of her perverted game.

CHAPTER 21

The Confession

(March 2000)

Grace pulled into the driveway quickly, screeching her tires as she threw the vehicle into park. The sound caught my attention, forcing me to peer out of the bedroom window. I didn't need Sarah to tell me the bad news. I could read it on both of their faces, even with the boughs and twigs of the huge maple distorting my view. The two of them hurried toward the front door, Grace fumbling with the number of keys on her chain, trying to find the right one that would open the lock. Mr. Russell followed closely behind in his own car, pulling up behind her into the driveway. He exited his vehicle and ran after her into the house.

The wind took hold of the heavy door, slamming it viciously behind the three of them. Sarah raced upstairs without a word to either of the Russell's. There was nothing left for her to say. Grace had done all she could, but her best efforts were not enough in the end. All she wanted at this point was to collect her things and make time to say a proper goodbye.

When Sarah entered our bedroom, I was already having a crying fit, lunging immediately into her embrace. We hugged without letting go of each other for several minutes, memories of the months past swelling our hearts. The room, like none other we had ever had, with fancy duvets, curtains, poster beds and cozy cotton sheets, had been our sacred place. A sanctuary where an intimate friendship was born, nursed and then matured into a relationship neither of us ever expected to find. Sarah regretted her initial restiveness in forming this bond, having wasted the precious moments we had had together, but there was no time for her misgivings. She had to pack. Miss Davies would arrive shortly to take her to Becky's place and Sarah didn't want to spend another minute of the few we had left shedding tears.

Sarah let go of me and wiped her nose on her sleeve. "Help me pack?" she asked, trying to muster a smile, lifting the gloom that hung heavily in our sanctuary.

"Of course," I answered, also making a concerted effort to end the floodgates.

As Sarah went over everything that had happened in the courtroom that afternoon, we worked arduously, careful not to leave anything behind until, finally, there were two crammed suitcases and one overnight bag where Sarah kept her most treasured items. There were greeting cards and small gifts of friendship I'd given her, including a locket, as well as a few things she had picked up at the mall on our shopping trip just weeks before. Perfume, some earrings, and a picture frame that she filled with the Polaroid we had taken together on New Year's Eve. In no time, Sarah's whole life had been stuffed into three bags, and it was time to bid each other farewell.

"What am I going to do without you?" I asked Sarah, my eyes heavy again with tears.

"You'll manage," Sarah answered, making a reasonable effort to sound positive. "Before you know it, there will be someone else filling that empty bed, and I will have been replaced," she joked.

"No one could ever replace you, Sarah," I replied with certainty, "You're the best friend I've ever had."

"I'm the only friend you've ever had," Sarah grinned.

"Shut up!" I sniggered, throwing a pillow at Sarah that hit her square in her face. We laughed out loud, rolling around on my single matress, forgetting our sadness for a brief moment.

Sarah wasn't wrong, however. She *was* the only friend I had ever, truly had. When the laughter settled, my eyes went distant, recalling a memory when we had gone to see a movie together months ago, the day we'd discovered Mr. Russell and Suzie in the alley.

"Do you remember the day we went to see *Clueless*?" I asked. "And we said we'd be friends for infinity?"

The recollection brought an efflux of warmth to Sarah, remembering our arms tightly entwined as we walked in the falling snow.

"I do," Sarah smiled broadly, "and I intend to keep that promise!"

"Well then why don't we make it official?" I asked, grinning impishly as I held up a stick and poke tattoo kit, including the needle, ink, some peroxide and cotton balls.

"What are you going to do with that?" Sarah questioned hesitantly and slightly confused. She had never known me to do anything risky before. It was so out of character.

"It's a tattoo kit."

"I know what it is. I asked what you were going to do with it."

I pulled out a sheet of paper from my back pocket and unfolded it for Sarah. On it, there was a small sketch of the infinity symbol I'd drawn, just large enough to fit on someone's wrist.

"Do you trust me?"

"With that? Where did it come from?" Sarah grimaced.

"I picked it up this afternoon on my way home from school. Well . . .?"

"I don't know Rita. Do you even know what you're doing?" she asked, sitting on her hands.

"There's only one way to find out." Shaking the ink, I raised my shoulders, indicating that I wasn't quite sure, but wasn't backing down. I smiled and grabbed Sara's arm from underneath her butt, rubbing her wrist with a cotton ball doused in peroxide.

Sarah let her shoulders go limp, still apprehensive and not fully convinced, but decided not to put up an argument. She turned her head and clenched her teeth. Carefully, with a bit of sweat on my brow, I drew the image on the inner portion of Sarah's wrist using the tattoo stencil. I filled a small dish with wet, black ink and dipped the needle. Then, with precision, I began to jab at Sarah's skin, staring at the area intently, careful not to make a mistake. Sarah held her breath, stifling back screams of pain. Still looking away, she prayed for the best.

Minutes later, when the image was finally imprinted, I removed the excess ink and smiled at my work approvingly. "There," I nodded, "not bad for a beginner. Now it's my turn."

Sarah turned her wrist up to her eye line, examining the finished work. She beamed at the mathematical image that would forever symbolize our infinite friendship. It was perfect. I performed the same procedure on myself, the second time more confidently. Our skin red and raw, we compared the identical artwork that would brand us forever. I decided that we should personalize them, suggesting we add each other's initials as well, to give the symbols a finishing touch. She agreed.

I forced the letters, *RM*, into her skin, and she laughed through the discomfort. I took the needle to my wrist just as we heard a bang at the door.

"Just a second."

I hurried the needle, making a bit of a mess before completing the task. Swiftly, I tucked the kit underneath my pillow before opening the door.

"It's time to go, Sarah," Grace announced in a gentle voice. She could not make eye contact with Sarah. Instead, she focused her gaze toward the forest green, plush wool rug, without raising her chin.

"Friends for Infinity," I reminded Sarah, trying to be strong, for her. "Call me every day, twice a day if you can." Sarah nodded her head in agreement.

We hugged a final goodbye, and Sarah, catching a glimpse of Grace still focused on the rug below her feet, whispered in Rita's ear, "Be careful."

Picking up her bags, one in each hand, her overnight bag slung across her body, Sarah exited their room for the very last time. And just like that, I was harshly propelled back to reality. Everyone leaves eventually.

CHAPTER 22

The Investigation

(April 2021)

Detective Hollis listened to Rita keenly and patiently for hours without losing focus. A good detective never interrupted, he thought, allowing his subject to speak freely, filling in the silence without the burden of disturbances. He'd always found he could extract more information that way. But as he sat unnerved at this latest development, he could no longer hold his tongue.

"Are you saying that it is Sarah Belmont you killed?" he queried, raising an eyebrow and tilting his head. Though relieved he finally had a name to put to his corpse, this new information sent a crawling sense of disbelief to wash over him. Once again, he questioned whether or not Rita was telling him the truth, certain that she could not be responsible for killing Sarah given how close they were.

Detective Hollis shook his head, "But you've told us that the two of you were great friends," he insisted. "How could you? I mean . . . why would you . . . possibly kill her?" He realized quickly that he was tripping over his words, losing control of the interview, and he immediately stopped himself from speaking any further. Rita looked to her husband, who gave her a nod of affirmation, permission to fill in the uncomfortable blank and answer the detective's questions.

"Yes, the woman in the park is, I mean was Sarah Belmont. And yes, we *were* friends," Rita answered, her head hanging remorsefully, the use of the word "were" being unquestioningly used in the past tense.

Confused, Detective Hollis asked, "Can you tell us what happened next? After Sarah left. Did you have a falling out?" He studied her face as he swigged his last sip of cold coffee. Nothing was making any sense. He knew the matching tattoos, more importantly, the initials *RM* had connected Rita to the woman in the park, but until a few moments ago, he figured the indefinable initials stamped on Rita's wrist could have belonged to anyone but not Sarah. He waited in suspense for her to pick up where she had left off.

"Can we give her a few moments, detective?" Rory intervened just then, likely wanting time to confer with his client before making any further statements. Perhaps even tutor her on what to say next, or more likely, what not to say. Either way, Detective Hollis agreed to put a pin in his questioning while he digested the new information. Besides, he'd felt the buzzing of his phone in his pocket several times in the past couple of hours and knew it would be Patti. After all, it was almost morning, and he hadn't arrived home yet. She would be getting worried.

Detective Hollis nodded his head, then announced the time for the sake of the recording, "0500 hours," before hitting the pause button. They all stood, except for Rita who looked spent, hunched over in the derelict chair. Detective Hollis left the room, immediately gripping his phone. He looked at the screen, three missed calls from Patti. He shook his head, unsure if he actually wanted to ring her back. Instead, he decided to send a text message, his hands hovering over the keypad as he scrutinized over what to write. He decided on just two words, "Still here," accompanied by a sad-faced emoji. That would do for now. He tucked the phone back into his pocket and, keeping his head down; he headed for the washroom to splash some cold water on his face.

On his way through the otherwise vacant hall, he ran into Officer Miller once again, who was changed out of her uniform and barely recognizable in her street clothes. He'd wished he would have pushed through the washroom door before bumping into anyone else, but these halls were rarely ever empty.

"Getting anywhere?" she asked curiously but breezily, careful not to sound too nosy.

Detective Hollis felt a sense of annoyance, not even having had a moment to process the recent development before being questioned about his case. Nevertheless, he raised his heavy head, revealing his creased brow and answered, "Slowly, but surely. Very slowly." Detective Hollis let out a measured, steady breath, tamping down his exasperation and growing fatigue.

"I guess that's a good thing. I mean, at least you're getting somewhere, right?" Miller said, her voice optimistic, attempting to mitigate the uncomfortable vibe that was diffusing the air between them.

"I suppose," he replied, the corners of his mouth rising a fraction, her positivity lightening his mood a degree or two. "Why don't you go home and get some sleep. You've had a busy day," the detective suggested, wishing it was him who was taking leave from the building instead of her.

"I mean no disrespect, detective, but are you feeling okay?" Miller asked with genuine concern, taking note of his sallow skin, dull eyes and obvious irritability.

"Never better," he answered with conviction, the baldest lie he had ever told. But in that second, he wasn't sure who he was trying to convince, Constable Miller or himself.

Staring at her left wrist which was decorated with a heavy-duty, black, digital watch, more suitable for a man than a woman, she said eagerly, "My tour ended five minutes ago, but I'd love to stay and help if there's something you need doing. I mean it, anything at all."

Considering her generous offer, he thought raptly about the many things that needed to be completed, starting from the top of his list. If he wanted to confirm that Rita was telling him the truth about the victim's identity, that would require someone scouring through the registries. Though the detective was usually of the proclivity to decline assistance, he had to concede defeat. There was no point in arguing the fact that he could use all the help he could get, and that she was it.

When the detective didn't answer right away, she took his silence as a flat out no and said regretfully, "Well, okay, if you're sure there is nothing I can do," slinging her bag over her shoulder, making her way to the door.

"No, wait," he begged, hoping she had not reconsidered. "You really don't mind hanging around for maybe one or two more hours?" he asked her with a sideways glance knowing full well the task would take at least twice as long.

"I could always use the overtime, boss. What can I do to help?" she answered, setting her bag back on the floor and removing her coat. Miller rubbed her hands together, an indication she was eager to sink her teeth into whatever the task. Detective Hollis was momentarily brought back to his early years when he had had the energy for these long, gruelling shifts and decided to take advantage of the young officer's enthusiasm.

Reaching for his mobile, Detective Hollis scrolled through his photos, clicking on an image of his corpse in the park. It was the photo from her locket that he'd snapped before entering into evidence.

"Here," he said and passed Miller his phone. "This is the woman in the park. I need you to compare this image to any and all Sarah Belmont's found in our databases.

City and state. And don't forget to check the station's paper files. Apparently you can find them rotting in the basement. I'm not sure where she's from, so check it all. Even Federal if you have to. She may not even be Belmont anymore."

"Right away, boss," Miller answered vigorously, sending the photo from his library to hers before handing the phone back. This was her first big case, and it made the detective happy he'd reconsidered. Newbies were ardent perfectionists, rarely known for cutting corners. Hopefully, she would be able to confirm what Rita was telling him was true.

Miller sauntered off towards a computer, re-energized, and Detective Hollis finally made his way into the restroom. He looked at the mirror and frowned, unhappy at the reflection staring back at him. He thought about the good old days when he was young, like Miller, full of piss and vinegar. When staying up all night to crack a case was exhilarating, like inhaling the pure oxygen they pour into the casinos that wills you to keep playing. He was beginning to lose his passion for the game, whether he wanted to admit it or not. He threw some cold water on his face and then put his mouth under the running tap, ridding himself of the sour coffee residue.

Detective Hollis let his head hang momentarily and then stabilized himself, grabbing onto either end of the sink. He had to appear alert for the next few hours though he felt quite the opposite. "I can do this," he assured himself, letting go of the porcelain as he ran both of his damp hands against the front of his shirt. He rubbed at his temples, nursing his building migraine, then tousled his hair, taking one last look at himself before he swung the door open.

This time, the halls were empty, and he relished the moment to himself. He took his phone in his hand once more and looked at his screen saver. The detective smiled. A photo of Patti on their trip to the Catskills wearing a chunky, knit hat stared back at him and in that second, a message popped up on the screen, "Good morning." It wasn't much, but it gave him the jolt he needed to steamroll on. He returned the message with a brief text, telling her that he would still be there a while.

He knew Miller would need some time to complete her mission and wanted to use those hours wisely. He needed to get this done. Standing at the door to the interview room, Detective Hollis grabbed the knob and turned it slowly. He gently but invasively pushed open the door and asked, "Are you ready to proceed?"

CHAPTER 23

The Confession

(March 2000)

A couple of weeks had passed since Sarah's untimely exit and as expected, we had kept in touch, not as much as promised, but we tried to talk to each other at every opportunity. Every two or three days I'd hand over gossip about the people at school and at the coffee shop, and Sarah brought me up to speed, for the most part, on what new things were happening in her life.

Sarah had made some new friends for which I was grateful but also a bit envious. I was finding it difficult to open myself up to new relationships, fearful of losing them too. But just the same, I was happy to hear Sarah's voice at each call, listening to her new adventures at school and at home, her new life with Becky. To Sarah's surprise, and slightly to my dismay, the two of them had gotten off to a great start. Becky had gotten a job, she was cooking and cleaning, doing all the household chores. Secretly, I was hoping Sarah would wind up back at the Russell's place, though I knew I was being selfish. For my friend's sake, I was always encouraging and mindful never to make Sarah feel guilty for her contentment and good fortune. Sarah was still my best friend, and I was happy for her.

In the meantime, with Sarah gone, the space that surrounded me seemed to grow more vast, feeling even lonelier than before Sarah first arrived, before I knew what it felt like to have a real friend. In time, I knew that I would come around, get out there again, and begin new friendships. But at that moment, I wasn't ready to extend any olive branches. I needed a project to keep me occupied, and in the back of my mind, I knew what that would be.

Though things seemed to have quieted down around the Russell's place in recent weeks, I had a foreboding hunch that whatever was going on in this house would eventually bubble over and explode. The proverbial calm before the storm.

Before Suzie could arrive back home and, like the day Sarah and I had tossed the room, I, again, trudged nosily through her space in our bedroom, hopeful that today, she had felt comfortable enough to leave the diary at home. Since Sarah's departure, there had been little to no friction between us and the diary, not to mention what she had said about Grace, had ever been brought up again.

Unknown how much time I'd have, I moved hastily. In hot pursuit, I rummaged through her stuff, lifting, probing and thirsting after the pages that would explain what

Suzie and the Russells were up to. There was no way she would carry that thing around with her every time she went out. It had to be somewhere in that room.

Though I combed painstakingly through everything, the diary was nowhere to be found. Eventually giving up, I leaned my back against the wall, using it as leverage. Slowly, bending my knees, I slid down until I came to a sitting position with a thud. Upon my butt hitting the ground, I felt a jouncing underneath the green rug. Thinking nothing of it at first, I let out a heavy sigh at my useless efforts. I took a deep breath, and I sat for another second until it hit me. I'm not sure if it was the oxygen infusing new life into my brain, but in that instant, I knew that I had found it. I jumped up and pulled back the carpet, gently lifting the floating floorboard, and to my excitement, there lay the item for which I'd begun the hunt. The red, leather-bound diary with gold ribbon and laminate trim was staring me in the face. I'd hit the jackpot. Under the floor board a steel box lay in hiding.

I opened it and I reached for the diary that sat among wads of cash and contraceptive pills. I curiously picked up all three items and marvelled at the cash. But pressed for time, I set the money and the pills down and sifted through the pages swiftly. I saw scribbled notes that were difficult to make sense of. I saw numbers and dollar signs. There were times and dates. I saw Grace's name, then Grant's, the names and locations of motels and hotels, and detailed descriptions of the unspeakable things that happened in those places.

Although I ripped through the journal with speed and immediacy, processing the information came at a much slower pace. Staring at the pages open-mouthed, I could not believe what I was reading. Gradually, and with great disgust, I was able to piece it all together. A carefully laid out scheme from which the three of them would benefit. I already knew that Suzie was sleeping with Grant and that Grace was well aware, but I didn't know why, until now.

A desperate and conniving Grace had asked Suzie to have sex with her husband, get pregnant, and have Grant's baby, for which she would be paid handsomely. I grimaced at the very madness of it, but I forced myself to keep reading. During Suzie's pregnancy, she would tell Miss Davies that she had chosen to give up her baby for adoption and that she had wanted her child's forever family to be with the Russells. Grace and Grant would file for adoption. It would be that simple. Grace would have been accurate in assuming that Miss Davies could not refuse them this opportunity after all they had done for the agency. Besides, Miss Davies thought highly of the Russells and knew that placing a child permanently in their home would open up a world of opportunity for a girl or boy. Unfortunately, until now, the Russell's time hadn't come; there simply hadn't been the chance. With such a small population to draw from in Lincoln County, it wasn't every day that a baby was given up by its parents.

Then, immediately after giving birth, Suzie would disappear and abandon her parental right to attain an access order. The Russells would get their baby and

Suzie would get her money. It seemed like a flawless plan, providing everyone stuck to the script.

However, while Grace knew that her husband would find the extra-marital sex extremely gratifying, after all, he was a man, she didn't count on Grant falling for Suzie, arranging his own plan to leave with her eventually, setting them in opposition.

To complicate the sick plan even further, unknown to either of the Russells, Suzie had no intention of fulfilling her end of either of these bargains. She had gotten the pill, careful not to get pregnant, and in the meantime, while accepting payment from Grace, Suzie was also tricking Grant into thinking that she was falling for him, each visit sifting through his pockets while padding her own. After accepting his assistance in getting her out of there, she would eventually leave him once she got her footing outside of Lincoln County.

It was a cunning deception, I believed, albeit extremely deranged. But I wondered how long it would take for Grace, or Grant for that matter, to realize what she was up to. They were obviously very sick people, but they weren't stupid. They could never allow Suzie, a seventeen-year-old girl with barely any education, to outwit them. But, with desperation driving them both, Grace finally getting her much-desired child and Grant getting out of his marriage, their judgement had become clouded. Eventually, the two of them would get what they deserved.

I wanted to continue reading, but knew that my opportunity was limited, that Suzie could walk through that door any minute. Besides, I had already accumulated more than enough information than I could stomach for one sitting and had pretty much gotten the gist of what was happening. There would be other moments to look at the diary again now that I knew its hiding place.

As I slid the journal, the pills and the cash back under the floorboard, I felt agitated and very much depleted. Though I was happy to finally gain the information that I'd longed for, I felt disturbed at the knowledge that Grace had not been keeping us out of the goodness of her heart, but merely using us as chess pieces in her well thought-out game. It may not have started out that way, but as they say, the road to hell is paved with good intentions.

Sadly, Grace's plan may have come to fruition, if only she hadn't chosen someone equally as greedy and deceitful as herself. The only comfort I'd felt in that moment came from the knowledge that Grace's plan would fail. Suzie was never going to become pregnant; better still, before long she would take off with Grant and they would be out of all their lives for good. Surely the agency wouldn't hold that against Grace; they would have no idea that she had set this plan into motion. They would likely feel sorry for her, and I would continue to live here, in the comforts Grace provided. Maybe I would even get some new roommates. As I said, I was young and selfish and I thought devilishly of how Mrs. Russell would react to finding Suzie and Grant had disappeared, without a trace. And, even worse, with a load of their money. The idea of it actually put a smile on my face momentarily.

"What is happening to me?" I questioned, thinking only of myself with zero regard for anyone else. I briefly imagined putting a stop to the whole thing, warning the Russells, but that came with a great risk. Grace would inevitably throw Suzie out, and she would go running to Miss Davies with her diary, which would undeniably land me in another home. Though so much evil lurked in the underbelly of this house, for the time being, it was far better than any of the places I had stayed before.

Self-preservation was best. I needed to do what it took in order to protect myself. And as I hammered down the rug over the loose floorboard with my socked foot, I began to feel a little of my old self start to emerge, the person I was before coming to the Russell's. Conniving, slick, doing what I had to do in order to survive. Maybe I would even help myself to a bit of that cash. I wasn't sure if I liked it, but what choice did I have?

I would fill Sarah in on my discovery at my nearest opportunity. She would agree with me, as she always had, and urge me to keep my mouth shut. Needing a little bit of fresh air, I made a beeline for the back door. I tucked my feet into my cozy winter boots and ran into the forested area behind the Russell's Victorian. It always made me feel better, being among the masses of towering, hundred-year-old black and white ashes, yellow birches and maples. I breathed in their sweet smells of mint and sugar, listening to the welcome sound of the returning birds chirping, and tried to forget about what I'd learned, at least for now.

CHAPTER 24

The Confession

(March 2000)

As it turns out, while I had been snooping, uncovering and hurrying through the pages that were off-limits, Mr. Russell had rented a fairly superior hotel room for himself and Suzie to share an intimate mid-afternoon rendezvous. A three candle, empire chandelier hung from the white, stucco ceiling, and a burning fireplace lit the room, lending to the romantic ambiance the suite already held.

Their bodies laid entwined in the dishevelled, Egyptian cotton sheets, covered with a heavy down-filled comforter. Even though spring was in the air, they were enjoying the warmth that the luxuries were bringing them as they watched the tree limbs sway in the gentle breeze outside the double-glazed, draft-proof windows. Neither of them thought of Grace during their afternoons together; at least Grant didn't. The only thing he thought of was when and how he could finally get Suzie out of town, away from Lincoln County and all of its prying eyes.

But while Grant fantasized about their future together, Suzie secretly dreamt of her escape from Lincoln County and, eventually, the Russells altogether. She wondered how much longer she could keep up this facade, the sight of both of them beginning to turn her stomach in equal measure. It wouldn't be long before Grace would catch on. Suzie was never getting pregnant, and Grace had already started to ask questions regarding their involvement months ago. Luckily, for a little while, Grace's attention had turned from Suzie to Becky's competency hearing which bought her a little more time. But now, she would be expecting this deal to get sealed.

Keeping Grant occupied was easy. Suzie knew how to distract a man from an early age. Besides, men never asked a lot of questions, and as far as she knew, Grant had no clue he was being duped. If he had been wondering why she wasn't pregnant already, he never mentioned anything. Notwithstanding, she needed to keep him onside. He was her backup plan, someone she could rely upon to get her out, put them up in a small place until she got her footing. He wasn't going to be her forever love. He was a means to an end.

Grant suddenly jolted from his preoccupation, squeezed Suzie tightly and gently kissed her forehead. "Any ideas of where you'd like to go when we get out of this place?" he asked, with a rapturous smile.

"I'm not sure. I haven't really thought about it," she lied. "New Hampshire, maybe?" Suzie suggested. "We could leave the state of Maine behind completely."

"Really? I was thinking somewhere a lot further," he replied, disappointed in her lack of imagination.

"Like where?" she asked curiously, propping herself up on one elbow.

"I don't know," he shrugged. "How about California. We could rent a place on the beach and get a convertible. We'll take weekend getaways and see how the other half lives."

If Grant was being honest, his motivation to move cross country wasn't only for the sun and the sand, although those two things would be a bonus. He simply needed to get as far away from Grace as he possibly could. He knew that she wouldn't accept this double-cross with a grain of salt and would likely want to tear him limb from limb. *"Hell hath no fury like a woman scorned,"* he silently reminded himself and shivered at the sentiment.

Suzie snatched up the blankets, pulling them firmly around her, glancing at Grant inquisitively. "California?" She questioned, a place that seemed so foreign to her; it might as well have been on another planet. She was never one to have big dreams, given her past, but the thought of it enticed her, briefly curious about what it might be like to travel so far away, Cooper's Mills a distant memory. At any rate, she knew that if she ever made it to the Golden State with Grant, it would not be for long. She would look for a new boyfriend, one with tanned skin and huge pecks. Grant wasn't unhandsome, he was just old and, truth be told, a little strange.

"Yes, California. The blue sea, palm trees, cocktails with umbrellas, I mean, when you're old enough to drink, that is," Grant said teasingly; the idea of it all, on its face, seemed euphoric to him. Spreading his limbs out wide like a starfish, his chest and palms facing upwards, he envisioned himself basking in the hot sun, thousands of miles away from Maine.

She snuggled into the crook of his shoulder, pasting on an agreeable smile, and told him that his idea sounded wonderful. Suzie allowed him this moment of satisfaction. He'd earned it, having been married to that stick-in-the mud for so many years.

Admittedly, she had felt a pang of jealousy on New Year's Eve, watching the two of them engage in a loving embrace. She could not explain it, but the emotion was fleeting, and she had thought little of it in the passing months. Maybe it was seeing Grant all dressed up in his fine suit or the vodka she'd taken from the liquor cabinet when no one was looking that brought on the untimely agitation. Either way, she needed to remain resolute. Grant was just a gateway, that's all.

Unburdened, Grant fell into a deep sleep, turning over onto his side, away from the pile of unleashed clothing on the floor. Suzie got up from the bed, careful not to wake him, and rifled through his pockets, her usual post-coital tradition. Normally, she'd wait until he was in the washroom cleaning up, but instead, she used this opportune moment to sneak through his wallet.

As she flipped the leather pocketbook open, neatly tucked into the insert, she saw a wedding picture of Grant and Grace wearing bright smiles, and scoffed. She also located several, crisp, one-hundred-dollar bills, which immediately withdrew her attention from the photo as she grabbed at one, figuring it would not be missed. She stared briefly at the portrait of Benjamin Franklin and nodded satisfactorily. It would do for now. She placed the wallet back into his jacket, counting on the idea that there would be more to come.

Suzie looked at Grant pathetically, rolling her eyes upwards. He was so relaxed and unknowing. She did not feel a single twinge of guilt, that gene being effectively erased from her body given her upbringing. Besides, he was as depraved as she was, even more so. He was an adult, not a teenager, without the forethought of consequences. He would get what he deserved.

She tucked the bill carefully into the back pocket of her jeans that lay on the ground and returned to the bed, her temporary absence going unnoticed. Suzie quietly crawled back underneath the covers laying her head onto the fluffy pillow when Grant suddenly opened his eyes.

"Sorry. How long have I been out?"

Suzie gently caressed his forehead with her fingertips as she looked into his blinking, apologetic eyes. Disguising her antipathy for him, she smiled sweetly and answered, "Not long."

CHAPTER 25

The Confession

(March 2000)

Eager to keep their affair a secret from the world, Suzie and Grant consistently used the same approach when entering and exiting a hotel, a strategy to ensure that they would never be seen together. Grant would arrive or leave first and then allow a few minutes to pass before Suzie would trail far behind. But, when Grant got off the elevator on the first floor of the swanky hotel that afternoon, he hadn't banked on running into Miss Davies in the lobby. I mean, of all people, what were the chances of meeting up with anyone that he knew, let alone Suzie's social worker, at a Lincoln County hotel, in the middle of the day? Hotels were for out-of-towners, invisible people visiting from other cities and countries, not locals helping themselves to a cup of complimentary coffee in a hotel lobby. His stomach dropped when he caught sight of the sign he'd obviously missed earlier, announcing a convention for social workers from the county.

He prayed in vain that he would go unseen and began hurriedly walking in the opposite direction when, suddenly, he heard his name being called out in a loud, unrelenting voice.

"Mr. Russell," Miss Davies shouted, all heads turning in his direction. Before redirecting his gaze from the revolving front door to her, he momentarily thought of ignoring her cry and heading briskly out of the hotel. Unfortunately for Grant, it was too late as she ran toward him, waving both arms over her head, eager to capture his attention, and suddenly, they were face to face.

"Mr. Russell, I thought that was you. How are you? How has Grace been feeling since the hearing? I've been meaning to get in touch with her, but you know, always on the clock," she went on, pointing at the pager strapped firmly to her belt.

"Hello Miss Davies, fancy meeting you here, of all the gin joints," he faltered, understanding full well how corny he must have sounded. Grant silently admonished himself for seeming so caught off guard. He steeled his feet to the ground for support, feeling slightly faint, as he answered her questions reluctantly. "I'm fine. She's fine. You know Grace, always finding new projects to keep herself busy."

"What are you doing here?" she asked, looking around the lobby, unsure if she would be expecting to see his wife somewhere in tow.

"I was meeting a colleague for lunch," he answered, trying his best to sound convincing, hoping his hair didn't look too dishevelled being in bed all afternoon with Suzie.

Miss Davies looked at the clock and commented sarcastically, "That's a long lunch," she paused. "It's three in the afternoon," announcing the time.

Mr. Russell, checking the face of his bejewelled wristwatch, desperate to sound unfettered, replied, "Oh, so it is. I didn't realize the time. We must have run late, so much to discuss. Anyway, I'd better head back to the office before they put an all-points bulletin out for me," Mr. Russell joked, mindfully trying to hurry her along. All he needed was for Suzie to walk out of that elevator while he was speaking to Miss Davies; his next stop would be Kennebec County Correctional facility.

"How has Rita been doing since Sarah left? Is she coping okay with the change, keeping up with her studies?"

"Sure, you know Rita, good as gold that one."

"That's true. If only all my girls were like Rita it would make my job a lot easier. And what about Suzie?" she continued her interrogation.

"To be honest, Grace would be the one to ask, you know, she has more of a connection incidentally, teen age girls and all. They don't involve themselves very much with me, you know, discuss their feelings," Grant answered, beads of perspiration forming on his top lip.

"Okay then, Mr. Russell, it was nice seeing you," she faltered, aware that Grant was trying to ditch her, figuring he was in a mad rush. "I'm glad Grace is feeling better. Maybe I'll check in with her this week. It's been a while since I've been to the house. You know, with the growing caseload." She motioned toward her canvas bag full of organized files, each folder containing a more depressing story than the next.

Just then, Mr. Russell heard the familiar chime of the elevator landing on the first floor. The Doors opened, and he saw Suzie standing in the car. The elevator attendant shouted out, "Lobby".

For a second, Suzie stood stunned, her eyes emblazoned at the two of them standing awkwardly in the foyer. She immediately darted behind the elevator attendant for cover, praying she's been missed. Miss Davies followed Grant's eyes toward the elevator, just as he thought Suzie had become invisible.

"Was that . . .?" she asked, her voice trailing off, sounding confused. As the elevator doors closed, Miss Davies immediately turned her inquisitive look back towards Grant, uncertainty in her glare.

"Was that who?" Grant asked surreptitiously, cramming down his panic.

"Hmmm, no one, I guess. My eyes must be deceiving me. I'm sorry, I should be going. Our break is almost over," she answered, giving her head a slight but visible shake.

"Well then, enjoy the rest of your conference," motioning to the sign posted only three or four feet away. "Have a good day Miss Davies, good seeing you."

"Likewise," she answered, her focus returning towards the elevator, practically willing it to re-open, as she walked slowly away.

"Fuck," Grant whispered, just audible enough for himself to hear. He walked out of the hotel without a backwards glance, moving swiftly toward his car. He put his key in the door and immediately took refuge in the driver's seat. He slammed his fist on the steering wheel, "Damn that was close," he conceded before turning on the ignition and accelerating out of his parking spot. He drove erratically, travelling way above the speed limit back to his office.

When he finally arrived, he pencilled a fake entry into his journal, just in case Grace should somehow learn about his accidental meeting with Miss Davies. Somehow, he was sure that she would. He exhaled a huge breath and prayed that Miss Davies would let the whole thing go, that she was not convinced she'd seen Suzie behind the liftman. He yearned for the day that the two of them would no longer have to sneak around. The close call reminded him that he needed to hurry his get-away ploy along. He sat at his desk and slammed down his fist. He had gotten away with it this time, but deep down, he figured his luck would soon run out.

CHAPTER 26

The Confession

(March 2000)

Grace opened the refrigerator door and selected a cold bottle of chardonnay from the chiller shelf, pouring herself a healthy measure of the golden coloured liquid into a long-stemmed wine glass. It was almost five o'clock and she was having a good day. She carelessly filled the goblet to the rim, sitting down with the daily crossword puzzle from the local paper. Her worries about me becoming a problem seemed to have been in vain, Sarah's departure not propelling me to make a connection with Suzie. In fact, it seemed to Grace that Sarah leaving had had the opposite effect on me. I had been spending less time at home, deliberately staying out of Suzie's way, attending class, and studying at the library for my SATs that were around the corner. I wasn't interested in finding out more about Suzie. I'd done everything I could to stay out of her way. Besides, I already knew all there was to know, not only about Suzie but about Grace and Grant and their depraved undertaking, and they were none the wiser.

Grace took the glass in her hand and sat languorously at the kitchen table, nursing her glass slowly, enjoying the cool sensation of the buttery liquid descending smoothly down her throat as she filled in the clues with ink. But as the alcohol crept through her veins, relaxing her even further, the doorbell rang, jolting her upright, nearly causing a spill.

"Who the hell could that be?" she asked herself, raising an eyebrow as she set the glass gently back down on the counter, annoyed at the interruption. Making her way to the door, Grace peered out of the sidelight, clapping her eyes on Miss Davies' car. "What could she possibly want?" Grace said to no one in particular. She sighed as she unlocked the bolt and pulled the heavy door open with a synthetic smile.

"Sorry to show up unannounced, Grace. Do you mind if I come in for a minute?" Miss Davies asked, shutting her umbrella and shaking off the excess water from the canopy.

"Sure, please. I've just poured myself a glass of wine. I know it's a bit early, but it's six o'clock somewhere, isn't it?" Grace laughed at her facetious excuse for imbibing so early in the evening.

"No judgement here, Grace. It looks very similar to what my night will look like once I finally get home," Miss Davies laughed.

That didn't surprise Grace. She assumed that Miss Davies' job would be dispiriting, one that would call for or even require alcohol or prescribed medication to assist her in winding down after a bleak day, making her wonder why she'd have chosen her career.

"I don't suppose you want to start early?" Grace grinned, searching for another glass, opening and closing the cupboards anxiously. For some reason, Miss Davies' visits always made her feel uneasy.

"No thanks, Grace, I'm still on the clock. A glass of water would be nice if that's being offered? I'm actually here to speak to you about something important; if I could have a few moments of your time?"

"Of course." Grace fumbled for a tumbler, trying to keep her hands steady. She moved towards the sink and unscrewed the tap, placing the glass beneath the cold, running water. She would have splashed some on her face if she'd had the opportunity. "What is this about?" Grace asked, motioning towards the table, a wordless invitation to join her.

Miss Davies pulled out a chair and sat down as she grabbed a file from her bag and asked curiously, "Is Suzie home?

"No, she hasn't come home from school yet. Why do you ask?" Grace's stomach was tied in knots. If she were to be honest with herself and with Miss Davies, the truth was that she had no idea if Suzie had been to school, as she rarely attended class. In fact, she had no idea where Suzie was or when she would be home but had a feeling that she was about to find out.

Opening the file that contained upwards of fifty pages, she replied with a sigh, "That's the problem, Grace. She wasn't at school today. I called the principal, and he told me Suzie was truant, and this behavior was not unusual for her. He also said that he has brought this to your attention on more than one occasion." Miss Davies took a sip of her water and returned it to the coaster with a clunk, protecting the solid oak table and carried on. "Grace, I'd be lying if I said that I wasn't concerned. You know that Suzie is one of our problem foster girls. It's your responsibility, and Grant's, to make sure she's making it to class. Are you positive you're up to handling a case like Suzie? I mean, she can be a bit of a handful, even for our more experienced foster parents."

"Of course I am," Grace protested, her voice beginning to give rise. "Sure, she's not exactly easy, but don't you dare think for half a second that I'm not up for the challenge. I'll be sure to speak to her the minute she gets through that door. I'm sorry, Miss Davies, we will certainly be more vigilant in the future." Beads of sweat made their way from Grace's brow, threatening to drip directly into her wine glass. She dabbed gingerly at her forehead with a napkin, hopelessly trying to mask her discomfort. She feared that Miss Davies was coming to take Suzie away, but nothing could prepare her for what came next.

Putting aside Grace's promise to run a tighter ship for a moment, Miss Davies said with a pause, "Listen, Grace, there's something else I need to talk to you about." Grace wasn't sure if she could handle another scolding from Miss Davies today and grimaced, but Miss Davies continued. "I had the pleasure of seeing Grant today at the Beaumont Hotel in midtown. I ran into him in the lobby this afternoon."

Grace's mind was dizzy with confusion. She didn't understand where this conversation was leading.

"Is that so?" she managed to get out with great effort, keeping a lid on her powder keg of emotions threatening to explode. "That's interesting. Did you have an opportunity to speak to him?"

"I did," Miss Davies nodded and sat up straighter, tilting her head. "Were you aware he had a lunch meeting at the hotel today?" she asked in a solicitous tone, her impertinent stare gauging Grace's reaction.

Grace's head spun wildly at the question, her speech beginning to falter. "A lunch meeting at the hotel? Why, no, I didn't, but he doesn't always make me privy to his schedule."

"There's more," she went on, biting at her lower lip, appearing nervous, and then releasing the news. "Well, I'm sure it's nothing, perhaps just as likely a figment of my imagination, but I thought that I may have seen Suzie at the hotel as well."

"Suzie?" Grace responded aghast. "I'm sure your eyes must have been playing tricks on you, Miss Davies. I mean, what would Suzie be doing at a hotel in midtown?"

Miss Davies took another sip of her water before locking eyes with Grace, "I'm not sure. I was hoping you could help me to answer that question?"

"With all due respect, Miss Davies, as I told you earlier, I thought Suzie was at school where she should have been. I have a lot going on here, two children to look after, appointments, and parent council. I can't know where each girl is every second of the day, but surely you did not see Suzie at that hotel. I mean, what are you even implying?" Grace was becoming slightly hysterical, pushing her chair back with a loud scrape as she rose to her feet.

"Calm down, Grace," Miss Davies said, gently reaching for Grace's forearm, willing her to sit back in her seat. It alarmed her to see Grace become so upset, and she made a strategic decision to back down from her line of questioning, releasing her hold. After all, Suzie was not the only child Miss Davies had to worry about, she had dozens of kids on her roster, and she couldn't afford to lose the Russells as a foster parents altogether. Besides, for all Miss Davies knew, she had made a mistake, she hadn't seen Suzie at the hotel at all, and Grant was telling the truth about his meeting.

"I'm not implying anything, Grace. Perhaps I've misspoken," Miss Davies backpedalled, but in an abundance of caution, she added, "I'm sorry if I was out of line, but the truth is, well, I'm worried about Suzie, given her bleak past, you know, with men," Miss Davies said, lifting an eyebrow. "Maybe you could watch her more closely, at least for the time being."

Grace knew what Miss Davies was referring to, the prostitution, the back pages. Perhaps Miss Davies never meant to insinuate that Suzie had been with Grant, but, instead with a 'client'. That certainly was a possibility, and the idea relaxed Grace somewhat. At the same time, she knew she had to alleviate Miss Davies' misgivings regarding their parenting abilities if they wanted to be considered for adopting Suzie's baby once it arrived.

"Of course I will, Miss Davies. I'm glad you have brought this to my attention,"

Grace replied, instantly relieved she was not implicating Grant in any wrongdoing.

"Thank you, Grace. I knew that you would understand. Look at these files," Miss Davies frowned, lifting her bag of manila folders. "There are so many kids I have to keep track of, ensure that they are abiding by our rules and staying safe."

"Absolutely," Grace conceded.

"Before I go," she lingered at the table, "I've been wanting to ask, how is Rita been doing? Has she been ok since Sarah left? I know that they were good friends."

"Yes, fine, perfect actually. She's been studying hard for her SATs that are coming up next month."

"That's great. I wish all of my kids were like her," Miss Davies nodded satisfactorily, the corners of her mouth slightly turned up.

"Indeed." Grace returned a cordial smile, meeting her eyes.

Finally, she took the last sip from her glass and moved swiftly toward the door, her questions answered, her concerns, to all appearances, alleviated.

"Good day, Grace." Miss Davies petitioned as she turned the brass knob clockwise, letting herself out.

"Good day, Miss Davies," Grace replied, closing the door securely behind her. When she was satisfied that Miss Davies had driven away, she ran toward her wine glass and slugged back the remaining contents in one, long swallow. She threw the glass into the stainless-steel sink, shattering it into a hundred small shards, slicing her hand in the process. She grabbed at a dishtowel and wrapped it tightly around the wound. Miss Davies had finally confirmed her suspicions. How naive she had been.

CHAPTER 27

The Confession

(March 2000)

Grant arrived home that night, unaware of what he was about to meet at the other side of the door. He had had no idea about Miss Davies' visit with Grace earlier that evening. At the office, he had wrestled with the likelihood that his wife would somehow find out about him being at the hotel; he just wasn't aware that the news would travel this fast.

He casually entered his home, assuming he would find his usual dinner on the table, but instead, when he made his way into the kitchen, he was faced with an inebriated Grace, the towel still bandaging her bloody hand. He stood confused for a second and looked around the room, no doubt searching for us girls who might bear witness to this woman whose face he recognized, but not her behavior. He stared uneasily at the nearly empty wine bottle on the counter and braced himself.

"They're out," she said in a slurred speech before he even had a chance to ask.

"What's going on?" he questioned Grace sheepishly, now already quite aware of what beheld him.

"You were at the Beaumont this afternoon," Grace answered, her voice more even this time.

It was exactly what he had feared; that Miss Davies would run straight to Grace, even if it was only to plant a seed of doubt in her head. Immediately, he was grateful that he had the wherewithal to etch the made-up entry in his calendar before leaving the office.

"I was. I had a meeting. I thought I'd mentioned it," he answered wistfully, picking up the TV converter and turning on the nightly news.

"No. You didn't. I think that I would remember something like that . . . a meeting at a fancy hotel."

"Well, you know how preoccupied you have been. You've probably just forgotten."

"Stop bullshitting me, Grant. You weren't at any business meeting. You were at the hotel with Suzie. How long has this been going on?"

Grant was taken aback by Grace's choice of words. She rarely cursed, and he knew he had to think fast on his feet. Deciding to play dumb, he answered, "Suzie? What would give you that idea?"

"Miss Davies popped by. She was concerned that Suzie had skipped school today. She thought she may have seen her at the hotel."

"That's preposterous," Grant insisted, standing up taller to appear more commanding. "I wasn't at the hotel with Suzie. I was at a meeting. Call my secretary. She'll verify what I'm telling you."

"You've been taking advantage of our little arrangement, haven't you?" Grace returned, still unconvinced of Grant's alibi.

"That's ridiculous, Grace, I was at a meeting, and I'm not going to say it again," he rebelled, his voice amplifying.

"Liar!" Grace spat, her eyes shaming him.

Knowing that nothing he could say would convince her he had been at the hotel for a meeting, he shrugged his shoulders in defeat, giving up his facade.

"So. I was at the hotel with Suzie. So what? I'm busted. Who cares anyway? You were the one who asked for this Grace," he reminded her, rudely pointing his finger in Grace's direction.

"This is not what I asked for and you know it! It was only supposed to be a few *scheduled* visits. But now you're shacking up with a teenager in the middle of the afternoon when she should be at school? How many other dates like this have there been, Grant? How many other swanky hotels have you taken her to? I want the truth."

"Just a few," another lie told, happy he had paid cash. "The question is, why do you care so much? We haven't had sex in ages, and besides, you should be thanking me. I've been doubling our chances," he said with a smirk on his face.

Grace picked up the first thing she could get her hands on, a spatula, a corkscrew maybe, and threw it in Grant's direction, nearly missing his head as it clanged against the wall behind him before landing on the ground.

"I need to be in the loop, Grant. This wasn't part of the agreement."

"Fuck your agreement, Grace. Since when do you make all the rules? You started this, and I'm going to finish it. You still want a baby, right? Then stop making a fuss."

Again, Grace was made to feel like a scolded child. She was no longer in control. She'd pushed her husband into this affair and Grant was right; it was all her fault.

"Do you love her?" Grace sniffled, knowing full well she wouldn't get the truth from him.

"Don't be absurd, Grace. A man has needs, that's all."

But she wasn't interested in hearing about his needs. At this point, she was only concerned with her own. Now outplayed, her eyes oozing with tears of hot betrayal, she conceded and roared, "For God's sake Grant, get this thing done once and for all. And next time, don't be so fucking careless!" She poured the remaining wine into her glass and drained it quickly.

Refusing to react to her tears, Grant asked, "Does Miss Davies know?" His original concern about getting caught by Grace immediately shifted to whether he'd been found out by the social worker.

"I think I've convinced her that she was seeing things. It's over, for now," Grace answered, trying to assure him, as well as herself.

And just like that, the argument between them was over. Grant had been caught red-handed, and Grace would just have to accept his infidelity if she truly wanted a baby. She debated with herself, deciding on what was most important to her, saving face or having a family? But now, with her pride disintegrating and her mind made up, she let the whole thing go. Suzie wasn't a permanent fixture, she was just a passing fancy, and her husband would eventually lose interest, especially after she became pregnant. She didn't believe that that sort of thing would be a turn-on for Grant.

Just as Grace had decided to weather the storm and the battle had concluded, I walked into the house, having heard the shouts from outside of the door. I figured I knew what they had been arguing about but couldn't make out what was being said.

Grace looked disheveled and out of sorts, but she quickly reined herself in as she caught sight of me in the doorway.

"What happened to your hand?" I asked, the shouting and the vision of a polluted Grace haplessly bringing me back to my days with Ray and Laura.

"Nothing dear, just a silly accident," said Grace, removing the towel and wiggling her fingers. "Look, it is fine," she assured, offering me something to eat as she staggered about the kitchen. She worried how much I'd heard before coming through the door but decided it was just the alcohol that was fuelling her anxiety.

"No, thank you, I'm not hungry. I think I'll just head to my room, if you'll excuse me." I bowed my head and quickly took my leave.

"I think I'll head up too, have a shower and get to bed. It's been a long day," Grant said cool-headedly, making his way in line behind, leaving Grace alone in her quiet, but sad contentment.

While the warm water cascaded over Grant's body, releasing the tension he'd built up during his altercation with Grace, he decided then and there that it was time to make his exit. Considering his close encounter with Miss Davies, and Grace now being in the know, he figured the sooner the better. His brain turned relentlessly as he actualized a meticulous blueprint of what his subterfuge would look like. He'd thought about it many times before but he wanted it to be seamless, taking Suzie, his work, and finances into careful consideration. "Just another week, tops," he thought as he shut off the water and stepped out of the shower. He was almost ready, and his timing couldn't be more perfect.

CHAPTER 28

The Confession

(March 2000)

After arriving home to the to-do in the kitchen and excusing myself from the very uncomfortable situation happening downstairs, I made my way to my bedroom feeling slightly overwhelmed. Several hours had passed since I'd learned the truth about Suzie's liaison with the Russells and what was really going on between the three of them, but I hadn't let the enormity of it sink in, until now. The wheels were falling off, and I was desperate to tell someone.

I had made several attempts to contact Sarah in the past twenty-four hours, leaving messages on their answering machine to call me back, urgency evident in my voice. I started to wonder if I should be concerned as she would usually call me back straight away. I wondered if something was wrong. Perhaps things weren't working out as Sarah had hoped, but I decided to give it a little more time before raising any red flags. I called one last time and when there was no answer, yet again, and no more room to leave messages, I slammed down the handset back on the receiver and huffed. I needed to speak to her, pining to get this information off my chest.

I sat on my bed cross-legged and opened a maths book. I wasn't really in the mood for quadratic equations, but I took a crack at my homework anyway. Grabbing a pencil, I got to work, simultaneously listening for the familiar ring of the telephone to clamour, longing to pick it up and hear the soothing voice of my best friend on the other end of the line.

After sifting through functions, variables, and sequences, an hour later, I was done and still no call back from Sarah. I sighed heavily as I threw my books back into my school bag and placed it on the floor beside my bed with a thud. That thing had started to weigh a ton. Sarah would always laugh at me when I'd need to take a rest halfway home from school. But she didn't take any maths classes, so she wasn't toting around the heavy textbooks, making her load a lot more manageable. I decided to close my eyes for a few moments, the formulas having given me a dull headache. I rubbed gently at my temples and tried to clear my head of everything, at least for just a few minutes.

But suddenly the door swung open, and it was Suzie, standing still in its frame. She stared blankly at her end of the bedroom without a word, likely ensuring that it was exactly how she had left it, that no one had been snooping into her things. No doubt she had just come from seeing Grant; I mean, she wasn't at school, and where else could she have been? I shuddered at the very thought of them together. But, I have to admit, I did look forward to reading that diary tomorrow once her newly dated entry was complete.

For a brief moment, it irked me inside, thinking of Suzie's treachery, her betrayal of Grace's trust, never having seen her in such poor condition before tonight. But I quickly gave my head a good shake, reminding myself that neither of those two could be trusted and that each of them was equally to blame. So instead, I took comfort in the knowledge that soon, Suzie would be gone, as well as Grant. Grace would lean on me for comfort, her husband having left her behind, and my position in this house would be secured.

Suzie made her way to her bed, jumping and landing on it with a resounding bang which startled me. She looked at me with a disapproving face and laughed, "Did I scare you?"

"No, you didn't scare me," I replied, even though she surely had. "You surprised me, that's all. Do you always have to be so loud?"

"Chill out roomie. You've been a bit agitated since your friend has been gone. By the way, have you even heard from her? Or has she dropped you like the hot potato that I knew she would?"

"She hasn't dropped me, Suzie. She's just busy settling in." As my reply fell off my tongue, I wasn't sure who I was trying to convince, her or me. "You'll see," I went on, "that phone is gonna ring any minute now."

"Sure it is," she falsely reassured me, rolling her eyes. "Listen Rita. It happens, she's met some new friends and has moved on. And maybe you should do the same instead of pathetically ogling that phone, willing it to ring."

Even though I was angry and hurt by Suzie's suggestion that Sarah had *dropped* me, I was starting to believe that she wasn't wrong. Maybe Sarah's new friends were chewing up all her free time, leaving little to none for me. But what about our tattoos? The markings in permanent ink that branded us friends for infinity. Certainly, she hadn't forgotten her oath so quickly. I didn't want my mind to go there. After all, it had only been a few days, so I decided to ignore Suzie, rolling on my side, positioning my back towards her.

"What is it? Have I hurt your feelings? Grow up Rita. Surely this isn't the first time anyone's forgotten about you . . . let you down. I mean seriously, you're here, aren't you?"

Suzie's words stung, causing me to wince at the very sound of her voice. As usual, she was malicious and unkind, but sadly her statement was not untrue. I had been abandoned before, but I hadn't wanted to be reminded of it, least of all by Suzie. I wanted to shout at her and curse her, but after taking a couple of deep breaths, I thought better of it.

When Sarah was around, I could handle Suzie's obnoxious behaviour, I didn't cower when it was two against one. Sarah would always be prepared with a great four-letter comeback for Suzie, willing to take her on, verbally and physically. But alone in this room with one of the most vial people I have ever met, I felt out of sorts and decided to keep my mouth shut.

An unexpected wash of empathy must have cascaded over Suzie at that moment, seeing me cocooned in my blankets with nothing left to say. She sat up in bed and in a less bitchy tone, she said, "I know you're hurt, and I know you're lonely, but you have to get used to it. Kids like us have to deal with this all of the time. Have you ever heard the expression, 'What doesn't kill you will make you stronger'? Well, it's true."

And with that said, I threw on my earphones and put a tape into my portable player, something I had picked up on my shopping trip with Sarah. I didn't want to hear any more of her nonsense, though in her own right, she was, at the bare minimum, attempting to be nice for a change. I hit the play button with the intention of simply drowning out her voice, but as a bonus, the melodies provided comfort. With the beat of the music assuaging my sadness that had been looming in Sarah's absence, I closed my eyes and let sleep take me.

CHAPTER 29

The Confession

(March 2000)

The music must have been more soothing than I had bargained for as I woke up unsettled the next morning, surprised at finding I had slept all through the night. A restless sleep mind you, filled with dreams of Sarah, so vivid, I almost thought that when I finally opened my eyes and looked around, I might find her in the room, back in her old bed, the pillow covering her head. I quickly threw off my duvet, swinging my legs from the mattress, making my way toward the answering machine, worried that I had missed her call. Unfortunately, when I pressed on the button, I was abruptly faced with what I had always dreaded hearing, "You have no new message . . . beep."

My shoulders slumped in disappointment, and I wondered if I had done something to upset her. I picked up the phone and dialled Sarah's number which I now knew off by heart, but again, there was no answer. However, this time, there had been newly made space for messages to be left, proving she had heard and ignored my earlier pleas to call me back. I was angry but mostly hurt. Hanging up the phone without leaving another message, I got myself into the shower, hoping that a splash of warm water would revive my spirits a bit. I had a test to study for, but that could wait a few minutes while I ran the shampoo and conditioner through my tangled hair. Slightly rejuvenated from a good scrub, I stepped out of the shower onto the plush rug beneath my feet and wrapped a soft terry towel around me.

"It's possible she just doesn't want to talk with Becky around," I reasoned with myself, "or maybe Becky is blocking my calls," conjuring up excuses in my head for Sarah's failure to respond as I dragged the comb through my wet hair. I didn't want to be so simplistic, but maybe it was truly that simple.

It was Wednesday, the weekend ahead with no plans, the norm since Sarah had left the Russells. I crumpled at the recollection of those precious days we'd spent together. Anyone with their head on straight would think the memories of us, having had these unforgettable times with one another, would incite feelings of weightlessness and appreciation, but instead, they made me feel heavy, burdened by the idea that they were in the rear-view mirror.

I needed to pull myself together, to think of something, some way, that I could mend the fracturing relationship. I bounced lightly on the bathmat beneath my feet, thinking of ways to get Sarah's attention. I had already told her that I had something important that I needed to tell her, and it hadn't gotten me any response. Suddenly, my hand flew to my mouth, feeling a unexpected redness spread over my cheeks. *Perhaps an impromptu visit to Sarah would be just the thing to breathe some life into our dying friendship.* I smiled at the idea of surprising her. Certainly the visit would be well received.

So, Saturday after work, still not having heard a peep from Sarah, at precisely two-fifty-eight pm, I boarded the bus to Waldoboro, experiencing frenzied emotions of both fear and excitement. In half an hour, I'd see my friend again which should have made me happy, but as they called to board, I began to feel nervous, immediately questioning the grand gesture. My hands became damp as I forced a few calming breaths, desperately attempting to push away my irrational trepidation. But helplessly, I continued to circle back to the distinct possibility that maybe she wouldn't feel content to see me, but at the very least, I would get an explanation for her silent treatment.

Either way, I was now on route, and it was too late to turn back. I tried to think positively as I nibbled at the snack I'd packed from the coffee shop for the journey. A chocolate croissant, stale now, but it would have to do. I took small bites, but the dryness in my mouth was making it impossible to swallow. Besides, I didn't really have an appetite.

I spent the drive up to Waldoboro thinking about what I'd say once I arrived, unannounced, on their doorstep, but once they called out my arrival, none of the words seemed fitting. Sarah would see right through a rehearsed speech, making my visit look planned and not spontaneous. I decided to just let nature take its course. I knew that once I saw Sarah, I would know exactly what to say.

I followed my map to Sarah's place, just a one-mile walk from the bus station. There was still a chill in the air and the wind almost took the sheet from my hands as I clutched to the directions for dear life. I followed all the side streets in, through the puddles, wishing I'd worn a smarter set of boots. Getting dressed, I selected a more stylish pair, the ones Sarah and I had shopped for together, the ones that would make me look cool once I reached her front door. I knew she had new friends and I was steadfast in my desire to measure up.

With the map still in my death grip, I had finally made it. 150 Appleby Avenue. This was it; I was here and I was pleased with my decision. I folded up the map and placed it in my backpack, walking with determination through the white picket gate toward the painted blue door. It was a small house, rickety and old, but charming all the same. It wasn't the Russell's Victorian, but it was a home that anyone could be proud of. If I was being honest, I wasn't sure what to expect, but it certainly wasn't this. If anything, I was impressed.

It was getting dark, so without hesitation, I rang the bell and waited for signs of life. Minutes passed, and just before I was about to try the bell again, a flicker of light appeared above me. I heard some shuffling before I saw a dark pupil staring right at me through the peephole. I smiled and gave a slight wave, hoping I would not be turned away.

"Who is it?" A gravelly voice asked from the other side of the door, one that I had recognized as Becky's from her untimely arrival outside of the Russell's place.

"It's me, Rita, from the foster home. I'm here to see Sarah. Can I come in?" I petitioned from the veranda, the wind starting to pick up. I heard a heavy sigh as she turned the lock and opened the door just a crack, failing to unhinge the chain.

"What are you doing here?" she asked, sounding slightly annoyed at the intrusion. After what she had pulled months ago, showing up out of the clear blue sky, you'd think she would have been a little more understanding of my plight.

"As I said, I'm here to see Sarah."

"Well, does she know you're coming?" she mumbled, her speech slightly garbled, a whiff of alcohol on her breath.

"No, I mean, I thought I'd surprise her," I answered, trying to remain optimistic even though I could sense that Becky was alone in the house, no signs of Sarah in the background, validating my trip here had been a useless idea.

"She's not home, Rita. She's out with her boyfriend. Jake I believe his name is. Yes, Jake or maybe Mark, I'm not sure." Becky pursed her lips and turned her eyes upward, trying to jog her memory. "Anyway, they're at the movies, at least that's what she told me."

It didn't come as a surprise to me that Sarah's own mother wouldn't know the name of her mystery boyfriend, the one whom I had heard nothing of, or where they were currently hanging out. She didn't strike me as someone who would provide much supervision, given her past parenting skills.

She began to shut the door in my face when I pushed back gently, "Do you know when she'll be home? I don't mind waiting."

"She didn't say. It could be hours, who knows. It's Saturday night. Look, I'd invite you in, but I'm kind of busy."

Peering through the door that was barely ajar, I could see what her idea of *busy* meant. Becky's gaze followed mine to the old, woolly blankets smothering the couch, next to a half-empty bottle of wine that stood open on the end table. I shuddered as my thoughts, for the second time this week, trailed back to Laura, wasting away on the sofa with her own bottle of whatever she could get her hands on.

"Okay then," I said. "I guess I should be heading back to Cooper's Mills before I miss my bus." My head hung as I turned and walked away from Becky, making my way back towards the gate.

"Listen," Becky called out unlatching the door chain, and following a few steps behind. She grabbed my hand and wouldn't let go, forcing me to listen to what she had to say. "Don't worry about Sarah, okay? She's fine;

we're both fine. What you saw back there was nothing. It's just . . ." Becky stopped to think before speaking again. "I'm trying to unwind after a long week, that's all. Just some *me* time, you know? It's not easy having a kid in the house again. It's been an adjustment, having someone always underfoot."

I took a step back, my heart hammering at her words that I tried desperately to make sense of. She'd moved heaven and earth to bring her daughter home, turned Sarah's world upside down and just weeks in, she was complaining? How dare she? Becky had no idea how her comment burned at me, how I would have given anything to have Sarah back, to even just speak to her for five minutes. I tugged my hand from hers without speaking and walked hastily toward the bus station before I could say something I'd regret.

Making my way to the terminal by memory, I could still hear Becky calling out to me, desperate to have me hear her out. But no longer willing to listen and not being able to get away from the nasty woman fast enough, I took the corners rapidly and blindly, the fur lining of my hood obstructing my vision. Completely preoccupied, I found myself colliding with someone, knocked backwards by the jolt. I pulled my hood back, about to warn the person to watch where they were going, when I looked up and saw the familiar face that virtually sent my heart soaring.

"Sarah," I cried, reaching with both arms with the intention of giving her a big, barrelling hug, but instead was offered just a casual embrace before she quickly let go.

"Rita? Why are you . . . I mean . . . how did you get here?" Sarah stuttered, looking from one side to the other, presumably for Grace's car.

"I took the bus. I came to see *you*," I answered cheerfully, hoping she would share in my excitement.

"You should have called first," she answered tightly, staring at the ground.

"I did call. Several times. I've left tons of messages for you, but you didn't call me back. Besides, I wanted to surprise you."

"Mission accomplished," Sarah faltered.

"Don't worry about not returning my calls. It's fine. I know you've been busy. But I'm here now and we can talk all we want. The last bus doesn't leave until nine-thirty pm. Why don't we go back to your place, where it's warm?" I took her arm in mine like I used to, pulling her towards Becky's. "Come on. I'm freezing out here."

"No Rita, really, now's not a good time."

"Are you worried that I'll see Becky drinking back there? Don't worry, I've already seen her, and I have half a mind to tell Miss Davies that she's in need of bumping up that bi-weekly visit."

"Rita, no. Please, that's not necessary. You don't have to do that."

"I don't mind, Sarah I'd be happy to. Maybe it'll give you the opportunity to come back," I grinned.

"Rita! Stop! Just stop it!" Sarah ordered.

"Stop what? Stop caring? Stop worrying? What exactly would you like me to stop? I've come out of my way to see you, and it seems like you don't even want me here."

Sarah fixed her jaw, and without thinking she yelled out, "You're right. I don't want you here. I never asked you to come," unlinking her arm from mine.

I stood stunned, time seeming to slow for a few seconds as my ears tried to absorb what I'd heard. The one thing I had feared the most had come true, my best friend didn't want to see me, but I had no clue what it was all about.

"But why," I asked, my chest caving as the harsh words dug deeply into my sternum.

"Because Rita, I'm starting a new chapter in my life. I have new friends. A boyfriend. I'm getting settled, and I don't need you ruining things for me."

"What are you talking about? How would I ruin things for you? All I wanted to do was talk. To reconnect. You've been very distant lately."

"By doing what you are doing, getting into our business. By running to Miss Davies, telling her what you think you saw. You've got the wrong idea Rita. No matter how much you'd like to believe it, Becky isn't Laura," Sarah exploded, her face so close to mine.

"I never said she was. And just because you have new friends and a boyfriend, it doesn't mean you should disregard your old ones. Seriously Sarah, what is this about?" I begged as Sarah turned away in a huff. Desperate for answers, I grabbed at her sleeve, unintentionally pulling it upwards, the infinity tattoo now exposed to the brisk air.

Sarah glanced apathetically at the ink on her wrist and quickly covered it back up. "This was your stupid idea," Sarah reprimanded me, waving her hand in a frenzy above her head.

"Stupid? But we swore, friends for infinity," I whined, my voice starting to become irritating now, even to me. I didn't expect to have to beg for Sarah's friendship. I had earned that relationship over the months and countless precious moments we'd spent together. For the life of me, as hard as I'd tried to understand Sarah's point of view, without a valid explanation, I could not put together what was happening.

"Listen Rita, I've moved on. Shit happens, ok? It's been a couple of weeks and I'm happy here. I'm trying to put my past behind me and move forward, and that includes you and the Russells and every foster home I've been in along the way," Sarah answered, more calmly, but with conviction. "I want to forget that the last six years ever happened."

There was little, if anything, left for me to say. Sarah had made up her mind. I gave her a long, hard stare, forcing her to look into my eyes. I thought I might see something, some hint of remorse for her cruel treatment, some other explanation for why she was discarding me this way. But there was nothing, just an empty stare. The same girl I met last year. The lost person she'd been before we became friends.

Notwithstanding, in that moment of helplessness, I decided to play my last hand and spouted off what I had learned, trying eagerly to get her attention.

"Grace is paying Suzie to sleep with Grant, to give them a baby!"

Sarah's interest was momentarily piqued, her eyes opening noticeably wider. This excited me, thinking she would ask more questions, and invite me back to her house where I would be able to finish my story. But instead, after a second's pause, she simply shrugged. Sarah was no longer concerned with anything that had to do with me, Suzie, or the Russells, that much she made perfectly clear. She remained silent, her face, once again, neutral, offering no verbal reply, just a shrug, and definitely no invitation back to Becky's as I'd hoped.

I immediately sank at the idea that I had no more cards to play, tears of resentment freezing to my face in the bitter wind. But angry at being rejected, I instructed forcefully, "Listen, forget about what I told you, and if you can't forget it, just keep it to yourself, please. Regardless of what is happening at the Russell's, I'm comfortable and want to stay. Besides, none of it is our business. Maybe it's time I think about moving forward too, about what's best for *me*."

Sarah nodded, indicating that she understood before turning back towards home. I watched her go, my anger being replaced with a sour resentment, the same way I'd felt when Ray had left us with no real explanation. Suzie was right I should be used to being left behind, first my parents and now my best friend. But while I learned to forgive Ray, I could never forgive Sarah for treating me like something she'd stepped in. When I had finally reached the bus, I was exhausted and screamed unabashedly, falling to the concrete until I appeared like nothing more than an inconsolable child who hadn't gotten her way. The stares came in droves, and it wasn't until a uniformed officer from the terminal came and picked me up off the ground that I was able to gain some composure.

"Where are you going, miss?" he asked in a concerned, but agitated voice, lifting me to my feet.

"Cooper's Mills," I managed to answer as he threw my arm over his shoulder and gently guided me to the correct platform.

CHAPTER 30

The Confession

(March 2000)

I must have dozed off on the bus home, as when the driver called out, "Cooper's Mills," I sat up with a start, thankful I hadn't missed my stop. I stood and walked to the exit as the bus came to a chugging halt, carefully taking one slippery step at a time toward the platform. My head hung lethargically, and I was flooded in disappointment as I waded my way through the slush, taking in gulps of fresh air.

As I reached the Russell's front door, I thought fleetingly about not going in, about turning around and disappearing into the night, finding a new life as Sarah had, moving on from the past and the present while setting up a future of my own. But something stopped me. I had obviously lost Sarah, but I still had this place that brought mild comfort with its familiarity and truthfully, I had no way of starting over anew, at least not yet. Sarah had managed to get out of Cooper's Mills, and Suzie was well on her way, but unfortunately, my opportunities were limited. I needed shelter, people. I needed to finish my year, take my SATs and get into a good college.

Conceding, I turned the doorknob and crept quietly inside, wishing not to be heard, and definitely not seen, my face stained with salty tears and my eyes puffy from crying. I removed my coat and stepped into the foyer. Unfortunately, my wish had not come true as I was met head-on by Grace who appeared genuinely concerned.

"Rita?" she asked with an abundance of care. "What's wrong? Where have you been? I've been worried sick."

For some reason, though, I knew that the person before me, someone I had once admired and grown close to, was truly sick and undeserving of my attention, in the moment, with Grace's arms stretched out wide upon seeing my distorted face, I immediately reacted. I fell into them without thinking, knowing it was the only consolation I would be getting after the unsettling meeting with Sarah. I momentarily took comfort in the knowledge that we were two souls commiserating, both of us being left to the wolves to feast on.

"I've been to see Sarah."

"What happened?" She asked with an abundance of care, unravelling our embrace and grabbing my hands firmly.

"She told me she doesn't want to be friends anymore. That she is moving on," I answered, nearly sobbing.

"That's ridiculous," she said as she let go of my hands, her arms crossing over her chest inquisitively. "It's not even been a month. You two were a great pair."

"I know," I answered as I ran my sleeve over my nose, which was dripping from the combination of tears and the dampness outside. "I'm still in a bit of shock."

"Come with me," she said, guiding my shoulders towards the kitchen. "I'll make us some hot chocolate, a house special, and you can tell me everything."

"If it's all the same to you, Grace," I said, taking a step back, unwilling to rehash the very unpleasant meeting. "I think I'll just go upstairs and get some rest."

Reining in her disappointment, she responded dolefully, "Okay then, go on up. Maybe you'll feel better in the morning."

"Thanks, Grace, I'll take a rain check," I replied, turning my back on her and heading towards my bedroom.

Grace watched as I climbed the stairs. Painfully aware of her eyes following me, I had the urge to turn around and tell her what I knew, that Suzie and Grant had a plan to disappear, feeling a tug of obligation in light of how kind she'd been. But that, I thought, would be insane, the confession only being forced in a split second of indebtedness, a knee-jerk reaction to my despair. I mean, really, what did I have to prosper from telling her? All hell would break loose, and realistically, the longer I could keep this thing quiet, the more I would have to gain. I'd get to stay and in the meantime, keep a fancy roof over my head until it was my decision to leave, instead of being forced out.

While I began to see reason, now thinking a little more clearly, I marched on with resilience and kept my mouth shut. I'd been knocked off my feet, but I didn't want to fall any further than I already had. Aside from having a nice home to live in, I still had my school and my job, and with Sarah officially out of my life, I didn't want those things snatched away from me too.

Unequivocally deciding that I would bide my time under the scandalous roof where everyone was depravedly profiting from one another, I shut the door behind me, excited at finding the room empty. I went straight for the loose floorboard and picked up the diary that Suzie now felt comfortable enough leaving behind, blazing through her most recent entries.

As it turned out, I was right. Suzie had been out with Grant last Tuesday afternoon, this time at a fancy hotel where she took the opportunity to add to her stack of cash that was tightly enclosed in rubber bands. She had also written that she may have been seen by Miss Davies in the elevator of the hotel, but so far, this was unconfirmed. "This is what the Russells must have been arguing about the other night," I thought.

With the current entry read, I closed the book and slid it back into place, covering it carefully so it would appear untouched. Only moments later I heard the door close noisily downstairs and was pleased with my excellent timing.

I hurried quietly to my bed and tried to act as normal as possible, my face still unwashed having run out of time, pulling a teen magazine from my nightstand and pretending to read. When she came inside, she, as Grace had, noticed I'd been crying.

"Still no call?" she asked flatly.

"No, no call, but . . ." and in that second, without thinking, I blurted out the entirety of my visit to Sarah, sure that the crude details of my trip to Waldoboro wouldn't extract empathy from her.

But surprisingly, she asked, "Are you okay?" removing her wet jacket and throwing it onto the floor next to her bed.

Suzie's motivation to have this conversation being unclear, guarded, I answered, "Not really, but I will be."

"Well, if you need to talk about it . . ." Suzie stopped speaking, continuing on about her business.

"I'll manage, but I can't help but wonder . . . why all the sudden preoccupation with my life? You've never shown any interest before, why now?"

"Forgive me for trying to be nice. I'm sorry I asked," she answered, taking up her usual post on top of her bed, and turning off her light.

"That's not what I meant . . . I'm just . . ."

"Forget it," Suzie interrupted, "You're right. I don't know why I asked," abruptly trying to put an end to our conversation.

I reached for my light as well, it was very late, and I was grateful the awful day was finally coming to an end. But before exhaustion could take me, feeling spiteful at being cut off, I asked, "Anything exciting happening in *your* life, Suzie?"

***

Suzie listened keenly for sounds coming from my end of the room. When she heard deep breathing resonating from my bed, sure that I was out, she peeled back the carpet and lifted the food board to ensure the safety of her journal following my unsolicited inquiry. To her dismay, but not to her surprise, the book wasn't how she had left it, she was sure of it. The satin string Suzie usually tied tightly around it was loose, the pages falling open. She knew then and there that I had been snooping, and read its contents while she had been out. But without any solid proof backing her theory, she tried to calm her increasing heart rate. Just the same, Suzie grabbed at the journal and tucked it underneath her for protection with the promise that she would never again leave the pages unattended.

"That bitch!" Suzie exclaimed as she glared to the other side of the room, plowing a fist into her mattress and screaming into her pillow.

CHAPTER 31

The Confession

(March 2000)

"Rita, can you come down here for a moment please?" Grace yelled from the bottom of the stairs, dressed in a very smart, cream-coloured blouse and a skin-tight pair of jeans. She slung a bright blue, cross-body purse neatly over her chest looking very polished, ready to prance the catwalk. No one would ever guess that she was nothing short of a maniacal sociopath, just a typical spoiled housewife with a platinum card who spends big bucks at expensive stores and salons.

She had woken up early, deciding to surprise me with a day of shopping after seeing me in pieces following my journey to Waldoboro. She had already called the school, making an excuse for my absence. Besides trying to be consoling, the winter was coming to an end, and she desperately wanted to cast an eye on the summer fashions that were now donning the display windows of every store in Cooper's Mills. Grace found this activity very soothing, running her fingers over the soft and silky materials of all the new sweaters, blouses, dresses, and slacks that hung in the fancy boutiques.

Leary at the prospect of skipping class, but tired of spending time alone, I agreed to join her. This was not the first time we had ventured out together, and I knew I was libel to get more than a few nice items for my wardrobe. I didn't want to seem too eager at first, so I let a few moments pass before I answered with a simple, "Sure," from the confines of my room. I grabbed my jacket and made my way downstairs with a smile. "I'm ready," I said, my voice coming from around the corner.

That afternoon the pair of us masked our inner quandaries with mindless retail therapy. We strolled aimlessly as we took in the fresh scent of the spring foliage, gripping the handles of the designer bags that held all this coming season's trends and styles. My mood began to lighten at the thought of showing off my new things at school. With Sarah having cut me off, I would soon have to start thinking of making new friends as she had, and being contemporary couldn't hurt.

We were out there for hours, pounding the pavement leaving no shop unvisited, when finally, spent and out of steam, Grace suggested, "How about some lunch?" pointing to a fancy tavern on the corner. "I'm famished."

I grinned, approving the invitation, my stomach starting to pang hours before. We walked in unison to the glass door that read in frosted letters, *The Bistro*. As we pulled the door open, we were met by the maître d' who wore a starched white shirt and a pair of pressed black pants finishing the look with a burgundy bow tie and an apron tied around his waist. He asked if we preferred to dine 'al fresco', which at the time, I did not know meant open air. Seeing the blank look on my face, Grace nodded and took the lead, walking ahead as I followed her toward the outdoor patio.

As we passed through the restaurant, it was difficult not to gawk at the pristine tables, set with tablecloths and napkins, floral centrepieces, and so much cutlery I couldn't guess what it was all used for. I marvelled at the sight, touching the linens, likely lingering a fraction too long as other guests began to stare.

The weather was warmer than expected for late March and the sun was beginning to peek through the overcast sky. The maître d' led us to a large, round table set for two and pulled out our chairs. As we sat, he set the menus down in front of us, but not before grabbing at the napkins and placing them in our laps like we were royalty. I smiled at Grace and she smiled back. I hadn't felt this content in a long time, almost forgetting about my meeting with Sarah yesterday. I picked up the vase and put my nose to what looked like carnations, taking in the fragrance of cinnamon and cloves. I set it back down and turned to Grace, "So what's good here?"

Grace immediately looked at the waiter who appeared at once. As he poured icy water into our glasses, we listened to him spout off the daily specials from memory. When he reached the end of a long list that included Maine's iconic culinary delicacies like fish chowders and fiddleheads, a man I had never seen before approached our table, his arms wide open.

"Grace Russell. Is that really you?" The stranger's voice barrelled as Grace looked up to meet his face with an obvious stare of recognition. He grabbed at Grace's waist, pulling her from her chair like a rag doll. He was a burly man and he hugged her exuberantly, scooping her up off her feet and then twirling her around like a ballerina, nearly knocking the other patrons from their chairs.

"Put me down, Arty Abbot, you old flirt," she laughed and returned to her seat, retrieving her napkin that had fallen to the floor. Before she could ask him to join us, the man pulled out one of the vacant chairs and made himself comfortable, motioning for the waiter to bring him a drink. He was tall with broad shoulders, and he had a deep voice. He had a little grey showing around his temples, but still, he was handsome.

"How long has it been?" he sputtered in excitement.

"Too long," Grace answered as she patted him gently on his knee. "And how is Barbara? I haven't seen her since the last mixer at the sorority house. That was a crazy night." They giggled and winked at one another as though they were sharing an inside joke.

"Oh, the old gal is great," he grinned, looking pleased. "We married over three years ago," he continued, tapping his jacket pocket, presumably searching for his wallet. When he'd found it, he reached inside, producing a wedding photo of the two of them with gusto.

Grace took it in her hand and joked playfully, "That's funny I don't recall receiving a wedding invitation," passing the photo back to him.

"Oh, it was quick," he answered defensively, "you know, shotgun quick."

"Oh, she was pregnant?" said Grace, deciphering his code.

"Yes, with Elizabeth, our oldest," he answered, handing her another photo. "That's her there, and this is Laura," pointing to each of his children as he spoke. "Elizabeth has just turned three years old, and Laura is one."

Ogling the photo, Grace gave a stoic half-smile, fighting back tears, eagerly disguising her emotional distress. Everyone had kids but her. However, determined to keep their chance meeting upbeat, she decided to change the subject.

"Are you still in Cooper's Mills?"

"No," he replied as he replaced the photos back into the picture flap. "We moved out to Westport after Elizabeth was born, and we've been there ever since. It's better for families."

"I see," Grace answered, her body tensing while bile rose in her throat. "Where are my manners? Arty, this is Rita, my..."

"Sister?" Arty completed her sentence.

Flattered and now blushing, Grace answered him back, "Don't be silly Arty. This is my foster child, Rita."

"Child? You don't look like any child I've ever seen," he commented wryly, sizing me up from head to toe as he took my hand. I stared blankly at this man whose prurient smirk was beginning to creep me out.

"Yes, Arty, child," Grace answered back defensively, batting his hand away from mine, instantly irritated by the idea that all men were the same. I was just a teenager, but then, so was Suzie, and that hadn't stopped her from asking her to sleep with her husband.

"Well it's nice to meet you, Rita," Arty answered back, less salaciously picking up on Grace's reproach. "Funny," he remarked quizzically, tilting his head noticeably to one side. "I didn't think the two of you wanted kids."

"What would have given you that impression?" Grace questioned, confusion washing over her as she placed her hands on her hips. She didn't think that that was a conversation piece Grant and Arty would have explored back in their fraternity days.

"Well, you know . . ., the . . ." he stopped, immediately regretting bringing up the topic.

"The what?" Grace asked light-heartedly, though his hesitance to finish was making her feel uneasy. Whatever was on his mind, it was more than obvious he did not want to say the words out loud. Grace stared at Arty in anticipation; her hands trembled while she fidgeted in her seat. "What, Arty? What on earth are you talking about? Tell me now!" She hissed through clenched teeth as she tugged forcefully at his sleeve.

Again, the cat had gotten Arty's tongue, so instead of using his words, he removed his sleeve from her stronghold and, slowly, with two fingers placed strategically near his groin, he mimicked the gesture of something being cut with scissors. "You know . . ." Raising his brow, again, he left his sentence hanging.

Grace gasped openly. She had pieced together what he was trying to say without him actually *saying* it, but she couldn't believe it. Her mouth hung open as the colour drained from her cheeks. *How? When? And why was Arty privy to this piece of personal information that Grace was not?* So many questions trampled through her mind. She shook her head back and forward for several seconds as she let the suggestion sink in.

"It's not possible, You're mistaken Arty!" Grace finally blurted out, taking loud, long breaths as she waved her hand at Arty's erroneous suggestion.

"Well maybe I am," he replied apologetically, though it was apparent he wasn't sorry at all, and that what he had said, he was certain to be true. It was so obvious; he quite simply knew something that she didn't.

I sat silently in my chair as I watched the exchange between them unfold, the corners of my mouth dropping expeditiously. I thought about the diary, what was going on between Suzie and Mr. Russell and Grace's hand in all of it. It was a massive slap in her face. This plan she had put together, the risks she had taken orchestrating it, the peril she had put her marriage into by its very suggestion, it was all for nothing, as Grace was now fiercely aware. And putting all that aside, as if that wasn't enough, all of this time the couple had remained childless, she was made to believe that it was entirely her fault. It was the ultimate betrayal.

With her last bit of dignity intact, Grace rose to her feet, placing the napkin from her lap gently onto the table.

"It's been a pleasure Arty," Grace bristled, as she bent over and lifted her shopping bags. "Let's go Rita. Suddenly I've lost my appetite."

"Grace . . . wait," he begged, but it was too late. She brushed by him violently before running toward the door.

I was disappointed, but I didn't argue. I knew it was time to get out of there, and I didn't waste a moment saying goodbye to this clueless individual who couldn't quit while he was ahead. I grabbed my packages and dutifully fell in behind Grace, who clearly could not get out of there fast enough. She hurried to the car, slamming the door behind her. When I finally caught up, I could see Arty falling well behind, giving up his chase.

Now, seated in the car and safely out of his earshot, she turned her tortured face to meet mine. Looking at me sternly, she said, losing her breath, "You don't mention what you heard at lunch today to anyone, do you hear me? No one is to find out about this! Don't even mention Arty's name. Especially to Grant. Got it?"

I nodded wordlessly, pledging allegiance to Grace. When she was satisfied that I understood her demands, she turned the ignition and roared out of the parking lot. Throwing on my seatbelt, I braced myself for the massive explosion that would undeniably take place once we reached home.

CHAPTER 32

The Confession

(April 2000)

While Rita and Grace were out shopping, figuring Suzie had played hooky as well, Grant snagged his opportunity to call her at home, something he'd never done before. He didn't fancy the idea of risking a phone call, figuring any one of us could listen in, and, unlike Suzie, he certainly never put anything in writing. All their arrangements to meet had been made in person, brief and indiscernible conversations, careful at being discreet.

"Hello," Suzie answered in a husky morning voice after the phone had rung loudly several times, Grant nearly giving up. She didn't realize that she was alone in the house, and she never liked picking up. She sounded annoyed as she waited for the person on the other end to start talking.

"Suzie? It's Grant," he said, speaking urgently. Is everyone still out?" Barely giving her time to look out of the window to see if Grace's car was parked outside, he demanded, "Suzie, answer me!"

With her upscale vehicle absent from the driveway, she answered, "I guess so. Why?" Suzie took note of the time. It was already after twelve, but she had been up all night, tossing and turning, deciding whether or not I had read her diary.

"We need to talk. It's important. When can you meet me?"

"I'm getting up now. I don't know, half an hour? You don't sound good. Is everything alright?"

"No, I mean, yes," he grunted, "I need to see you. It's important. Meet me in the alley in thirty minutes. I need time to settle some things up at work."

"Sure, but you're scaring me. What's going on?" Suzie asked.

"I'll explain when I see you. Just meet me there. Can you do that, please?"

"Yes, I guess. I'll see you then," she said and heard a click on the other end.

Agonizing over having to make her way downtown, she stretched and yawned with abandon while she made her way to the closet. Half an hour wasn't long enough to have a shower and get herself to the alley. Aware of her time constraints, she decided to skip the shower and instead, she brushed her teeth and ran the deodorant stick under each of her armpits. She threw on her usual garb, a hoodie and dark jeans, completely forgetting to grab the diary on her way out.

Suzie made her way on foot through town, rushing to their meeting spot after consulting her watch. She didn't want to keep Grant waiting. She knew that whatever he had to tell her must have been important, calling her on the house phone. She pulled her hood over her head, prudent not to be seen after the close call with Miss Davies and ventured toward town. She thought momentarily of the first night they had gotten together and how far she had come since, from the seediness of the alley to fanciful hotels, and she was pleased with herself. When she finally arrived, just a couple of minutes late, she saw that Grant was already waiting for her, standing covertly behind the garbage bin.

"Where's the fire?" Suzie asked jokingly, though her grin quickly fell off when she caught sight of Grant's pale face.

"It's time Suzie," he said with suggestions of excitement and fear in his tone.

"What do you mean, it's time?"

"It's time to go, the two of us, like we planned," careening her in his arms.

"Now?" she asked, pushing him away, partially annoyed he had made these plans without consulting her first. "But . . ."

"She knows!" He interrupted before Suzie could protest further.

"Who knows?" Suzie asked.

"Grace." He answered, becoming mildly fed up, time not being on their side.

"She knows what?"

"Stop being so coy, Suzie. About our affair, what else?" Grant raised his voice, exasperated by the question.

"How does she know?"

"Miss Davies believes she saw you in the elevator at the Beaumont. She told Grace, and she pieced it together. I've been trying to warn you for nearly a week."

"But you denied it . . . right?"

Grand exhaled loudly and answered, "I tried, but she wore me down."

"Hmmm, but, wait . . . if Miss Davies saw me . . . how am I still here?"

"There's no time for a long explanation. Let's just say Miss Davies thinks you're up to your old *tricks*, so to speak," he answered, clearing his throat.

Suzie was calmer than Grant imagined. He figured this would upset her more than it had. But for Suzie, it was not a surprise. She always knew that Grace had

had her suspicions, but it was not like she would run and tell anyone. As for Miss Davies and her thoughts of her, she wasn't thrilled, but it was better than her thinking she had been with Grant that afternoon.

"So, what are we going to do?" Suzie shrugged carelessly.

"We need to catch a bus today! Everything is in order," he answered, showing her a knapsack full of crisp green bills.

Her eyes wide, she gasped and happily acquiesced. Suzie had always been greedy, so tamping down her earlier protests, she conceded, "No time like the present, I guess." She had planned for this moment and waited patiently for the day that she would leave this place for good, and it had finally come.

Without necessarily meaning to, she added to Grant's ruffled state and blurted out, "I think Rita knows too."

"What?" He asked breathlessly. "How do you know?"

"I just know, okay. Forget it. When do we leave?" Suzie asked, changing the subject. She didn't want to worry Grant further by telling him that I had seen them together months ago, and she certainly didn't want to mention the diary. Admittedly, she had initially started the journal for insurance until she was paid by Grace after giving her a baby. But even after she'd changed teams and took up with Grant, she'd kept it going, intent on getting a payout from one of them, she didn't care who. But, to her surprise, she wouldn't need it after all.

Grant was standing in front of her, ready to go with a bag topped full of cash, and he was taking her with him, as promised. But all the same, she didn't need it falling into the wrong hands and thought wistfully of the promise she'd made yesterday never again to leave it unmanned.

"Then it's settled. We leave this afternoon. It's only a matter of time before Rita goes blithering to Miss Davies. Meet me at the terminal at four pm. We'll make a quick stop, lay low, just a couple of weeks; until the smoke clears, and then we'll start making our way south from there. But in case something goes wrong, take this," handing her a piece of paper with an address on it. "That's where we'll be staying for the time being."

With Grant's mind made up and Rita and Grace still out on their 'mother, daughter' shopping expedition, Suzie tucked the paper into her back pocket and kissed him goodbye.

"I need to run back home and pack some things. I'll see you at four."

Suzie turned and started to run, Grant watching her disappear in the distance. Tired but determined, she gathered speed, making a mental note of the few things she wanted to take with her, including the box tucked safely, she believed, beneath the floorboard. Winded, she still managed a smile as she huffed, and thought, *"I'm finally getting out for good."*

With his office cleared out and the daunting trip to the bank behind him, Grant exhaled and checked the time. It was just one o'clock and he had a few hours to kill. He decided that he would get a much needed drink to steady his nerve, making his way to a seedy bar at the edge of town, not far from the terminal. As he walked, he imagined what his new life with Suzie would be like. At the same time, he grinned at the thought of Grace's expression when she would learn that he'd quit his job, cleaned out their bank account and that she was to blame.

Putting one foot in front of the other with no thoughts of turning back, he felt a buzzing coming from his belt line. It was his beeper, paging him to call the office.

He wondered what they could possibly want from him, his contract terminated, and his final cheque cut, including a little bonus for his dedication and hard work. Perhaps he had left something behind. The idea of disregarding the page crossed his mind, but he felt that he owed them the courtesy of a call back, given how understanding they had been about him leaving so suddenly. He blamed Grace, relaying to his bosses that since their dream of having children had been all but quashed, his wife was eager to get out of her hometown and explore new networking opportunities while she reignited her career in fashion. "New York," he told them, the team of bosses feeling sorry for them and instead of talking him into staying on, they offered him letters of reference.

He peered around for the nearest phone booth, throwing a quarter into the slot and dialled the office's phone number. When Beatrice answered the call, the blue-haired secretary who had become a relic in the office, celebrating her fortieth anniversary last fall, she said apologetically, "Sorry to bother you Grant. I know you are very busy with the move and all, but you have an urgent call."

"From whom?" Grant asked apprehensively, his stomach dropping as he waited for the answer.

"He says his name is Arthur Abbot."

CHAPTER 33

The Confession

(September 2000)

Shortly after learning about her husband's vasectomy and his ruthless betrayal, Grace was on a mission. She yanked on the steering wheel hard as she let out a vitriolic scream. She looked possessed, while sweat dripped from her brow, and her face warped with an expression of disgust.

We rode in silence aside from the bestial whines coming from the very core of her belly. After she arrived home, I stayed out of her way, cowering in the family room as she went furiously through Grant's wardrobe, searching through his pockets, boxes, and old files, finding nothing to confirm what she had learned.

If Grant had really had a vasectomy in college, that meant that he'd been lying to her all these years, that he never intended on having a baby with her, or Suzie, for that matter. It would explain why Suzie hadn't gotten pregnant yet after all the extra-curricular sex they were having. She was enraged and couldn't help but wonder if this was something that he'd been keeping from everyone or if she was the only person being duped. It was possible that Suzie knew about his deeply hidden secret and had kept the initial payment, making false promises, knowing full well that she could never carry through with what they agreed to.

She went to our room next, rummaging angrily among Suzie's things. She ripped apart her bed, stormed through her closet and emptied her drawers until it looked like a storm had blown through, and figuratively speaking, it had. She didn't know what she was looking for, just something that would give her assumptions some oxygen. Raging at finding nothing to implicate Suzie, she stamped her foot in frustration, hearing the creak of the floorboard beneath her. She immediately looked to her feet, remembering the loose plank and her unfulfilled promise of having it fixed. Conceding that it would be a perfecting hiding spot, she rolled back the rug and lifted the board. To her delight, right in front of her laid the items she had no idea she'd been looking for, a steel box that enclosed the answers to her many questions.

She grabbed at the diary first, with confusion and fury, skimming the pages with great speed, her breath heaving rapidly. Aside from the fact that it contained several dark secrets that would ruin them both, it also confirmed her deep-rooted fear that Suzie hadn't any intention of fulfilling her end of the bargain. Next, she took lifted the second item in her hand, the pills, and squeezed them tightly in her palm, screaming bloody murder. The only ounce of solace she felt in that dreadful moment, while the rug was being pulled from beneath her, were two things. One, that she had not been the only one kept in the dark about Grant's little secret. The birth control pills confirmed that. But more importantly, she had found the diary before Suzie had the opportunity to use it against them.

Finally, she took hold of the money and counted it. Her deposit was all there, and then some, which she gathered from the journal, the excess had been stolen from Grant when he was distracted. With his head in la la land, he was essentially paying her for sex, just like her previous John's. She scolded herself for trusting either of them, never for one second blaming herself for even believing that she could pull off the operation.

Returning the items securely back into the box, Grace ran out the door, screaming Suzie's name. When Suzie wasn't home, she took a deep breath, barely able to hold it together as she considered her next move. With her discovery, it was all over. Her plan to have a baby had been quashed again. But these two, they would get what they had coming to them. Having taken ownership of the diary, she could never be implicated. She would get rid of it, and no one would believe it was Grace who had sent this ball rolling should someone point the finger in her direction. It was payback time, having played the fool for long enough. She would tell police that her husband was having sex with one of their foster children, that's all the authorities needed to know, and they would likely accept her at her word. And even if they didn't, Miss Davies had all but seen the two of them at The Beaumont Hotel, which would support her accusation.

When she landed in the kitchen, it was just in time to hear the mud room door open, and Grace braced herself for the unpleasant encounter that awaited them. When Suzie turned the corner, she grimaced at the twisted look on Grace's face as she carried the metal box over her head. She smashed it on the counter with a heavy slam, knocking the diary loose. Suzie immediately took up a fighting stance, planting her feet firmly, her hands ready for Grace's attack.

"You fucking bitch," she yelled, drivels of saliva landing on Suzie's face. "I trusted you!!!!" She screamed, her lips pulling back, baring her teeth as she poked her finger in Suzie's face.

"Well, that was your first mistake, wasn't it?" Suzie said, unflinching, never losing Grace's gaze. Though she tried to appear unruffled, the sight of her diary falling loose burdened her. She needed to get at it before Grace could.

But before she could make a move, Grace barrelled towards her, ready to wring Suzie's neck. She made a noise so shrill; it shocked the two of them equally, disturbing Suzie's artificial calm. No longer able to ignore the commotion, I ran from the den where I had been hiding out since we landed in the driveway, careful to stay out of Grace's way. I knew that Grace uncovering Grant's secret meant the end of the baby-making plan and that the fallout wasn't going to be pretty, but I didn't imagine that she would locate the ammunition she needed to prove Suzie's double-cross. And definitely not on the same day, adding insult to injury.

But, apparently, judging from all the shouting, she surely had located the box, confirming that Grace's determination should never be underestimated. My chin quivered as I popped my head into the kitchen, watching on. I clapped my hand over my mouth, ardent to remain quiet, though I wasn't sure if I was even capable of making a sound.

She screamed into Suzie's face, trapping her in a corner, "I will make you pay for this, you and Grant. He'll be finished in this town, everywhere in fact. He'll go to jail. No one will want to employ anyone who has sex with children, and that's if he ever see's the light of day again! I will tell everyone who will listen and let them know the predator he is. Have him, he's all yours! Oh, wait," she back-pedaled teasingly, "that's right, you don't even want him," she said, taking a few steps back. "Well I can hardly wait to tell him what you've been up to," Grace shouted as she listened to the thrum of her own pulse pounding in her ears. It was pure indignation propelling her and believe me, she would have made good on her threats.

Back at the counter, Grace grabbed at the wad of cash and insisted, "I believe this belongs to me," fanning herself with the bills before placing throwing them carelessly back into the box. Next, she clenched the round, plastic pill dispenser in her hand and howled again before throwing them directly at Suzie. "And these belong to you. You'll need them when you have to start taking up with your *clients* again now that you'll be broke and homeless."

Suzie let the pills hit the wall, shattering the contents all over the floor. She wasn't concerned with the pills just then, her sights set firmly on the diary that lay at Grace's feet. Grace reached for it, taking it tightly in her hand as she dangled it in Suzie's face. She continued screaming at an ear-piercing volume and assured Suzie that she wouldn't have a leg to stand on with the authorities now that the diary was in her possession. The jig was up. She would have no solid proof of Grace's proposition, only her accusations that would basically mean zilch considering her reputation.

Grace began rummaging through the junk drawer that was conveniently within her arms reach. She moved the contents back and forth until she pulled a long barbeque lighter from the clutter, determined to set the drivel alight. She held up the red book, the only catalogued evidence of Grace's baby-making project, and pressed the igniter, holding the flame close to the pages.

"You wouldn't dare," Suzie insisted, her arms crossed tightly against her chest, her face menacing at the idea that Grace had secured the upper hand. Her journal contained solid details, facts and figures; it had evidentiary value she would not be able to recall from the top of her head. Hotel names, dates and times. Sadly, Grace wasn't wrong. No one would ever take her at her word. If only Grant hadn't rushed her out the door this morning, she would have remembered to take it with her.

I begged them to stop yelling, cowering in the corner, nearly scared to death by the pandemonium taking place before my eyes. I was powerless to cease the turbulence and thought briefly of calling the cops should I have found the courage to move a single muscle, when suddenly, there was a loud bang at the front door.

"Grace, are you home? It's me. Please open the door."

Stunned at the horrible timing, Grace stood aghast at the sound of Miss Davies' voice calling out from the other end of the door.

She set down the lighter and moved quickly to the living room window. Still clutching the diary in one hand and pulling back the curtains gently with the other, she could see Miss Davies, with Sarah in tow, standing on the porch. Suzie lunged, taking one more swipe at the red jacket to no avail. Grace had the diary firmly in her grip.

"Grace, I see your car. I know you're in there. Just open the door. We need to talk. I've already called the police." The pounding on the door continued as Grace started to panic.

"You did this, didn't you?" Grace turned her sights away from Suzie for a brief moment, her gaze landing directly on me. "If you knew about this, why didn't you come to me first? You went to Miss Davies? How could you?"

"I didn't go to Miss Davies, I swear!" I told her, my voice shaking. I begged Grace, "Just open the door. We'll straighten this out. I'm on *your* side."

Ignoring my pleas, Grace implored, "Well then, you told your friend, and *she* told Miss Davies. That's it! And don't try denying it, she's standing right outside."

"No," I groaned, flatly denying the accusation. But Grace was right. I had told Sarah about what I'd discovered, at least part of it. Only I hadn't counted on her telling anyone, I just wanted to get her attention. Before we parted company, I had told her it was none of our business, and now, sitting in the midst of the frenzy that was unravelling, I wished that I had kept my mouth shut.

However, knowing Sarah had come for me and, in her own way had tried to help me by telling Miss Davies the truth about the Russells, allowed me to gain some courage as I tried to lift myself up and run for the door. But in my moment of fortitude, I suddenly felt the pain of Grace's sharp kick at my gut, leaving me winded and back where I started, amassed in the corner, unable to move. As she lifted her foot to give me another good kick, I admitted guilt, pleading with her to hold her fire.

With the interminable knocking at the door, Grace lowered her leg to the ground. She had to think fast. She immediately gave up on me, focusing solely on what had to be done before she could open that door. She had to get rid of that diary. She pressed the igniter one last time and turned the burning flame to the pages of the book.

Suzie was outraged, seeing her written words starting to crumple, her backup plan literally going up in smoke. She would surely tell Grant what I had been up to. Out of the corner of her eye, she spotted a shovel in the mudroom that was just a few feet away. She reached at it cunningly, and with a solid grip on the wooden handle, she lifted it high over her head, intending on striking with as much force as she could muster up. She lowered the shovel and heard the crack as it met the top of Grace's skull. Her body shriveled to the floor, a pool of blood forming around her head like a halo. The burning diary had flown from her hands, taking instantly to the linen curtains, the blaze spreading fast and furiously through the kitchen.

With the pungent smell of smoke wafting through the clean spring air, and no one coming to the door despite the fact Miss Davies had told them the police were on their way, in that moment of urgency, she used all her strength, ramming her body into the solid wood. One slam, then another and then with a final, good push, she barged through the front door, shattering the lock.

"What the hell is going on in here?" Miss Davies coughed, the thick smoke already overpowering her lungs. The sight of Grace lying helplessly on the floor shocked her, and for a brief second, she questioned her abilities as a social worker. She admonished herself. How could she have allowed things to go this far? She had had a gut instinct that something wasn't right. But with flames engulfing the better half of the main floor now, there was no time for self-doubt. She ran to her, checking for signs of life, but she was already gone. Knowing there was nothing more that she could do for Grace, she haphazardly bounded toward me, still immobile, in pain, and screaming for help.

Sarah stood mutely for a moment, confused at the sight of the smoke-filled room, unable to help anyone inside, except herself. While Suzie tried, in vain, to save the diary, Sarah's attention focused elsewhere. Through the fog that was now blurring the pathways to escape, she glanced at the cash box on the kitchen counter and somehow mustered up the courage to run at it. Suzie, finally giving up on the diary followed closely, the two of them tussling over the box. But Sarah had surprisingly overpowered her. Taking it in both hands, she knocked Suzie hard, causing her to become unbalanced, briefly losing her footing as she tumbled to the ground.

Sarah could see that Miss Davies was having trouble getting me to my feet, but her fight or flight instinct took over, and she made a quick decision, a choice that she thought she could live with. Instead of helping, the two of us desperately looked on as she ran with the cash, taking careful strides through the rising heat and pyrotechnic flames. Feeling her way through the kitchen to the back door, she finally found refuge, and her breath, in the forest behind the burning Victorian home. She ran as far away as she could into the woods, and gulped in the fresh air greedily, dropping to her knees. She was thankful as guilt-ridden tears soothed her burning eyes, rolling down her face, washing away the ash.

Losing sight of Sarah in the smoke, Suzie knew that she had somehow made her exit, and had taken the cash with her. She forced herself up and rummaged blindly toward an egress, well aware that she couldn't let Sarah get away. Sirens coming quickly in the distance, she lent no effort to help anyone remaining in the uncontained, infernal blaze. She needed to go after Sarah, but not before reaching for the shovel still lying next to Grace, whose gruesome image had thankfully become hazed.

With a hardened focus, she made her way out as well, quickly spotting Sarah in the distance with her back turned to her, gasping as she tried to clear the sludge from her lungs. Suzie, hot on her heels, only about a hundred yards away now, quietly gathered up the last bit of strength that she needed to launch her forward, allowing her to catch up to Sarah, whose head was still tucked towards the ground. She took a silent sip of air, and without saying a word, she lifted the shovel, as she did with Grace, and struck her with just enough force to incapacitate her. Suzie watched in satisfaction as Sarah toppled over, her face blank of expression, her eyes shut. She didn't check for a pulse; she didn't even know how to. Besides, after what she had done to Grace, she figured the blow had done the trick.

Relieved, she hurriedly dug a hole, just long and wide enough to fit Sarah's body in and buried her in a shallow grave. Glancing around, she covered her with a bit of wet dirt and fallen leaves with the intention of returning later to complete the job properly. She grabbed at the cash that had spilled from the box and tucked it back inside.

Suzie looked towards the burning house, still unsure if either Miss Davies or I had escaped. Even with the money, she knew that she wouldn't be able to get very far if we were to tell the police what we knew. The proposal, the murder. The authorities would start a manhunt, and her face, as well as Grant's, would appear on every news channel in Maine. She couldn't take that risk.

But what Suzie didn't know, as she headed back towards the flames, was that I had already gotten out of the house, for which I was, and still am, eternally grateful. Miss Davies, struggling to breathe, was able to make her way to the faucet, grabbing a dish towel and soaking it under the running water. She clambered back toward me as the flames spread throughout the entire house, handing me the towel, urging me to cover my face and make a run for it.

While I was frightened and completely shaken by the events that had led us to this moment, trapped in a fire that was now closing in, I gained new determination at the idea that I was not alone, that someone had fought for me, that I hadn't been abandoned this time. With the towel over my face, I took the path of least resistance toward an exit, waiting for Miss Davies to fall in behind. But she never did. To this day, I still envision her with that shoddy canvas bag, full of files, the legacies of all the girls and boys she had helped, burning along with her in the fire.

Waiting for the police to arrive, I hid behind a huge oak where I saw Suzie barrel back into the house, covering her face with her sleeve. Apparently, her desperation had no limits; perilously urgent to finish what she had started. But sadly, as the cavalry pulled up in front of the house, her image faded in the heavy exhaust, and that was the last I ever saw of her.

I looked briefly for Sarah, but I didn't see her anywhere. Figuring she was long gone with the cold hard cash, I ran to the front of the house through the side walkway and waved my hands furiously, trying to get someone's attention. When the authorities caught up with me, I told them my name and that there were three people left in the house. After braving the raging blaze with gallons of water poured with abandon from the closest hydrant, the fire fighters eventually pulled the charred bodies from the house that day; Grace, Miss Davies, and, Suzie.

CHAPTER 34

The Investigation

(APRIL 2021)

Grateful that this long interview was coming to an end, Detective Hollis rose to his feet, his legs becoming numb having sat in his chair, listening and combing through every detail Rita had to offer for hours. It was late in the morning, nearly noon, and he seemed to have gotten nowhere. He couldn't, for the life of him, understand how Rita could have killed Sarah last night if she had died twenty years ago. Frustrated and ready to keel over once he made it to his feet, he demanded an explanation.

"Okay, so what you are saying is that Sarah rose from the dead and arrived in Greenville twenty-one years after the fire, and what? What happened, Rita? Who was in that park? Tell me, I mean really, I want to help you, but I can't, not until you have told me the truth."

"I'm getting to that, God. You think you're the only one who is tired? Fuck, I'm about to give birth in this chair, and you're exhausted?" Rita was starting to unravel, but then, so was Detective Hollis.

The three of them decided to take one last break before putting this confession to bed, affording all of them a final opportunity to get their ducks in a row. Detective Hollis made his way to the door, itching for another coffee or at least the opportunity to speak to his wife before she put an all-points bulletin out on him.

When he twisted the knob and pulled the door open, he found Constable Miller rushing toward the interview room door, a stack of papers in hand. He had all but forgotten he had sent her on this fact-finding mission and was grateful to see her teeming down the hall. Her timing could not have been more perfect. None of this was making any sense. He needed to know for sure if it was, in fact, Sarah's body that was found in the park or if Rita was just making it all up as she went along.

"I'm sorry, Miller. This has gone on longer than I expected."

"No problem, boss. I just got here," she answered, panting as though she'd just run a marathon.

"Well, what did you find?" Detective Hollis asked curiously, eager to get his hands on anything that could validate Rita's confession.

"I've located Sarah Belmont's driver's licence in the New Hampshire's database, along with a mug shot taken last year, a misdemeanor possession charge. I've compared them with the shots of the girl in the morgue.

They're a match, sir. I also located her old file in the basement and had forensics compare fingerprints. They were a match as well. It's definitely Sarah."

Confused and growing impatient, Detective Hollis said, "Why do I get the feeling that there's more," pulling the documents from her hands.

"Those are the canvassing sheets submitted by all the officers at the scene last night. From what I could gather, several people saw Rita in the area of the park yesterday afternoon, and no one else sir. There's also surveillance video of Rita out front of the hardware store, likely minutes before the murder took place. The shop is around the corner from the park."

"Good 'ol Mrs. Havasham," he said, remembering her suggestion to look for video at Nick's. He shook his head, once again acknowledging that she had been the person responsible for shedding the light on this entire case. Perhaps he would recommend her for a community award, some Good-Samaritan trophy if it existed.

"Also, the results came back from the lab. Constable Moran sure did put a rush on things. The samples from underneath Rita's fingernails match the DNA from the body at the morgue. She definitely killed Sarah. I hate to say it, boss, but it seems like your intuitions were wrong this time," Constable Miller said with remorse, returning to the conversation they'd shared many hours ago.

"I guess so," Detective Hollis replied, feeling a bit stupid for doubting Rita's admission of guilt. I mean, after all, what did she have to gain by confessing to a crime she didn't commit?

"If there's nothing more, boss, I think I'll be heading home to get some shut-eye. I'm due back later this evening. Are you alright?"

"Yes, Miller. I'm fine," he assured her. "By all means, go, and thank you for your help," he answered back, rifling through the pages in his hands as Miller's image became faint, the halls now bustling with officers.

Detective Hollis tucked the sheets under his arm as he reached for his phone, hoping to find another message from his wife, but there was nothing. She was most likely asleep after spending the entire night worrying about him. He typed in a quick message, "I shouldn't be too much longer," hopeful that the rest of this investigation would be quick and dirty. He was almost there.

***

Detective Hollis put the phone back in his pocket and went back inside the confessional, tired and slightly fed up. He decided not to pull any punches, that the Mr. Nice Guy routine had dragged on much longer than it should have.

Placing the documents on the table, he took his seat once again turning the chair around and used its top rail for support and pressed record.

"Rita, please, let's put this investigation to rest. You've already confessed. Just tell me how Sarah, who you claim perished over two decades ago, ended up in the park last night," Detective Hollis begged, aware that he was losing his professionalism. The long, drawn-out story had drained him, and he'd just about had it with the 'I'm pregnant act', practically demanding an explanation.

Rory prompted her with a weary nod while massaging her back, something he'd learned in their Lamaze classes.

"Well? I'm waiting . . ."

"I'm getting to that!" Rita snapped.

Detective Hollis quickly clammed up, resorting back to his usual 'silence is golden' handbook, and waited, this time, more patiently for Rita to carry on.

"Sarah obviously didn't die that night. I'm sure your investigators have already figured that out," Rita responded sarcastically, taking a pause and then continuing. "The next morning, after the fire, Sarah climbed out of that hole, alive and well but in awful shape. She made it to the police station, dirty and dehydrated, repeating what I had already told them. How Grace was killed, about the diary and about her despicable plan to pay for a child. And, finally, how Suzie had attacked her and how she'd made it out of the shallow grave, lucky to be alive."

Detective Hollis nodded, silently urging Rita to carry on.

"Following her near-death experience, and in the wake of her guilt, and greed, she could not find the strength, or courage to face me after what she had done, leaving me to suffer while she grabbed the money and ran. She was simply relieved that I had gotten out intact, and, in the weeks following the fire, she refused her opportunity to make things right. She was just comfortable knowing that somewhere, there was a girl named Rita Morrison, a girl with whom she shared an identical tattoo. A girl who she had tried to help but eventually had left for dead. A girl who was deeply etched in her heart and on her wrist, her friend for infinity, even if I no longer felt the same way. Sarah replaced her guilt temporarily with feelings of pleasure, knowing that wherever I went, I would eventually be happy and find a better existence without the horrible Russells, without the *friend* who had left me behind, and she had made the decision to close the book on her past, this time, for good. She told her story and never looked back."

"And you never wanted to confront her? I mean, in spite of everything, no one could have blamed you for reaching out "

"Really, detective, what more was there to say?"

"So why the sudden appearance in Greenville?" Detective Hollis asked, forgetting his vow of silence, again urging her to answer his questions.

"She got in touch with me about a week ago, begging me to meet her. She said she had something important to discuss with me, that she had to see me immediately and asked me to meet her in Toddler's Park. She had tracked me down from a photo in the Greenville newsletter and wanted the chance to talk things out between us."

"And then?"

"And then I relented and agreed haphazardly to put my feelings about her aside and hear her out," Rita sighed. "We arranged to meet in the park at two-thirty, before the kids got out of school, so that we could be alone."

"So, you both arrived at the park. And then what?"

"Yes, we did, and as I had imagined, Sarah begged me for forgiveness, for shunning me on my trip to Waldoboro, for snagging the money and running, for leaving me the day of the fire. But something in me snapped. She wasn't sorry. She was just looking for absolution. She only wanted to put her mind at peace."

"Why now?" Detective Hollis asked, his interest piqued.

"She told me that for several years she had wanted to get in touch, that she had searched, but she just didn't know where to find me. She had gone to the agency and asked where I had ended up, but they wouldn't tell her anything."

"What do you mean by *snapped*?" Detective Hollis asked, sitting up straighter in his seat.

"You want me to say it again, fine. I will. I killed her. I grabbed her by her throat after her feeble attempt to explain herself, after her lame apology for being a total bitch when I needed her most, after choosing the money over helping me. With the wretched feelings of abandonment flooding back, this time in waves of anger, I squeezed her throat as hard as I could, and when she fell to the ground, I left her in the park. The same way she'd left me the day of the fire."

"Only *you* didn't die."

"And neither did *she*, not until yesterday, that is."

"Okay, so what you are saying, again, for the sake of the recording, is that seeing Sarah again triggered a rage inside you that had been building for the past two decades until it finally erupted having seen her for the first time since the fire?"

"Talk about putting words in my mouth, detective. But, yes, that about sums it up," She answered, her neck barely able to support her head that was now threatening to fall flat onto the table.

And finally, that was it. Rita had told Detective Hollis all of it, from her upbringing, how she landed in the foster system, how she had come to be at the Russell's house of ill repute, to the proposal from Grace, the fire, and how Sarah ended up being in a park in Greenville yesterday afternoon, ultimately meeting her demise.

"Is that it? I mean, is that everything?" He questioned, ensuring she hadn't left out any important information. Detective Hollis crossed his arms securely over his chest as he waited for her answer.

"Yes, that's everything," she replied in an apologetic, solemn voice, her temperament filled with despair, aware of what would happen next.

"Okay then, let it show that Rita Morrison has completed her statement of confession at exactly eleven-hundred and ten hours, on April twelfth, two-thousand and twenty-one years," and enthusiastically hit the stop button.

Placing a stack of paper in front of her, topped with a pen, the detective asked, "And are you willing to sign this confession?" He held his finger out to the large X he had drawn on the line where her signature would fall. It was nearly done, just sign, and it's over. She would have her baby in jail, serving fifteen to twenty years, but she would *eventually* get out and be free. Maybe the judge would go lightly on her sentencing, being pregnant and having a family who needed her, the whole thing not being premeditated.

She looked at Rory, but he could not meet her glare. He simply nodded towards the papers, tears pricking his eyes. She had told Detective Hollis what he needed to hear, and now there was only one thing left to do, sign her name, Rita Morrison.

Rita hesitated, rubbing her belly, thinking of what this would mean for Benjamin and her unborn child. She took one final moment, drew a large breath, and picked up the pen. She signed on the line, threw the pen back on the table in front of the detective and exhaled.

"What happens next?" She wept openly, waiting for the detective's response.

"You'll go in front of a judge at four o'clock. He'll ask you for your plea, and in the presence of your lawyer, Rory, you will plead guilty. You'll be taken to the local women's prison, where you will wait for your sentencing which will likely be next week."

She shuddered at the word 'sentence' and then nodded at Detective Hollis who looked spent, two dark, fluffy clouds hanging heavily from under each eye. It was obvious that he was dealing with a lot more than just this investigation. He was a good detective, he listened and didn't jump to any conclusions. He didn't make assumptions. He allowed Rita to finish her story, for the most part, without being rushed, though clearly, he was wrestling with his own demons. His eyes were not merely tired but also sad. She'd given the detective what he needed to hear to close this case and now he could go home and put this one behind him. He'd gotten another bad guy, another notch on his belt, and would, with any luck, leave this case in the past without giving it another thought.

Two largely built armed guards entered the room, taking each of Rita's elbows in their grip. But before they could place the handcuffs on her, they allowed her to hug Rory one last time. He furrowed his head into the crook of her shoulder, crying relentlessly as they said goodbye. Finally, they shared a peculiar look at one another and kissed hard on the mouth. This niggled at Detective Hollis, but he immediately dismissed his interest, grateful to put a lid on this investigation, thankful to go home to his wife where he knew she was waiting for him. Besides, his intuition had already failed him once over the past twenty-four hours, he couldn't be bothered feeling like a fool again.

As she was escorted out of the room, Rita felt new unfamiliar air fill her lungs. It was the type of oxygen only sipped by a mollified individual. A person who was no longer looking over her shoulder. Sure, she reasoned, it was going to cost her a several years of her life, unable to watch her children grow up and live happily ever after with her husband. But Sarah was gone, the one loose thread that could no longer be pulled, unravelling the maze of strands that still held her secret together.

CHAPTER 35

The Truth

(April 2021)

Four weeks following my confession to Detective Hollis, I gave birth to my son Joshua, relinquishing my parental rights after pleading guilty to a murder charge. I couldn't be someone's mother while stuck in a place like this for the next fifteen years, ten with good behaviour. That was the sentence the Honourable Judge Max Levy had handed down. It was the best he could do under the circumstances, murder in the second degree.

I urged Rory to never bring the children here, to make up some story of where I'd gone. Joshua would never be the wiser, and even Benjamin would be too young to remember his mother, ironically, the same way I grew up.

The parturition went as smoothly as it possibly could have, one arm and one leg shackled to the hospital bed as if in the throes of giving birth I could run anywhere. In prison, you suffer so much indignity, unable to perform any of life's natural functions without being monitored. You must eat, sleep, and use the toilet under someone else's eye. There are no private moments. Even in childbirth, it was protocol to have burly guards positioned outside of my hospital room's door. Rory was not permitted to coach me in the delivery as planned, and even with the tiny human inside of me whom I'd grown so close to, I'd never felt more alone.

Joshua was born at six pounds and four ounces, they said. The nurse wrapped him in a blue blanket and let me hold him for a few moments before I pushed him away. I didn't want to be reminded of what it had felt like to hold a newborn in my arms, but I needed to be a mother, if only for a few seconds. It was a euphoric high. I looked into his eyes, so much like mine, a deep-set blue, encompassed by Rory's face with broad cheekbones and a prominent chin, and then I said goodbye.

I'm sure Rory will take good care of both of our boys. He has always been a great father to Benjamin, though he never wanted children, something he decided years ago, well before we'd met. Besides, I had insisted on a divorce, so I'm sure one day, not long from now, he will remarry, and some lucky woman will inherit an instant family.

Now, six months into my sentence and donned in my orange, prison issued jumpsuit, I sit in my cell where I spend twenty three-hours a day, and am forced to think of the past. Surrounded by three walls and a row of secure steel bars, I laugh at the irony. Caged in my environment, I feel no different than I did for the twenty years I spent after the fire when I was able to roam at liberty. Secrets have an odd way of making a person feel trapped, entangled in their web of deceit, pulling tighter around you until the day when the squeezing becomes so tight, the pressure forces you to explode.

For me, it was Sarah's arrival in Greenville that triggered this tipping point. It is a fallacy to think that sleeping dogs will lie because eventually, whether we like it or not, they always wake up.

Today, sharing this space with two other inmates after cutting a deal with the State's Crown Attorney, I peer around my cell, which is reminiscent of where my secret all started. Sharing a room with two foster girls and an offer that I wasn't in the position to refuse. Twenty-five thousand dollars was a lot of money for someone who arrived at the Russell's with barely the clothes on her back. Of course, I never received the full sum, but with the five thousand dollars I insisted upon initiation and the money I had absconded from Rory's, I mean, Grant's pockets during our meetings, it was more than enough to get me some new clothes, identification, and a bus ticket, leaving a chunk left over. I would never make it to California on what remained but had more than plenty to travel three towns to the east, Greenville, where I've spent the last twenty plus years, hiding in plain sight and doing a pretty good job of it until now.

What I told Detective Hollis in my interview was mostly true. The day of the fire, yes, someone did make it out, but it wasn't Rita. When the police found me in front of the Russell's Victorian, I quickly formulated my plan, strategically running interference. If I couldn't get out of Cooper's Mills, what with the police now invading the entire surrounding area, at the very least, I thought, I could leave my identity behind. I had killed one, maybe even two people, so in that split second, I stole the moment to start afresh.

With the charred bodies inside likely being completely unrecognizable, and all three of our files, mine, Sarah's and Rita's, disintegrating in Miss Davies' canvas bag, our true identities would be conveniently erased. No pictures of us, lists of distinguishable features or even addresses of where we'd been or where we'd come from would be left to find. And, of course, no parents had been searching for Rita or me. Cunningly, I thought there might be a chance to get away with this, to actually become someone else, a chance to be a better person, so I seized the opportunity. I looked around quickly and, almost sure that no one else besides Sarah had gotten out of that house, and with nothing to lose, I told him, "My name is Rita Morrison."

The following morning, after I'd left the station, I'd heard that somehow, Sarah had gotten out of her grave alive. When Sarah woke up and pulled herself to safety, she swore that I would pay for all of this but was relieved when she'd heard I had been killed in the fire. I'm certain that she figured I had gotten what I had coming to me. Miraculously, like I told the detective, she had opted not to meet with 'Rita', still eager to move forward, my true identity remaining safe.

I was whisked away from the house of horrors and placed in a new home, away from Cooper's Mills, and as luck would have it, away from where anyone would recognize me, far from anyone who would know Rita. I waited on pins and needles for the day that someone would have pieced this all together, when someone at the placement centre would have that *'a ha'* moment, but they never did, which was a miracle really, or just a benediction that they really just didn't care. Eventually, like footprints in the sand, transiently in the tides, all traces and thoughts of Suzie had gratefully washed away.

As for Grant, as irony would have it, the day of the fire, as he'd planned, he disappeared in a puff of smoke. After our meeting and his unwelcomed conversation with his old friend Arthur, he tried to warn me what I might be walking into, furiously making his way through the avenues on foot towards home. But when he arrived at the Victorian, he was shaken at the commotion, the smoke, the inferno, and selfishly, he made a run for it, making his four o'clock bus to Greenville.

The next day, desperate for information, he ran to the corner store to snag a newspaper, hopeful to learn something, anything about what had happened at his home. And there it was, smack on the front cover of the Herald and several other national papers, 'Three People Dead In A House Fire', is what the caption read. He sped through the article hopelessly needing to uncover the names of the three deceased. 'Grace Russell, the homeowner, Annie Davies, a local social worker, and a minor whose identity cannot be revealed at this time, perished in the fire, the cause of which is still unknown at this time'.

"Shit!" Grant yelled, frustrated and guilt-ridden. He hadn't meant for things to get this far, definitely not for anyone to die! He had so many unanswered questions. What the fuck happened at that house? Who was the third person? And why had Miss Davies been there at all? He continued skimming the article, which had little to no details, until he reached the last line, 'Police are seeking any information on the whereabouts of Grant Russell for questioning'.

"Fuck!" Blind to what the police had been told, and unsure of whether or not to turn himself in, Grant paced the linoleum floor of his new apartment, a far cry from the luxurious hardwood finishing he was used to. Then, calming himself, he decided to lay low, to bide his time until he could find out more.

For weeks after, he scoured the papers, watched the news, but apparently, three dead people in Cooper's Mills weren't making headlines anymore. He had learned nothing new, and as time passed, and there was still no sign of the girl he'd moved mountains to be with, he figured I'd had been the third victim.

Being Rita Morrison, I had to play by the rules, do what Rita would do, stay in the foster system, go to school and work hard, and be amenable to house rules. But on Rita's eighteenth birthday, now technically mine, August 1st, 1992, I became of legal age to go out into the world on my own, gripping the opportunity deliberately with both hands. I kept the address of where I could find Grant, hopeful he hadn't flown the coup, unknowing whether or not I had survived. I took hold of my bag, said goodbye, and headed straight to the bus station. "One ticket to Greenville, please," I said as I handed over the cash.

Following my arrival, I walked for what seemed like hours, putting one foot in front of the other, when finally, I had made it to my destination. I looked up at the door, scared and unsure about what I'd find on the other side. Even if Grant were there, maybe he wouldn't want to see me after Grace's death. But there was only one way to find out.

Taking a deep breath, I knocked gently at the door. Once, twice, three times, when suddenly it opened, and there he stood, his face smothered in surprise, relief, and guilt. The fire had taken its toll on him. New worry lines attacked the corners of his eyes, his posture withering. To my surprise, he welcomed me in; with open arms, grateful someone he cared about had made it out of that fire alive.

In the tiny house, I broke down and told him everything, about the diary, my original plan, about what I had done to Grace, to Sarah, about my new persona. He told me about his vasectomy, about how he had fooled both Grace and her into thinking he could give anyone a baby. How he had seen the house burning and didn't react.

The two of us feeling exposed, raw, and completely depleted after the long and pitiful conversation, we asleep on the couch, tucking into one another's and for the first time in a long time, we slept the whole night through.

Then, weeks after settling into to my new surroundings, something strange happened, something I was not expecting. All my earlier thoughts of using Grant to widen the distance between Copper's Mills and me started to fade. Life became comfortable, leaning on one another for support. I needed him and he needed me too. It wasn't love, not at first, but we had only each other, and the bond between us grew. Grant changed his name to Rory Rogers. He heard it in a movie once and liked the sound of it. He took the money I'd managed to hang on to and paid for a false law certification. Grant had always been a good lawyer, just a lousy husband. He started up a practice in Sangerville, something small and low profile but fruitful. He took on several divorce cases, and that procured more money than we ever imagined. Soon afterwards, we got married under our pseudonyms.

At the beginning, we laid low, keeping mostly to ourselves, but as time passed, we started to thrive in our new identities. When the money began to pour in, we moved to a more generous house on Sycamore Lane where I started to get involved in community programs out of sheer boredom, arranging the crossing guard schedule at our local school, community barbecues, and the neighborhood watch.

And then, at thirty-two years old, and Grant not getting any younger, I approached him about starting a family which I figured was a long shot. He didn't protest, but he knew, as it stood, he couldn't father any children. We contacted a specialist in town, someone who could reverse his vasectomy but was warned that there was little to no chance of this succeeding. However, not long after we started trying, miraculously, Benjamin was conceived. When he was born, we welcomed him with such enthusiasm we decided to have another.

Until six months ago, we lived quietly in Greenville. We had become a normal family, blending in with society's norms, all the while flying under the radar with our ad-lib identities, avoiding travel and social media. In our twenty-one years together, both of us had grown. We had become different people. I believe it was Rita's identity that forced me to make the change from conniving little bitch to someone who felt worthy of love. Looking back, Rita *was* a wonderful person, always doing the right thing and yearning for acceptance. I guess I decided to follow in her footsteps. and to some degree, though I was partially to blame for her death, I was happy to keep her memory alive.

As for Grant, deep down he had always been a decent person. After all, it was Grace's plan that sent their world spiralling. In his mind, he couldn't be blamed for falling in love, but he would always feel remorse for what happened at that house.

Then, one day, that stupid Mrs. Havasham had taken a picture of Grant and me at a community fundraiser and posted it to the local paper. There we were smack dab on the front cover of Greenville's weekly news rag. I figured it would do no harm, that no one would see it, and if anyone did, that no one would recognize us now. But, to my consternation, my worst fears had come true.

Months ago, Sarah had reached out, asking if I would meet with her. She had figured out who we were after seeing the clipping. She wanted money for her silence. Sarah, unlike myself, had not landed on her feet. Through the years, her guilt over the fire had consumed her and she had taken to drugs and alcohol to numb the pain brought to her by the memory of that fateful day.

I put her off as long as I could but knowing full well that she would never go away, I agreed to meet. I had gone to the bank after discussing it with Grant. He told me to give her what she wanted, whatever it took to make her go away. We had way too much to lose. I was only seventeen when I started sleeping with Grant, and he was my foster dad, in a position of authority. Once the police found out who he was, he would likely go to prison. Never mind the fact that he had been evading questioning for over two decades.

And then, of course, there was the even larger matter, I had killed Grace and had buried Sarah alive. Our children would grow up without parents. I withdrew the cash, twenty-thousand dollars, and met her in the park, hopeful we could be civil, a one-time exchange and she would be gone from our lives. Grant insisted that he go instead of me, being pregnant and all, but I assured him that I would take care of it.

When I saw her standing there in the park, the two of us alone, her eyes sunken, face pale and shrouded in contempt, I knew then that meeting wouldn't go as easy as I had hoped.

"You fucking bitch!" Sarah cried. Her appearance was as filthy as her mouth was, and always had been. She lunged at me, ripping the duffle bag from my hand, and warned me that this was just the beginning.

"You've done pretty well for yourself, I see. Fancy clothes, jewelry, and now a baby!" Sarah said, sizing me up. "There will be a lot more from where this came from! You ruined my life, you stupid whore! You killed Rita!"

I felt the uncontrollable urge to fight back, to be more like my old self, the person who would not take anyone's shit. Beginning to lose my cool, I shouted back, "I didn't kill Rita! *You* did!" Rubbing it in her face more than I had meant to. "You had to tell Miss Davies everything," I yelled. "You brought her to the house! You had no business doing that! And don't think for a second that I've forgotten how you took my money and left Rita in the burning kitchen, choosing the cash over your so-called *friendship.*"

Sarah clamped her hands around her ears. She didn't want to listen to what I had to say because, without a doubt, deep down, she knew that I was right. It wasn't until she saw the photo in the paper that Sarah learned the truth about Rita's fate, but the reality of the situation remained the same, She had never tried to help Rita escape the fire, and, now, with the knowledge that she had not survived it, though Sarah had tried to shift the blame, she felt a hundred times more guilty than she ever had.

"Stop talking!" Sarah shouted, slapping me so violently across the face, it caused me to fall backwards on my ass. It wasn't a surprise; this is exactly what Grant had warned me about.

I padded my throbbing cheek, trying to steady my legs as I picked myself up from the ground, slowly, holding my very round belly. "I won't stop talking! You know the truth as well as I do! Rita is dead because of you!"

Shaking off my claims, she shouted back, "It doesn't matter anymore, does it? She's gone! But *you* killed Grace and *you* tried to kill me! That ought to be worth more than a measly twenty-thousand dollars! If I go to the police and tell them who you really are, they'll lock you up and throw away the key. I want more! A lot more! I made a vow that you would pay for what you'd done to me. And believe me, you *will* pay!"

Just then, she caught sight of my wrist, furnished with the infinity tattoo I had duplicated as soon as I arrived at my new foster home. If I was to become Rita, I needed to do everything I could to create the illusion, and that included imprinting the tattoo, even if it was a botched job.

Sarah wailed at the reproduced image. She was enraged and came at me with murderous eyes. Grabbing my wrist hard, she pulled me towards her, meeting face to face. "You don't deserve to wear that tattoo," she spat. "That was for Rita and me. You don't deserve any of this," her hand gesturing towards my swollen belly and my fancy clothes. Sarah pushed me backward, for a second time, causing me to lose my footing, with no regard for the baby. She didn't care that there was a life growing inside me. She was angry and out for revenge. She was much stronger than she looked, and it had caught me off guard.

But even in my diminished capacity, petrified for our future, our children, and knowing that this extortion would never end, I lifted myself up once more, with explosive energy, and attacked. At first, she fought back and we grappled, scratching at each other and she frantically pulled at my hair. But I over-powered her and I wrapped my hands around her throat, squeezing her neck tightly. She tried to scream, but nothing came out, her cries muted by my strong hold. She kicked at me, hard, but I wouldn't let go. I continued to squeeze until finally the life in her was extinguished. She fell to the ground like a sack of potatoes I quickly looked around to see if anyone had heard us yelling or witnessed the murder, but I saw no one. I went for her wrist to ensure that, this time, she was really gone. When I couldn't feel anything, I picked up the bag of cash, and her purse, moving as quickly as I could toward home.

Once I arrived, out of breath and out of steam, I fell to the cold marble floor and wept uncontrollably. I had killed again. I had finished the job I had started twenty-one years ago. Sarah was not wrong. I did not deserve any of this, the house, the money, my family, even Grant. But now that I had it, I couldn't have let it go!

I should have known that it wouldn't take much for Mrs. Havasham to piece together my involvement. She was always bragging at our local book club that she could have been a detective in another life. In that instant, backed into a corner, I couldn't stay silent any longer. And then, like the day of the fire, I was forced to think quickly on my feet. Together in the interview room with Grant, we concocted my story while the Detective watched on from behind the glass. It wasn't all false, mainly lies of omission. I could stomach going down for one murder, but not two. Besides, I couldn't leave my children without any parents. I couldn't bear the thought of them ending up like I had, in the foster care system, my boys, in turn, repeating my fate. I tipped my hat, eager to take my punishment.

CHAPTER 36

The Fall-Out

(October 2021)

Six months following the unprecedented chaos that had muddied the tranquil waters of Greenville, Constable Miller had been given the dubious task of transposing the precinct's paper archives into their digital system, their department desperately trying to catch up with the twenty-first century.

The boxes had sat in the catacombs of the police station for years, becoming damp and mouldy in the building's underbelly. The command had been waiting for a keener like Miller to turn up, a new recruit whom they could dump the unwelcomed chore onto. She had been introduced to the files when she assisted Detective Hollis with the Rita Morrison investigation, so they could think of no one better for the job.

Miller, constantly eager to please, happily accepted the opportunity, and now, she regretted saying yes, as if she was given the choice. She could almost hear the laughter coming from the rest of her squad as they pictured her toiling in the dank basement. But, hoping that completing the assignment may earn her some brownie points with the department, she reluctantly got to work. Trapped in the eerie setting, lit only by a dim, flickering sixty-watt bulb that hung from a wire in the centre of the room, she let out a roar as she heaved the first of several heavy boxes from a huge mound.

She started sorting the files, putting them in chronological order, separating the men from the women, the living from the dead, meticulously going through each box.

For hours, she tore through the documents, scanning each mug shot, their fingerprints and entering personal data, like birthdays and last known addresses, into the digital folders. She even entered the phone numbers, though she knew this information would likely prove useless, everyone moving to cell phones in the past ten years. However, Miller wanted to be thorough so she worked industriously, with only the occasional curse word, until the particulars from the last folder in the 'living' stack had been entered.

With a heavy sigh and a pang of relief, all she had left to contend with were files of the deceased. Thankfully, Miller was told that these could go into the shredder, saving the easiest part of her job for last.

One by one, she passed the sleeves of paper through the sharp blades, the mindless, repetitive task beginning to have a calming effect on her. For a few moments, she found herself enjoying this ritual, seeing the portfolios of the dead turn to confetti, absolving them from any wrongdoing.

When she was nearly done, and just as she was about to send through one of the final rap sheets, she took notice of to whom the jacket belonged. Though the name on the front cover was partially obstructed by a large, red slash, it surprised Miller that she had missed it during her sorting.

Six months ago, this file would have ended up in the shredder like the rest of them without a second thought. But currently, after hearing the details of Rita's confession from Detective Hollis last April, the name on the file was one that she wouldn't forget. She opened the folder, pulled apart the pages that were slightly stuck together and whispered the name, "Suzie Hutchinson," as though it was a secret she didn't want anyone to hear.

In the file, she saw what she had expected to find, being well in tune with Suzie's history. Lists of convictions for solicitation, theft, and fraud lined its many pages. But it wasn't Suzie's criminal record that had piqued her interest, it was her mug shot that caught her attention, strategically attached to the top left-hand corner of the page.

For a moment, Miller thought her eyes had been playing tricks on her, the dim light likely blurring her vision. She immediately rubbed at them with her knuckles, blinking a few times to clear out the cobwebs. But after having a second and then a third look, she knew she hadn't been mistaken. She could never forget that face, but more notably, those piercing blue eyes. Yes, the photo was old and tattered, but she knew, without a doubt, that the person staring back at her was, undeniably, the woman who sat in that interview room six months ago. The one who identified as Rita Morrison.

Constable Miller ran from the basement with the file in hand and didn't stop, or even slow, as her colleagues yelled out, "I think you've lost them Miller!" She kept running through the halls and up flights of stairs until she reached Detective Hollis's office. With the discovery of the photo, she finally felt like a trained investigator, and she couldn't wait to show him what she had found.

She burst into his office without as much as calling out, finding it difficult to gain her breath.

"Ever heard of knocking Miller?" the detective questioned, staring at her, bent over at the waist, grabbing her knees for support. She breathed in through her nose and out from her mouth until she was able to steady herself and was ready to speak.

"Look at this," she told Hollis, throwing the file onto his desk, still slightly huffing and puffing.

"What is it?" he asked, taking it into his hand.

"Just look at it. Please."

"Okay, okay. I will," he said. "Calm down. Why don't you take a seat and catch your breath?" Detective Hollis offered.

"No, thank you," she responded, "I'd rather stand," excitement giving her jolts of electricity.

Appeasing her, the detective picked up the folder and flipped through the pages one at a time before Miller stopped him.

"Not the record, God damn it, look at the picture," she begged. Instantly regretting her choice of words, she apologized for her language and pointed to the photo. "Is that who I think it is?"

His eyes stared intently at the mug shot at the top of the page until he slowly started to nod. His head slightly swimming in disbelief, he answered her. "Yes, I do believe that it is."

"Hinky, isn't it sir?" Miller grinned.

***

Detective Hollis took the file and made his way hurriedly to his car. He drove quickly to his destination, the Women's Correctional Facility, his foot heavy on the gas.

When he arrived, he made his way through security, locking up his Glock before he could be let through. "It's standard protocol," the guard said, reminding him that the prison would not allow entry with any weapons. He used his wife's birthday as the temporary combination, something he knew he wouldn't forget, and found his way to the visitor's room.

On the other side of the prison, a guard called out, "Rita Morrison, there's someone here to see you. Open cell fourteen."

As the bars clanged open, Rita asked him, "Who is it?"

"I don't know. Why don't you come with me and find out for yourself?"

Her hands and ankles shackled, Rita followed the guard awkwardly, and nervously. She was concerned that Rory hadn't taken her request seriously. Perhaps he had come to visit, or worse, that he had brought the kids with him. But when the door opened to the visitor's room, it wasn't Rory who was visiting her after all. Her stomach dropped at the sight of Detective Miller waiting for her, coolly in his chair.

But before she could say anything, he beat her to the punch. He met Rita's gaze and catching sight of those unmistakable blue eyes, he said, "Hello Suzie."

EPILOGUE

(October 2001)

Back in his office with his feet elevated comfortably up on his desk, Detective Hollis chose a cigar from an ornate humidor he'd picked up at a bodega nearby. He kept these for special occasions, so he figured today was as good as any. Reaching for the single-blade guillotine that was hiding in his top drawer, he cut one end pristinely and lit the other with a match, spinning the cigar, allowing it to burn evenly. It was his ritual, something he learned in Cuba on holiday with Patti. He inhaled deeply, blatantly ignoring the state of New York's smoking in the workplace ban.

For the last time, he scolded himself for his shoddy investigation. He had known something was off, and he let the rookie cop talk him out of it, but he had only himself to blame. After Miller had shown him the photos of Sarah and the lab reports, he was convinced that he had been grasping at straws, looking for something that wasn't there and was firm in putting an end to the investigation. He had flagrantly disregarded his instincts that were telling him something was amiss, but, at the very least, he acknowledged, he *had* put the right person behind bars, just under the wrong name.

Regardless of his error in judgement, he had decided to forgive himself this one mistake and opted to put the whole event in the history books, for good. He now knew everything, and this time, he had it right.

As he puffed slowly on his cigar, enjoying hints of wood and vanilla, Hollis smirked at the thought of Suzie Hutchinson being arraigned on a whole new battery of charges, a second count of murder, one count of attempted murder, impersonation, and several others that would be among the long list read aloud by the Crown, asking for life in prison. Suzie was awarded a court appointed attorney to represent her this time, her husband's services having been deemed a conflict of interest. Notwithstanding, he was about to find himself unavailable for the task.

At the same time Suzie was being flanked in front of the judge, Grant would receive an unexpected knock at his door. Suzie had, once again, confessed. She had told the detective everything, but this time, it was the truth, not the lies she and her husband had concocted in the interview room under his nose.

He wondered how much jail time Grant would serve, if any, for his crime, sexual interference, sleeping with a seventeen-year old girl to whom he was in a position of authority. Probably none, he conceded, his crime surpassing the statute of limitations for his particular offence. But the bar would definitely revoke his licence as a practicing lawyer and he likely be hounded out of town. It sounded warped and unfair, but in the grand scheme of things, he did end up marrying this woman and spent the next twenty-plus years with her.

But then, there was also the matter of evading a police investigation for two decades, but as it stood, they would soon learn that Grant wasn't anywhere near that house the day of the fire and would be exonerated of that as well. This didn't sit right with the detective, believing that Grant deserved a harsher punishment for his sins. But he thought of their boys and what it would be like for them, both of his parents serving years in prison, and he let his animosity toward Grant float away with the smoke.

Feeling more relaxed than he had been in months and ready to call it a day, he swung his legs from the desk and snuffed out his cigar, just as there was a knock at the door.

"I knew I smelled Cubans," the man smiled as he entered Hollis' office and shut the door behind him.

"Care to join me?" Hollis asked, holding out the box to his old friend.

"No, thank you, trying to quit," Detective Sergeant Banks answered, waving off his generous offer.

"Suit yourself," tucking the humidor back into the top drawer of his desk.

"Good work on the Hutchinson case," he said, giving Detective Hollis a friendly pat on the back.

"Talk about coming out of left field," he replied, but not wanting to take all the credit for the slam dunk, he said, "Constable Miller was a big part of it, Wade. Maybe she deserves some kind of reward, a few days off with pay, perhaps. It really was a great discovery."

"I'll look into it," Banks said, acknowledging his suggestion, but Detective Hollis had a feeling it would leave his mind the minute he threw on his coat and called it a day. Another officer would do some good police work tomorrow, and his recommendation would go by the wayside. It was common practice in most police stations.

"Well, please accept my apologies, once again, for the disjointed inquisition. I guess I haven't been in the right frame of mind."

"You've had a lot going on, John. Why don't we enjoy the win and move forward, shall we?" Detective Sergeant Banks paused, staring at Hollis, square jawed, barely able to meet his eye.

All at once, Detective Hollis had the crawling sense that congratulating his old partner on a job well done was not the only reason Detective Sergeant Banks had made his way up to his office. With the sweet scent of cigars fading in the office, Hollis was beginning to feel ill at ease with the small talk and asked Banks outright, "Is there something else you wanted to speak to me about, Wade? If so, I'm all ears."

"Listen John, I have some news," he said, the frown lines around his mouth deepening as both corners dropped considerably. Hollis recognized this look as he had worn it many times while delivering notifications to unsuspecting families, *Your daughter's been in an accident . . . your wife's car has turned over on the freeway . . . your husband has had a heart attack.* He'd considered it the most difficult and unpleasant part of his job, giving people dreadful news.

Detective Hollis sat up straight in his chair, and although he literally had had enough surprises for one day, he braced himself for one more whammy.

"John, we've been friends for a long time, so I'm not going to jerk you around, and I'll come straight to the point."

"Well, what is the point? Please, just tell me," Detective Hollis demanded, his shoulders immediately tensing at the sound of Wade's voice. His friend was about to pull the rug out from underneath him. He could feel it in his bones, he could hear it in his inflection.

"You're required back in Los Angeles immediately."

"What? How come? I thought they had reassigned all my cases."

"Yes, you're right, they have, but that's not it."

"Then what is *it*?" Hollis asked, holding his breath.

Detective Sergeant Banks looked at his old friend justly in his face before answering him as gently as he could. "They've found your son, John," he answered and then paused before extinguishing Hollis's last hope that his boy would one day turn up alive. "I'm sorry, John, but he's been murdered.

Detective Hollis buckled. Inconsolable, and a literal puddle on the ground, he groaned, "Nooooooo!"

Detective Hollis wept openly, leaving Wade speechless as he watched John fall apart, and while he didn't expect anything less from a man who had waited two years for his missing son to finally turn up, it made him feel marginally uncomfortable. Notwithstanding, he watched on quietly for several minutes while he waited for his friend to gain some composure.

Slowly picking himself off the ground, he held on to his desk for stability and said, "Call Patti and book us on the next flight . . . we need to see our child!"

Thank you for reading Friends for Infinity.

Please watch for the second book in the Detective John Hollis Series . . .

Enemies for Eternity

Manufactured by Amazon.ca
Bolton, ON